# Peace, Quiet and a Little Justice in a Lawless Place

## A Black Cowboy Story

# Peace, Quiet and a Little Justice in a Lawless Place
## A Black Cowboy Story


By Mark T. Sneed

# Table of Contents

# DEDICATION

To my mother, family and friends who continue to inspire, encourage and challenge me to be a better person.

# THANK YOU

To the various minds that continue to thrive despite the lack of resources, equipment and education.
We carry our future on our backs.

Peace, Quiet and a Little Justice in a Lawless Place
A Black Cowboy Story

Peace, Quiet and a Little Justice in a Lawless Place
A Black Cowboy Story

By Mark T. Sneed

# Chapter 1.

Kate
California, April 1877

Marshall Darryl Dunnigan stood on the other side of the barred wooden door, armed and ready for trouble. Beside him was his loyal deputy, James Boyd. "Kate," the Marshall said, a little out of breath, a gun in his hand. "This don't have to end wit us in a shootout." He looked to Boyd and mouthed: This is gonna be a shootout. The Marshall had initially gone to where Kate Rawlins was supposed to live. She wasn't there.

The Marshall and deputy talked to her neighbors and one suggested that Kate might be down by the riverside in one of the shacks there. On that hunch the two lawmen rode down to the riverbank and found Kate sitting near the river.

Dunnigan had approached, calm and collected and before he could get close the girl had bolted carrying an oversized clothes bag. Boyd had drawn his pistol, but Kate had ducked behind one of the ruined remains of a building there near the riverbank and the chase was on.

The chase, if it could be described as a chase, had weaved around the dozen shacks on the waterway and ended up with the two lawmen winded and outside the shack they had seen the woman run inside. The two lawmen stood at the ready with their guns drawn.

The shack that they had chased Kate to was on the outskirts of old Sacramento. There were easily two dozen other small shacks that stood in memory of one of the once booming ghost towns that had sprung up during a gold rush gone by. The pair of lawmen were out of breath, but they knew they had tracked down the elusive Kate Rawlins.

The small wooden shack had two doors. There was a front door and a back porch rear door. There were four windows in the house. One window sat on each wall of the shack. No window was bigger than the front window.

Boyd gestured to the Marshall to get his attention. Boyd, a long-faced man with a broom brush mustache and stubble covered chin and jaw, was wearing a slouch hat, collared shirt, canvas pants and cowboy boots. On his hip was a gun belt. In his hand was a Colt Model 1860 revolver. The deputy made a gesture to himself and then pointed toward the corner of the house.

Dunnigan, bearded and wearing a ten-gallon hat on his blockish head, nodded. The lawman watched as his deputy cautiously moved quietly to the side of the shack and disappeared. He was going to make sure Kate Rawlins did not slip out the back of the shack.

Inside the shack Kate, armed with a modified pistol, looked to the front door where the lawman had knocked politely.

"Kate, I'm Marshall Dunnigan and I was lookin' fir you 'bout a shootin' someone said you might know 'bout," the lawman said.

The pouty teen looked at the front door and then the rear door. They were the only exits. She adjusted the beaten-up clothes bag in her hand. It was the only possession she carried. The clothes bag had been her mother's and the only thing she had to remind her of her lost family.

The daughter of Marcus and Cindy Rawlins, dressed in a heavy coat to fight off the unseasonable cold of Sacramento, looked to the back door as a possible exit. She had come to this shack to hide, for a few moments, after losing her temper in Sacramento and shooting a man that thought he could do whatever he wanted to her. Thankfully, she had her two guns with her.

In her clothes bag was the loaded belly buster derringer that Freeman gave her when she was nine. There were also two dresses, a heavy jacket, a scarf, a Bible, a leather purse and nearly five hundred dollars in gold coins in her durable bag.

In her right hand was the modified Colt 1860 that sat on the lighter 1873 Peacemaker frame. Kate had picked up the frame for ten dollars. She had modified the Colt Model 1860 to chamber a bigger .45 ACP cartridge.

Kate had bought the frame and older Colt 1860 as men decided to go to Alaska or back East. The boom of Sacramento had ended, but there were still hopeful gold miners roaming and panning for gold without much luck. They remained in the new capitol and told stories of their brushes with gold, bandits, robbers and their partners.

It was during a night, just a day or two before Marshall Dunnigan showed up, that two men saw Kate and tried to get her attention.

"Hey, lady, you know that it's not safe walkin' the streets at night, alone?" One of them asked.

"Yeah, I'll walk you home," one of the two men in the dark said.

Kate ignored them. Kate figured that was it. The teen girl had been talked to before and though it made her feel uncomfortable and she was hyper alert, nothing had come of it.

But two days before Marshall Dunnigan showed up the two men followed Kate. They followed the daughter of Marcus Rawlins down the gaslit streets and made rude comments.

"You shouldn't walk by yo'self, little lady. Anything can happen," one of the men said from behind. Kate tried to keep an eye on the men to avoid them getting too close.

"Don't walk so fast," one of the men said.

"It ain't a bad look though her walkin' the way she do," the other man said with a snicker.

Unlike most unaccompanied women in Sacramento, Kate did not fear the men that night. Kate had learned long ago to protect herself.

The three were near the dark side of Sacramento, Kate remembered. The gaslights that were lit on each block in Sacramento, went down to one gaslight for maybe every four or five blocks where Kate lived in Sacramento.

"Little one," one of the men said from behind and reached out to grab her shoulder.

Kate spun and knocked the man's hand away.

Kate stared at the two men and thought then and there to give the one grinning like he had done something a piece of her mind but chose to scowl and walk away. Saying something only would give them a reason to hurt Kate. She pushed on and hoped that being on the edge of her neighborhood would make the men turn around.

The girl walked only to find one of the men in front of her. She frowned at the man.

"Don't be that way," said the other man coming out of the dark behind her.

It was then that Kate pulled her pistol from under her blanket jacket.

"If you've got bad intentions, you picked the wrong woman," Kate said, aiming her pistol at the man trying to grab her.

Kate had the modified Colt pistol aimed at the smiling man. Seeing the pistol in her hand he raised his hands in surrender.

The other man who was circling Kate, she watched carefully.

"You spicy," the circling man said with a smirk.

"Do you want to die?"

The man smiled. "You look like one of those bitches that snap 'n bark, but you pet 'em 'n they jus' a big ol' pussycat."

The second man, who had his hands up backed into the dark. Kate still watched him, but her attention was on the talker. The more he talked the more she paid attention to him. He seemed to be ramping up for action.

He stepped forward and reached out to grab Kate's gun hand. Instantly, without thought, she pulled the trigger of the Colt pistol. The kickback was not unexpected but in the night and open of Sacramento the sound of gunfire, so close to her, was thunderous.

The loud talker recoiled and fell back into the street, holding his arm.

He was shot but he wasn't dead.

"Take your friend 'n get," Kate said to the other man lurking in the darkness.

He raised his hands and gathered up his wounded friend. In the dark of the night, Kate watched as the two men stumbled and then ran away. They ran to the first busy street. As they reached the busy street, in that same darkness, Kate disappeared.

So, as the Marshall blocked the front door, Kate decided to sneak out the bedroom window. Kate grabbed her clothes bag and slipped out of one of the squares where a window should have sat. As the Marshall talked, Kate slinked away into the night hoping her luck held.

She ran and thought that her temper had gotten her in trouble again. Kate ran, never looking back, knowing that letting her temper get the best of her would be the ruin of her. At seventeen, Kate found herself running from her home in Sacramento, wanted for shooting a white man who might have done anything to her the night before.

Kate ran into the night and as she put distance between the Marshall and whoever else was looking for her, Kate wracked her brain thinking where she could go and be safe. She couldn't go to the Stokers. They did not like Kate. They had good reason. They believed Kate killed and buried her first husband, their dear Donald the year before but they could not prove it. There were all these rumors but no evidence.

It was true Donald Stoker and Kate married. They seemed happy for the first year and then there were cracks in paradise. Kate married Donald with the hope that he was the man he said he was before they wed. By the second year being married to Donald Stoker was intolerable.

Despite all that Kate refused to go to her father's people. They were nice enough, but she always felt like she was a bother to them just by being around. Kate had come to them as a needy nine-year-old but she had been transformed.  Kate was no longer a whining brat but a hardened survivor.

With that in mind, Kate headed to the outskirts of Sacramento and the unclaimed ghost towns, just on the outskirts of downtown. Though Sacramento downtown was thriving, outside of those two or three miles it was still mostly farmland. Kate crossed the corner of the downtown and found herself in rolling fields of green.

A few minutes later Kate found a wooden structure that might have been a store a long time ago but had fallen into disrepair years ago. The store was just the shell of what it once was. There Kate hid and hoped that the next day she would be able to return to the city center and secure a wagon train heading north.

# **Chapter 2.**

Kate
California, 1877


The next morning Kate woke and walked to the center of town with her clothes bag and booked a spot on a freedman wagon heading to Oregon and eventually Coffeyville, Kansas. It seemed a stroke of luck that there was a wagon heading to Coffeyville and that of all places she knew of that Kansas town.

Her plan was to get away from Sacramento and the lawmen looking for her. Kate didn't have a plan beyond that. The wanted woman found a livery station and purchased a ticket to Oregon. That morning, she waited that morning for the freedmen wagon which would take her back to the Kansas territory and Freeman and possibly Kaiyote, the two plainsmen that had shepherded her from the edge of Coffeyville to the Kansas territories and Thaddeus Monroe.

Kate could not escape the feeling of irony as she stood near the bustling downtown of the still growing city, much like she had nearly a decade before when she arrived looking for her family.

Yet, it was the idea of her waiting for a wagon, much like she had with Freeman and Kaiyote in Garrett, in the Kansas territories, to transport her from a place of danger to the hope of family and a brighter future that made Kate chuckle.

All around Kate were men and women moving up and down the walkways. Horsemen trotted through the streets as well. On the streets were wagons, covered and uncovered.

Wagons had caused hope to spring up in Kate and her family as they fled Missouri and made their way to Kansas. Wagons had been the source of joy and expectation as her family and six others had attempted to find the Oregon trail.

As Kate arranged transport to Kansas, she knew that the return to the plains might not be what she expected. At seventeen, Kate knew most would not understand her desire to cross the territories and the plains to find two men that saved her life when she was turning ten.

The best part of living in a growing and bustling city was all the activity. Gunshots in Sacramento were not unusual. So, no one batted an eye when Kate shot and killed her husband. No one seemed overly interested when the next day she buried the body just two hundred yards from her house.

The only reason Kate had run afoul of the law was because she had shot a white man. The rules were different for them. They could shoot and kill almost anyone and suffer little to no consequences. Yet, if a black, Hispanic, Indian or anyone not white harmed them all the weight of the white judicial system came tumbling down on the heads of those criminals.

So, the morning after escaping the law, Kate found herself in Sacramento, in the midst of all this post-gold rush activity. Just a little after sunrise there was a buzz in the growing city. All around her there was building and movement.

At the town stable were five wagons with black men with beards standing near them. Kate walked toward the wagons and had flashes of her first wagon trip seven years ago. She blinked the thought from her head and nearly ran into a tall and oval-faced girl wearing a blue and green dress. Her hair was hidden beneath a matching blue and green scarf. Dangling from the rear of the scarf was a long thick black braided ponytail.

"Hi, you on the wagon train to Kansas?"

Kate nodded.

"I'm Elisabeth," the oval-faced sepia brown girl said. "Elisabeth Lawson." She smiled broadly and showed off her small teeth. "My dad is in charge." She spun around in the dozens of people moving up and down the street near the stable. She looked left and right and pointed toward a short and stocky black man wearing a bowler and dressed in cloth jacket and dark trousers. "Come on," the oval-faced girl said.

Elisabeth practically grabbed Kate's hand and dragged her to meet her father. Mister Reginald Lawson was a serious-looking man. He was just a foot taller than Kate, with dark eyes, bushy eyebrows and a full beard. He wore a button front shirt and vest. In the pocket of his vest was a chain that suggested he had a pocket watch in one of the vest pockets. On his hip was a gun belt and pistol. Strapped to his boot was a knife.

"Daddy, this is," Elisabeth began only to stop and turn back to look at Kate with her small eyes. She smiled at Kate and shrugged.

"Kate Rawlins," the teen said to Elisabeth.

"Kate Rawlins," Elisabeth Lawson, the daughter of Reginald Lawson, the wagon master, said. "She's comin' along wit us to Kansas. I am so glad she's comin' along. I thought it was goin' to be just me 'n a bunch uv boys 'n little Charlotte."

Kate listened and smiled.

Climbing on the wagon with the belly buster and the modified Colt pistol and all the money she could put her hands on before leaving. Though she had all she possessed or just the most essential it reminded Kate of her first visit to Sacramento.

Thaddeus Monroe had taken Kate to Sacramento to fulfill his promise to a friend.

"What are you goin' to do?" Monroe asked on the black side of Sacramento in front of the four wagons headed north to Oregon.

Kate shrugged her shoulders.

"Well, thankfully, I know someone who might be able to help you," Monroe said with a crooked smile.

Kate then, was introduced to a cashew hued woman with big brown eyes by Thaddeus Monroe. The woman, who was heavy-chested, wide hipped, broad nosed and thick lipped was ageless and seemed to be known by everyone. More importantly, Miss Jenny seemed to know everyone in Sacramento.

"We'll find your people if they live here," the woman dressed in a deep V-neck dress that showed off her ample curves.

A few days later Kate united with a family she had never known other than in stories from her mother and father. The Rawlins, Benjamin and Paula, and their four children welcomed Kate with open arms.

Her life had been a roller coaster ride. There were moments when Kate thought she was happy. Then there were moments when she felt as if all that she cared about was slipping away.

In that craziness and feeling of things slipping away Kate had moments of extreme violence. Initially, the violence was small and aimed at no one in particular. Yet, and still, as she found herself falling into despair more often Kate took her despair and turned it on others near her.

Kate thought absently that leaving Sacramento and heading back to Kansas might tame the violence brewing in her. She secretly hoped that she might find Freeman and thank him for all he had done for me when Kate was just a little girl.
Mister Lawson had a sheet of paper with writing on it and Kate presumed it was all the people signed up for the trip. He looked at Kate evenly.

"Welcome aboard Miss Kate Rawlins," Mister Lawson said in a gruff voice. "You can climb 'board any uv the wagguns. We'll be pullin' out soon as our last passenger gets here."

# Chapter 3.

Kate
Oregon, April, 1877

The wagon train rolled out of Sacramento and Kate looked back at the place she had called home for nearly a decade. The lawmen did not appear. No one shouted for the wagons to stop. Instead, the wagons creaked and squeaked and bumped along the well-trodden paths that led north and toward Oregon.

"We should be in Oregun in a couple of days," Elisabeth said at the first rest stop.

Kate nodded. Elisabeth pulled Kate away from her father and directed her to a covered wagon. Elisabeth helped Kate put her clothes bag in her wagon. Kate and Elisabeth climbed into the rear of the covered wagon.

"That's all you brought?"

Kate did not speak.

"We're goin' to be on the trail fir at least four months," Elisabeth said.

Kate nodded.

"I packed light," Kate said.

"Well, as long as you paid, we're goin' to feed you," Elisabeth said.

Kate nodded. She sat and tried to just take a moment to realize that she was heading back to Kansas and hopefully finding Freeman and Kaiyote. The idea was a bit overwhelming.

"Do you mind if we sit here quiet fir a little bit? I didn't get a good night's sleep last night."

Elisabeth sat and stared at Kate.

"No problem," Elisabeth smiled. "We have plenty of time to get to know each other."

"We're headin' through the mountains 'n then into the valleys before we reach Oregun," announced Elisabeth as the wagon and the four other wagons behind the lead fell in place. The wagons moved slowly east and toward the Oregon Trail.

Kate sat and watched the hijinks of the three Lawson boys, dressed in overalls, loose fabric collarless T-shirts. The three boys refused to wear shoes. They were always in various stages of undress.

Kate smiled and laughed at the boys' antics. Elisabeth smiled too.

"Your family is... int'restin'," Kate said, twisting her lips.

Elisabeth nodded.

"So, you have been on a wagon train before?"

"A long time ago," Kate said.

"Why you goin' to Kansas?"

Kate did not answer immediately. She had to decide what to tell someone she had only met. The teenager looked at the younger girl and hesitated.

"I am lookin' fir someone I owe thanks to," Kate said.

Elisabeth nodded and seemed to accept that as an answer.

The wagon train took off and headed north. The wagon bumped along the well-worn path toward Oregon.

Kate met Missus Lawson, little Charlotte, and the three sons of Mister Lawson. The oldest, Reginald Junior, RJ, was only nine years old. The three hung beside their mother and studied Kate quietly. After a handful of hours Ricky and Randolph were sleeping at Kate's feet. RJ had fallen asleep in the middle of the wagon floor.

The gruff teen closed her eyes as the wagon bumped along lulling her to sleep and found herself reliving the last time she had seen Freeman and Kaiyote in her nine-year-old past.

*"You ain't a killer Kate," Freeman said. "Don't let this life get ahold uv you. It will never let you go."*

*Kate looked at the dead man at her feet.*

*"Forget this," Freeman said. "Erase this. Don't look at this 'n let it haunt you. Believe me girl, this life ain't fir you."*

*Kate nodded.*

*"You got a pass today. No blood on your hands," Freeman said, holstering his pistol. The dark cowboy looked out into the*

*seemingly unending plains. "The plains has a way uv balancin'
things, by 'n by," Freeman said.*

Freeman, the dark and dangerous cowboy, and Kaiyote,
the Indian, who had saved her and protected her from men turned
monsters were indelibly etched into Kate's memories.

She hated to admit that all the men that she met and
engaged with were measured by how close they were to Freeman
or Kaiyote. For Kate, a real man, a man who could protect her was
going to resemble the best qualities of Freeman.

When she married Donald Stoker, she believed he had the
Freeman qualities to protect her from harm. Of course, he
projected those qualities until he drank. When drunk all those
outstanding characteristics faded and were replaced with
deplorable qualities.

It was Freeman's words in Kate's head that told her she
did not deserve to be mistreated. She deserved better. So, Kate
reached out and grabbed a handful of better. She had given
Donald Stoker a chance and he had chosen stupid.

Kate married Donald when she was fifteen and before
their second anniversary, he showed his true colors. The livery
worker began drinking and becoming mean for no real reason. The
meanness was there, but after working in the tannery he would
come home exhausted. He wouldn't talk to me. He wouldn't hold
me. Things got tense. Kater told Donald he needed to relax. He
didn't listen. Donald let the work and the stress of work affect him.
During the week he worked as a leather man, boiling, tanning,
stitching saddles and boots. During the work week he was devoted
to his work.

Yet, when the Friday arrived, and he had some money in
his pocket he would get together with his childhood friends and
drink and talk. Liquored up, he would come home, and manhandle
Kate. That only happened twice.

The first time Donald Stoker, her husband, put hands on
her she was shocked and surprised. For a moment, Kate thought
she had done something wrong to make her husband raise his

hand to her. Then she fought him off and made him leave the house.

Kate thought of killing Weaver the night her husband of one year thought he could put his hands on her without consequence. Freeman had taught Kate she did not have to accept harsh treatment from anyone. The dark and bearded cowboy had also, in a weeks' time taught her to handle the two pistols he had given her.

The next day, when he sobered up, he apologized profusely and told Kate it would never happen again. Kate did not follow through with her immediate thought and believed her husband. She wanted to believe her husband.

For a couple of weeks things seemed to return to normal. Then, one Friday, Donald showed up drunk and mean.

"Donald, you know I'm not goin' to let you touch me," Kate said, warning him. "I'm not goin' to let you treat me like a punchin' bag."

Donald laughed. He grabbed a chair and threw it in the direction of Kate.

Kate pulled her Colt pistol.

"What? You goin' to shoot me?"

Kate held the pistol in her hand as she had been trained by Freeman and Thaddeus Monroe. She took a deep breath and exhaled.

"Don't come any closer," Kate said.

Donald Stoker had frowned and scowled and against Kate's warning took another step.

The report of the Colt pistol was deafening that quiet night. Kate had known the gun would have a kickback, but the Colt nearly jumped out of her hands. She gripped the handle tightly and made sure the gun did not tumble from her hands.

On the floor lay her one-time husband. He held his chest and under his clenched hand blood darkened his dark blue shirt front. Kate stepped to the unmoving man who looked as if he was about to speak. She leaned down and listened.

There was nothing but silence in the small house Kate called home.

Donald Stoker was not the first man Kate killed, but he was the first man she had slept with and then killed. Kate had killed one other man, but Freeman had told her that he was already dead when Kate pulled the trigger. Of course, Kate did not believe Freeman, knowing that the dark cowboy wanted her to believe she was not a killer no matter what she wanted to think.

# Chapter 4.

Kate
Nevada, May, 1877

Elisabeth Lawson was a talker. She had an opinion about everything. Kate was surprised to hear the younger girl's opinion of slavery and the future for Negroes in the nation.

"Well, as I have seen in the short time I have been here, we not seen as anything but a burden," Elisabeth said. "It is a troubling situation. We did not choose to come here. We did not choose to be enslaved. We did not choose this path we are on."

Her mother, holding Charlotte in her arms, smiled.

Kate listened and thought about what Elisabeth said. She was not certain if she agreed with everything the girl had said but it was definitely something to think about.

Kate sat in the rear of the covered wagon and recalled the ambush of her parents and friends wagon train and the introduction to Freeman and Kaiyote.

The wagon train was days out of Kansas. They were headed to the Oregon trail. They were led by a curly haired wagon master who seemed friendly at first and became less friendly every day on the trail. The wagon train had left Coffeyville and was crossing the plains that seemed just an endless sea of green and yellow heads of wheat.

The wagon Kate was in was a hive of activity, as always. Her mother was in the rear of the covered wagon and making something to eat before we stopped for water or supplies.

Kate recalled the wagon train swaying and indicating a turn in the trail. They were moving north with trees on one side of the trail. Kate had thought the shade of the trees was a welcome relief, even though it was cool and days away from the first snow.

"Where we heading?"

"California," Kate's mother said with a smile.

"No," Kate said, shaking her head. "I mean I thought we were supposed to be headed west."

"We headed west," her mother said.

"I don't think so," Kate said, lifting her small handmade compass that indicated that they were headed north.

"The trail ain't always straight, my sweet," her mother said.

Kate was about to speak when her father spoke. His voice was more a screech.

"Hey. We got trouble," her father said, and the tone drew Kate's attention. Her father and big brother were sitting on the buckboard. John, her bigger brother, was the first to scream. Her father reached out for John as he pulled the reins and tried to stop the wagon.

Instantly, the Rawlins men were in action. Kate's mother who had been resting pointed to the area under the bench where she and her daughter were sitting. Kate scrambled and hid beneath the bench. The wagon rolled to a slow halt as the shooting began.

"Hide," her mother said, squatting fearfully.

Kate looked up from beneath the bench and saw the fear in her mother's eyes. Kate tried to make herself smaller beneath the bench. The first few bullets ripped through the canvas and her mother reached under the bench and Kate came out as bullets tore through the sides of the wagon where Kate had hidden.

Kate looked out of the wagon, toward where her father and brother had been only to see the two horses bucking, neighing and pawing at the dirt as three men on horses wearing blanket jackets rode by shooting pistols back into the wagon.

"Kate," her mother screamed. Kate looked back to her mother's gingham dress front as she crashed into her and then things went black.

Those thoughts flitted through Kate's mind as the wagon train rolled to a stop somewhere in Nevada.

"We're in Nevada and should be in the mountain pass soon," Mister Lawson said. The five wagons, as was the nightly plan, were positioned in a semi-circle with a fire in the mouth of the open circle. The horses were tied on a rope strung between two trees just a few feet from the camp. Two men volunteered to watch the camp during the night.

Most of the families slept in the wagons. Some of the men and boys slept on the ground outside of the wagons. Kate preferred to sleep in the comfort of the wagon with Elisabeth, her mother and Charlotte. The boys loved sleeping out of the wagon and proving they were tough with their older brother and father.

Kate, that same night, on the edge of the Nevada territory with the Utah mountains in sight, fell asleep thinking of how she had met Freeman and the Indian Kaiyote.

# Chapter 5.

Kate
Day One, Kansas Territories, 1869


The first thing to register in Kate's ears was the slapping of fabric and crackling of wood. The second thing the nine-year-old sensed was the acrid smell of smoke. She breathed in and there was something familiar in her nostrils alongside the smell of smoke, dust and things she did not know. Kate opened her eyes to find herself face-to-face with her mother. Her mother's face was resting against her forehead and her mother was just inches away from Kate. Her mother's hands were covering her ears. Kate wriggled beneath her mother. She freed a hand and was surprised that her mother had not opened her eyes. Instinctually, Kate imagined her mother was asleep.

"Mama," Kate said.

Her mother's eyes seemed odd all of a sudden. Kate squirmed and struggled as her mother lay atop her unmoving. Kate breathed and blinked and tried to move only to stop. The thoughts, the thinkings and understandings were creeping into her consciousness. The little girl twisted and reached up and gingerly touched her mother's face.

"Mama," Kate whispered, a bit confused. She pushed and wiggled from beneath her unmoving mother. She managed to free herself from her mother's upper torso. The first tear squeezed out of Kate's eyes at the realization that the woman on top of her was dead.

The little girl, not yet ten, once freed from the unmoving maternal protection, found herself and her mother on what would have been one side of the wagon's covering, instead of the wagon itself. All their possessions had shifted and been thrown over her and her mother.

To her left was the jumble of the family belongings tossed and flipped as if the whole world was upside down. Pillows, chairs, pots and pans, food, flour, rice and dresses and shirts were scattered everywhere.

There had been an attack. There was a familiarity in the jumble of the flipped on its side ripped apart canvas, the trampled personal belongings and the green and black gingham dress her mother was wearing the last time Kate could remember. With a push and another wiggle Kate freed herself from her mother.

Kate looked around the tipped over wagon she found herself in. Her mother's shiny black braided hair was divided into two hemispheres. On the one side the thick braids had come loose from the bunch and were hanging loose on the right side of her head like a black curly hair explosion of three dozen braids on her head. On the other side, the braids were still rolled together away from her unseen face to her neck. Kate felt her stomach lurch as she took in the blurred sight and distinct smell of her mother mixed with the acrid smell of blood, smoke and cordite.

Kate closed her eyes to the three bullet holes in the gingham dress. The vision before her was shocking. Kate opened her big eyes and confirmed the three holes that were grouped in the middle of her mother's back. The gingham dress below the bullet holes and to her mother's right side was blood soaked.

Kate reached out and looked for support. She grabbed and found the steel of one of the three metal support hoops that gave shape to the wagon cover. There were bullet holes peppering the wagon covering. The wagon cover was cut and slit to the outside. Kate blinked and tried to focus. The little girl remembered her father saying something before the shooting began.

Kate, big eyed, round cheeked felt a little pain on the back of her head. Hidden amongst the crown of black braids which encircled the top of her head was a tender and sore lump. The nine-year-old looked from her still mother to the latch purse her mother had hidden and protected from the curious eyes of anyone not in the family. Inside that latch purse, Kate knew, was the Rawlins wealth.

Her father had saved nearly one hundred dollars in gold and coins. The latch purse was where the gold and coins hid. The latch purse which had been hidden was now beside her mother.

Kate looked to the bench where she had hidden and realized that she would have been shot or killed had she stayed there. There were five holes in the side of their covered wagon. Again, Kate looked out of the wagon front. The horses that had pulled the wagon were gone. All around her was deathly still.

She looked back to her mother and in looking could not shake the sight from her eyes. Her mother lying face down dead, shot in the back four times. She reached out and stopped herself. Kate simply cried.

She closed her eyes and covered her face as the pain of the last time she would hear her mother's laugh sunk in. Minutes passed. Tears fell. Somewhere, nowhere that Kate imagined, she knew she must find her father and brother and possibly others from the wagon train who had survived and were still going to continue to California.

Kate turned away from her mother. She placed a small hand on the canvas and expected it to hold her. Instead, the nine-year-old fell through the distressed canvas and out of the wagon to the dirt and gravel outside. In the still bright of day Kate found herself near the trail's edge.

She climbed to her feet and scanned the wagon in front of theirs. Mister Logan and his family's wagon was on fire as Kate walked numbly back and away from the family's wagon and toward the rear of the ripped apart wagon train. The three wagons, the Clark's, the Jefferson's, and the Finney's covered wagons were silent and flipped onto their sides like the others. On the trail side where Kate found herself, she could see two bodies ahead of her. She took a few steps and found a single shoe on the trail. The shoe was worn and brown and laced up. Kate did not pick it up. Instead, she simply allowed it to sit in her head.

The Clark's wagon was turned over and there was a body between her family's wagon and theirs. There were no horses to pull the wagons. Where were the horses? Kate wondered. It was a relief to grab onto that question and not the horror all around her. In that momentary distraction the nine-year-old rested. She was all cried out, she imagined. She was looking for her brother and father. Find her brother and father. No one thing mattered. No thought stuck. Her mind flitted from one thought to the next. In the bright of day, not the night, monsters had attacked. There was no safety in the light of day, Kate realized. It, the pain, the attack, was the only real thought.

Whatever she expected or felt was missing from her. There was no feeling in her suddenly. There was no real emotion.

Being away from her family's wagon gave Kate a reprieve, emotionally. Kate looked up and through the leaves of the trees just beyond the ditch that bordered the trailside. The little girl looked and saw a squirrel sitting on a limb a hundred feet from her spinning a nut the size of its head in its small paws. Kate stopped and watched the squirrel.

The squirrel looked from the nut it had to the little girl watching it and surprisingly shoved the enormous nut into its mouth and looked left and right. Kate watched as the squirrel stood on its hind legs and jumped to the right and disappeared behind the trunk of the tree. Kate watched and studied the tree, but the squirrel never reappeared.

Not seeing the squirrel reappear the little girl turned back to the trail and continued walking toward the rear of the wagon train. Kate walked past the two bodies which had been a boy a little older than Kate. To her right was Joseph Jefferson dressed in camp shirt, overalls and work boots. He had two gunshots in his back. After Joseph, just a handful of steps from the facedown boy, sat Mister Finney, dressed in an over shirt, a shapeless blanket jacket, dark trousers and boots. He was sitting like he was asleep on the side of the trail against the buckboard.

The little girl, not ten years old, scanned the seated Mister Finney. His chin was resting on his bloody chest. There was a blood trail that began at his chin and led to his left hip. On the right side of his over shirt Kate saw a nasty wound that had ripped through his side.

Kate did not seem shocked or surprised by. either body or the gruesomeness of the gunshots. It seemed inevitable for some reason.

Her father had said as much.

"We can't live worried about dyin'," he said. "We ain't prisoners no more. We free. We goin' to leave Kansas 'n head to California," Kate's father said. "Livin' in fear ain't livin'."

"We safe?" Asked her brother John.

"We as safe as anywhere." her father said. "We got a right to protect ourselves jus' like anybody. We ain't goin' to let fear stop us from livin' 'n dream in'."

The little girl kept walking, thinking about what her father had said. Kate moved mechanically. Maybe as she walked toward the rear of the wagon train, she was hoping to find someone she knew to commiserate, hope and dream.

Kate stepped over the shoes and clothes that had been thrown out of the last wagon searching for any one left alive. She opened and closed her mouth thinking to call out and rethinking the idea for fear that whoever had killed everyone might still be around.

The little girl, reaching the rear of the wagon and finding hoped her father or one of the men had survived. She walked toward the last wagon and mechanically turned around and walked down the opposite side of the wagon train, closest to the hill. On the opposite side of the wagon train Kate Rawlins found more dead bodies. There was James and Jason Finney, the twins. They had all been shot. James was shot in the chest and head. His son had been shot in the back. Lying on the side of the Jefferson family wagon shot three times in the chest. She walked past three more bodies.

Surprisingly, the first heart pull came when Kate found her brother, John, dead, a few feet from the Clark family wagon. Seeing her big brother shot in the back, lying there like he was trying to hide was too much for Kate. Tears fell from her big red rimmed eyes. She looked down and saw he had on one shoe.

Without warning Kate's stomach twisted. She threw up for the first time that late afternoon. She could not say what triggered her retching. Was it her realization that her mother was dead? Was it seeing her brother face down and shot three times in the back? Was it her realizing that she was suddenly alone?

Everyone she loved and knew was gone. She had begun with her family and six other families. Now, the six families were gone. Everyone that she ever knew or trusted were gone.

The nine-year-old stopped and tried to gather herself. So much had happened in such a short period of time. Kate was overwhelmed.

Her brother was dead. He was only three years older than Kate, she recollected. He had been her protector on the wagon ride. Now, he was gone.

She searched the dead bodies and through her tears she found the familiar peppered Afro of her father dead near four other men who formed a loose semi-circle. Kate bawled uncontrollably finding her father and what remained of Mister Clark, Mister Davis, Mister Logan and one of his sons in the smoking remains of the ill-fated wagon train.

Her mother, her dear sweet mother was dead. Kate was mentally and physically exhausted. She re-entered the wagon and stopped. Kate cried and sat beside her mother. She reached out and held her mother's hand.

Kate did not notice, as she walked back to her family's wagon and her mother, the two figures on the ridge watching her actions.

# **Chapter 6.**

Freeman and Kaiyote
Day One, Kansas territories, 1869

The two horsemen rode into view. One was on a brown horse. The other was on an Appaloosa. The one on the brown horse wore a Hardee hat and carried a rifle. The other, the smaller of the two in the saddle, had long straight black hair and was wearing a buffalo coat and studying the trail. The one in the buffalo coat slowed. The stranger had a Smith carbine in the saddle holster. Across his chest, diagonally, hung a Colt Model 1860.

"What you see?"

"Wagons, bodies 'n no horses," the rider in the buffalo coat said.

"Okay, easy," the dark rider said, looking up and down the trail. He was cautious. He had learned not to be overconfident in seemingly wide-open situations.

The cowboy in the Hardee hat stood up in the stirrups and scanned the horizon looking for any signs of the horse thieves.

"No killin' 'less they try somethin'," the cowboy said and paused. "Looks like we're riding up on somethin' that jus' happened." He pointed to the fire smoldering from one of the wagons.

As the pair got closer to the wagons, the dark rider looked back at the reluctant rider still in the rear of the wagon train. The lone rider slowed his horse's progress. He looked at the cowboy in the Hardee hat.

"This your people?" The grim cowboy asked.

The long-haired rider looked at the dark cowboy curiously.

He spoke in a language that only he and the dark rider understood.

"No," the man with a visible ponytail said. "Jus' because someone is attacked doesn't mean that it was our people," the usually silent warrior said, with a smirk.

"You sure?"

"Not every attack is our people," the long-haired rider said pointing to the peppered covered wagons. The rider rode easily and with an incredible eye for detail. "We do not attack your people. Your... tribe not like... the demons," he added.

"But you ain't against us bein' in your tribe?"

The rider shook his head.

"They take 'n take until there is nothin' left," Kaiyote said. He spoke in an ancient language, a language that sounded like singing more than words.

The pair reached the trail and slowly moved toward the end of the tipped over wagon. The bearded rider directed the long-haired rider to the far side of the wagon. The two slowed.

The gruff cowboy was the first to climb off his horse with his rifle in hand. He paused seeing the number of black bodies and the wreckage. He replaced his Springfield rifle in his saddle holster as he noticed there were no horses for the wagons.

The bearded cowboy drew his heavier pistol and paused and looked at his silent and observant partner.

"So, remember we're searchin' 'n nothin' more," the cowboy wearing a Hardee hat said.

The long-haired rider nodded.

The dark cowboy nodded as well.

"Remember we lookin' fir gold 'n jewels or whatever we can sell off quick," the dark cowboy said to his partner.

"I think we try 'n save anyone, if they still alive," the long-haired rider said.

"Yeah, we'll look fir anyone alive, but we'll also look fir gold, jewels 'n the like," the cowboy said. "There's no reason we can't make a profit being helpful," the dark cowboy said.

The Native shrugged his shoulders at Freeman.

The cowboy drew his heavy Colt Dragoon pistol and moved cautiously from the rear of the wagon train toward the front, knowing that there was at least one person if not more alive there. The dark rider moved cautiously and quietly, scanning each wagon for signs of life.

On the opposite side of the wagon train, the long-haired rider moved cautiously, with his rifle in hand, headed toward the front of the wagon train.

When the dark cowboy came upon Kate, she was holding her mother's hand and staring blankly at him from the tossed interior of the wagon. Seeing Freeman in the rips and tears of the wagon the little girl's facial expression went from pained to a feral wildness. She reached out in the jumble near her and was suddenly holding a knife. Her eyes red from crying and a pained grimace on her face transformed and was replaced with an angry glare.

The dark cowboy did not falter. He looked at the girl, the still mother, the three bullet holes in her back and lowered his pistol, still six feet away. He smiled.

"Easy," the dark rider wearing a Hardee hat said.

"Who are you?" The little girl asked, waving the knife in front of her like a stick.

The bearded, dark cowboy did not speak. Instead, he raised his empty gloved hand and holstered his pistol and stepped back all in one motion.

"You can call me: Freeman," the cowboy said.

"Freeman?"

"What they call you?" Freeman asked, bending down and stepping cautiously into the jumble that was the girl's wagon. As he entered, he saw the dead body next to the little girl and the four bullet holes in her back.

"Kate," the little girl said. "Kate Rawlins."

"Please to meet you, Kate Rawlins," Freeman said with a concerned look. The inside of the wagon was topsy turvy. Clothes, furniture, pots and pans were everywhere.

He paused, thinking. He studied the girl and the dead body and the interior of the wagon. How was he to handle this situation?

"You shouldn't be in here, Kate Rawlins," Freeman said.

"I ain't leavin'," Kate said, angrily.

"Okay," Freeman said, with a crooked smile. "Where were you headed?" He asked, looking around the wagon.

"California," Kate said.

"Never been," Freeman said with his crooked smile. He knelt just out of reach from the knife. He looked around the jumble of the interior for any valuables.

"What do you want?" Kate asked, holding the knife in front of her defensively.

"Want? We saw the smoke 'n came to see if we could offer help," Freeman said.

"Help? Help? My family's dead," Kate said, tears welling up in her already red eyes, her voice trembling. "I'm all alone." Kate paused. "We?"

The long-haired rider reached out from behind Kate and grabbed her wrist and took the knife her. Instantly, Kate was twisted around and held firmly by Kaiyote. As soon as that happened Freeman signaled to his partner and the three stepped out of the wagon, despite Kate's protests.

"Let me go," Kate screamed.

Once outside of the wagon Kate found herself trying to break free from a strong and dark-eyed man. Kate kicked to no avail. She twisted and screamed again. Freeman shook his head. The Silent dark-eyed warrior narrowed his eyes to the struggling little girl in his hands.

"Let me go," Kate said, angrily.

"You need to calm down. We don't mean you no harm, girl. If there was anyone else here, you would be in real trouble. Me and Kaiyote here to help," Freeman said. He looked at the little girl and smirked. He took a breath. "Hell, girl, we're your only hope, right now."

Kate struggled with what Freeman said. The little girl pouted. She seemed to be angry, but her struggling eased up.

"We ain't gonna hurt you," Freeman said reaching out to Kaiyote and retrieving the knife he had taken from the girl. "We're jus' here fir a look see," Freeman said, smiling at Kate.

Kate pouted. She looked at Freeman like she wanted to beat him up. Freeman smiled. His partner held the girl firmly by her wrists. She struggled but without success.

"So, we gonna search these wagguns 'n move these bodies. You stay out the way or we gonna hafta tie you up," Freeman said. He paused. "Your choice," Freeman said.

"Let me go," Kate said, angrily.

"Anyone else here alive?" Freeman said in the language only he and Kaiyote spoke.

"Don't think so," The quiet warrior said.

"Think we should tie her up?" Freeman asked.

"She's jus' a baby," The quiet warrior said to Freeman.

"You see this?" He asked, lifting the knife. "If she cut you or me you wouldn't see her as a baby." He grinned. "Maybe she's a baby rattler?"

"She's scared. She lost ev'rythin'," the quiet warrior said.

Freeman shook his head. He looked like he might laugh. He looked to his dark-eyed partner and spoke to the man holding her. Kate listened.

"What you two talking about?" Kate asked, angrily.

Freeman looked at the little girl. "We'll let you go, but if you get in the way we goin' to have to tie you up, but we don't want to do that." He paused. "I don't want to tie up someone who looks like me." He paused again, looking at Kate. "Jus' stay out the way and let us check a few things and then we're gone."

"There's nothin' here," the little girl said.

Freeman looked at the little girl.

"Well?"

"Well? What?"

"Let you go? Or tie you up?"

"Don't tie me up," Kate said, pleadingly.

"Okay," Freeman said and nodded. Freeman looked at his trail mate. The quiet warrior released Kate. Kate shrugged and backed away from the two strangers and towards her mother. She looked at Kaiyote and the oddly placed pistol across his chest and then to Freeman angrily. She glared at the quiet long-haired man wearing a sombrero. She looked back at Freeman who was standing in her family wagon.

Freeman looked back at Kate.

"It's not right that that Injun grabbed me," Kate said, with a grimace.

Freeman smirked at the little girl. The quiet warrior bored, walked away, toward the smoking end of the wagon train.

"Why you with an Injun?"

"He ain't no Injun. He's Kaiyote," Freeman said.

Kate looked at the bearded cowboy and back to the retreating Kaiyote. Freeman stepped to the side and watched as the little girl entered her family's wagon and stopped and sat beside her unmoving mother.

Freeman placed a hand on the heel of his big pistol and watched the little girl sitting next to her dead mother. Freeman leaned on one of the wagon's supporting hoops and scanned the wagon for any conspicuous valuables.

"Anyone else here? Alive?"

Kate did not answer. The little girl just looked at Freeman with all the hate in the world behind her eyes. The dark-eyed cowboy studied the little girl in front of him and nodded.

"I'll let you be, for now," Freeman said. He pursed his lips, thinking what to say. Instead of saying anything.

The cowboy looked left and then right and walked toward the smoking wagon. Freeman rubbed his bearded face at the sight. Freeman walked to the front of the wagon train, rubbing his cheek.

He searched for Kaiyote. He found him at the lead wagon removing a body.

"Hey," Freeman said to his silent partner. "Can you help me?"

The quiet warrior stopped his work and headed to the smoking wagon. At the wagon Kaiyote paused.

"Where's the girl?"

"Back in the waggun," Freeman said.

The quiet warrior nodded.

Freeman pulled up his bandana and set to work. The quiet warrior and Freeman worked trying to remove the bodies before the fire engulfed the entire wagon. The pair dragged out two of the four bodies in the burning wagon. The quiet warrior managed to remove the other two before the fire swallowed up everything. Freeman finished his task and paused to catch his breath and pull down his bandana. The second wagon was a complete loss.

"What now?" The quiet warrior asked with the four bodies on the side of the trail.

"Try to put out the fire 'n make sure it don't spread," Freeman said.

He and Kaiyote kicked dust and shoveled sand up on the burning canvas and sparks. The fire slowly died out.

The quiet warrior went to the lead wagon to search for bodies and valuables.

After catching his breath Freeman went to the lead wagon to help Kaiyote. The pair made quick work of searching the interior of the wagon. There was mostly clothing and furniture inside. There were cooking utensils and pots and pans but nothing of real value. Perhaps the most valuable thing in the lead wagon was a small derringer that Freeman slipped into his jacket, thinking he might sell it the next time he was in a big town. Beside the derringer, there was a large clock wrapped in blankets. Freeman tried to lift it and the clock was heavy.

Freeman found a pair of cowboy boots, but they were too small. He looked to Kaiyote. The quiet warrior lifted a pocket watch on a gold fob. Freeman's eyes widened.

"Where you find that?"

"In this," The quiet warrior said, lifting a small jewel box that was now empty.

"What else you find?"

The quiet warrior showed his hand and the earrings, rings and a necklace in his hand.

"Good job," Freeman said.

The quiet warrior nodded and slipped the jewelry into his buffalo jacket pocket.

"Let's go to the last waggun," Freeman said. He pointed. "Skip the little girl's 'n work our way back."

The quiet warrior and Freeman walked past the smoking husk of a wagon talking in a forgotten language that only they knew, and the tribe Kaiyote came from. The two walked effortlessly to the last wagon of the train. The quiet warrior, the Long-haired rider, was barrel-chested and slightly bowlegged. Freeman was average height but strongly built.

"What you think happened?" Freeman asked.

The quiet warrior looked left and right and then back to Freeman.

"Looked like the wagguns got on this trail. Maybe they got lost? They got caught. They fought," The quiet warrior said. He looked around and nodded.

Freeman looked back toward the slight slope that descended toward the forest on the far side of the trail.

"They were hiding in the woods," Freeman said, scanning the ground. On the ground were dozens of bullet casings. Freeman bent down and picked up a couple of empty bullet casings.

"The men were killed first. Then the women 'n children," The quiet warrior said studying the area.

"Why?" Freeman asked, looking back at the hillside they had come down and the forest on the other side of the winding trail.

The quiet warrior did not speak.

"Tenderfoots?" Freeman asked. The bearded cowboy shook his head.

"Maybe," The quiet warrior said.

"Not too many waggun trains crazy 'nuff to set off on their own," Freeman said.

"Maybe," The quiet warrior said. "Some think they know when they don't."

Freeman nodded. The quiet warrior and Freeman stopped at the last wagon. Freeman looked down the trail that twisted and turned just one hundred yards from where they stood.

"More than four shooters? Right?"

"Look like five or six horses," The quiet warrior said.

"They took a dozen horses, at least," Freeman said.

The quiet warrior nodded and ducked into the last wagon. Freeman followed. The two men rummaged through the interior finding rings and some coins. Freeman slipped the rings he found in his coat's pocket. The two looked around and found a pearl necklace. The two after searching the wagon removed the bodies.

Freeman dragging a body from the same wagon, stopped and noted the bodies inside all had been shot in the back. The men who had tried to defend had been shot multiple times and left on the sides of the trail. The women and children were found in the wagons.

Freeman and Kaiyote searched the remaining wagons and took whatever they thought was valuable. They methodically removed bodies from the wagons after their searches.

"Cowards did this," Freeman said, decidedly.

"Not our people," The quiet warrior said.

Freeman nodded. He seemed suddenly reflective.

"So, what you thinkin' Dead Man?"

Freeman smiled at Kaiyote's words. He scratched his chin and looked on the trail at all the bodies the pair had recovered.

"The problem is...," Freeman said, stopping. "This ain't our bizness," Freeman said looking at Kaiyote. "We jus' 'pose to swoop in, pick up sum trinkets and ride out."

The quiet warrior looked up, curious.

"We jus' being decent," Freeman said, looking at the wagons and the trail.

"You talkin' a lot," The quiet warrior said.

"Yeah," Freeman said with a smile.

"Not goin' to leave her?"

Freeman did not respond. Instead, he looked down the wagon train and rubbed the side of his bearded face.

"It don't seem right, all uv a sudden," Freeman said.

"These your tribe?"

"No," Freeman said.

"But they like you," The quiet warrior said, pointing to Freeman's hair.

Freeman smiled and shook his head. "Tol' you don't know much about how we got here, but I do know we ain't all from the same... tribe," Freeman said.

The quiet warrior looked at the wagon where the little girl was hiding.

"She sort uv look like you," The quiet warrior said.

Freeman shook his head at Kaiyote. He closed his eyes to his silent partner. Freeman stretched and balled his fists. The quiet warrior grinned.

"We cannot fight the air, Dead Man," The quiet warrior said. "We live knowing we will be remembered by the footprints we leave."

Freeman listened and frowned. He looked down at his hands. Freeman chuckled at Kaiyote's attempts to teach the cowboy something.

The dark-eyed, bearded cowboy closed his eyes and tried to take a breath. Freeman stroked his mustache and beard. The quiet warrior looked again back at the last wagon needing to be searched.

"I'll take this last one," Freeman said.

The quiet warrior nodded and headed to the side of the trail to cover the dead that had not been covered.

Freeman entered the tipped over wagon and little had changed when he entered. Kate was still sitting next to her dead mother, holding her hand. Freeman knelt and crab walked into the interior of the wagon

"What do you want?"

"Well, need to get you out uv here," Freeman said. "We're gonna see what we can save, then leave," the cowboy said.

"Leave?"

"Yeah," Freeman said.

Kate looked suddenly confused.

"What?"

"Where will I go?"

"Where were you headed? Before all this?"

"California," Kate said.

Freeman smirked.

"You ever been?"

Freeman shook his head.

"We were headed to... Sacramento. My dad sed there was freedom there," Kate said. She looked from Freeman to her still mother. Freeman looked at the back of the woman riddled with bullet holes. The woman had black raven wing braided hair, pulled back into what would have been two ponytails of braids. The one side was loose and spread into a loose tangle of braids.

"Freedom?" Freeman chuckled. "Don't know what that is. All I know is you can't find it. You have to take it, hol' it and fight to hol' onto it."

Kate looked at the dark-eyed cowboy confused.

Freeman smiled. "You shouldn't be in here," Freeman said, looking at the little girl. "This is not good for you."

Kate frowned.

Freeman kneeled down.

Kate looked at the dark-eyed, rugged cowboy in the Hardee hat. She looked at the blue wool jacket, collared denim shirt, gloves, gun belt and two pistols on his hip and his comfortable cowboy boots.

"Why you here?" Kate looked at Freeman skeptically, all of a sudden. "There ain't nothin' here. This was a freedom train," the little girl said.

"Freedom?"

"Yeah," Kate Rawlins said.

"This is the worse day ever," Freeman said. He rubbed the back of his neck. Freeman looked at the little girl.

Kate looked at Freeman.

"You lost a lot today. I wish I had known my mother," Freeman said. "I didn't get that. All I remember is...bein' a baby and then bein' in the field." He paused. "I can't even remember what my mother looked like. All I remember is pain." Freeman paused. He looked at the little girl. "You lost a lot. But hol' onto the good. Bad memories will fade. Remember the good things."

Kate looked at Freeman, curious.

"What you remember 'bout your mother?"

Freeman did not answer.

"Hol' onto those good memories," Freeman said. "So, first thing, you shouldn't stay in here," Freeman said, with a shake of his head. Freeman reached out his gloved hand to Kate.

Kate did not move.

"The world keeps on spinnin'." Freeman paused. "You got to keep movin' too."

"Where? How?" Kate said, tears welling up in her eyes.

Freeman's forehead crinkled and he looked at the little girl seriously. He twisted his lips, thinking.

"There's an outpost jus' a day's ride from here," Freeman said. "I suppose we can take you there."

"Then what?"

"Let's deal with one thing at a time," Freeman said. "Life usually takes care uv itself."

He reached out his gloved hand again. Kate took it. Freeman pulled her out of the wagon with her bag.

The quiet warrior watched as Kate stepped out of the wagon and stood beside it.

Kate stood just on the outside of her family wagon watching silently.

"I'll be extra careful with your... fam'lee" Freeman said, looking back at Kate.

Kate watched as her mother was carefully removed from the wagon and wrapped in the remains of the wagon's canvas on the side of the trail.

As Freeman finished wrapping Kate's mother the cowboy looked up at the young girl. He studied the smaller version of the woman he had wrapped with her braided wreath of hair, gingham dress and comfortable lace-up boots.

# Chapter 7.

Freeman and Kaiyote
Day One, Kansas territories, 1869

Freeman hesitated, just outside of the little girl's wagon. He wiped his forehead and studied the hillside on one side of the trail and the bushes and trees on the other side of the path. Freeman had so many questions. Where was the trail boss? Did they have a trail boss? Where were the horses? At least two horses for each wagon. Were the horses branded? What was the brand? Did the little girl know the brand?

Standing on the trail, Freeman found he had questions as well. What was he thinking? Why was he even thinking about finding and retrieving the horses from the wagon train? Freeman hesitated. Was this even his fight? Was he willing to get involved in something that had nothing to do with him just because the people looked like him?

Freeman chuckled at the idea. Since he had escaped, he had looked out for only himself. Kaiyote and his people had tried to make him a part of their tribe and in four years he had struggled with the idea. Everything he knew about tribe and family had been turned on its head again and again with the prison masters. They had taught Freeman that nothing had permanence. Nothing lasted, not family, not friends, not life, not anything except death.

So, Freeman thought all this as he leaned against the little girl's wagon.

He paused. He was not in the business of helping others. He was a free man. He was a black man in the Kansas territory with peace and quiet, when loaded, on his hips and when he had the Springfield rifle in his hand there was justice.

Kate watched as Freeman crawled back inside her family's wagon and began to search the wagon for something. Kate looked and watched as Freeman rifled through the belongings of her family.

"What you lookin' for?" Kate asked from the trail.

"Well," Freeman said as he did a rough search of the interior of Kate's family's wagon. "I don't know. Did your family hide away any treasure?"

Kate smiled and laughed.

"Treasure? My father saved all he got to get us out the South," Kate said. "He took us from a plantation to Kansas."

Freeman listened. He studied the little girl.

"The fam'lees on this waggun train had to pay someone to take them from Kansas to California," Freeman said, looking at the little girl. "So, there had to be money somewhere."

"Why you askin' all this stuff?"

"Because nobody does anythin' fir nothin'," Freeman said. "That's lesson number one."

Kate listened. She frowned. "What you want?"

"What ev'ryone wants in this nation," Freeman said. He paused, looking at the little girl leaning into the wagon.

Kate did not know the two strangers or the man who said they were there to help. She was suddenly confused. Were they there to help? Were they just looking for things to steal?

"My family didn't have no treasure," Kate said, stepping into the wagon where her mother had recently laid.

The dark-eyed, bearded cowboy looked at the little girl and studied her and the interior of the wagon. There were pots and pans, clothes, shoes, boots and something that looked like beans and potatoes spilled in the wagon.

"When you and your family got to California," Freeman said, smiling without emotion. He paused. He smiled. "Freed prisoners or not your family needed money to stake a claim. So, did you see it?"

"See it?"

"Yeah, someone on this train had to have some money to pay or stake a claim," Freeman said.

Kate shook her head, confused. She felt tears welling up inside. The little girl pouted and looked down at where her mother had laid.

This man was trying to make a profit from the death of her family. Kate instantly did not trust Freeman. She refused to allow the man to make her cry.

The little girl looked up and toward Freeman the bearded cowboy with the two guns on his hips, sitting across from her. She tried to understand why he had come. She also found herself trying to decide if she could trust him or the Silent dark-eyed warrior with him. Freeman's talking about money that he believed was hidden somewhere on the wagon train made her smile. The idea of her family or anyone on the wagon train having a secret stash of treasure was comical.

"Why you smilin'?"

Kate shook her head.

Freeman looked at the little girl dressed like her dead mother and shook his head. He rummaged through the topsy turvy wagon looking for jewelry or gold. After a quick and rough search Freeman looked at Kate Rawlins with a stern look.

"Okay," Freeman said looking at the little girl. "If there's money here in this wagon train, you don't need it anymore 'n I do."

"Well, we didn't bring any... money. At least, I don't know anythin' 'bout no money," Kate said. "All I got is my clothes on my back and this bag for my clothes."

Freeman stopped his search for valuables in the wagon and studied the little girl and her clothes bag. Freeman reached for the clothes bag. Kate grabbed it instinctively.

"What you hidin' in there?"

"Nothin'," Kate said.

Freeman opened the bag and looked inside. He rummaged through the clothes and stopped frustrated. He climbed to his feet and stepped out and onto the trail.

Kaiyote seeing movement looked back at the two now on the trail.

Freeman walked away from the wagon and toward Kaiyote.

"I don't know what to do," Kate said, suddenly sitting outside of her wagon and looking at the bodies of her family lying on the shoulder of the trail.

Freeman looked at Kate and the small clothes bag.

"What are we goin' to do?" The quiet warrior asked.

"Leave," Freeman said.

"What about the girl?" The quiet warrior asked.

Freeman shook his head. The cowboy looked away.

"Four summers you shared our tents," The quiet warrior said with a shake of his head. "And still you have learnt nothin'."

Freeman looked at Kaiyote curiously.

"We are all connected, Wearing Dead Man's Clothes," The quiet warrior said.

Freeman winced. "You know I like to be called: Freeman."

"You lived wit us four summers, Freeman, 'n learnt nothin'," The quiet warrior said.

"I learnt lots," Freeman said.

The tall and noble Kaiyote looked away from Freeman and toward the horizon. The cowboy followed Kaiyote's look to the horizon. A single bird winged its way across the sky.

Freeman thought about all that Kaiyote had said as he stood on the trail and near Kate's family wagon.

"You 'n I tribe, Wearing Dead Man's Clothes," The quiet warrior said. "We look out fir each other. We don't do that because we made to. We do it because we wish to." The quiet warrior looked at the wagon where Kate was sitting. "This girl has nothin'. She like you when I found you. We brought you to our tribe... we must add her... to our tribe," Kaiyote said. He spoke in the ancient language. The quiet warrior looked at Freeman. "We help those in our tribe."

Freeman reluctantly nodded.

"You goin' to save her?"

"Save her?" Freeman said as he patted his horse's neck. "I don't know no one that can save her from what's ahead?"

"What's ahead?"

"The same things ahead fir all us, a hard road," Freeman said.

"You can be like a day wit'out sun'," the quiet warrior said.

Freeman looked at Kaiyote and then to Kate. He shrugged his shoulders.

"We could put her out her misery right now or leave her 'n know she won't survive more than a few days alone, if not end up disappearin' 'n never bein' heard of again."

Freeman looked at Kaiyote The quiet warrior stared evenly at Freeman. Freeman rubbed at his bearded cheek. He adjusted his Hardee hat on his head. There was a long pause.

"So? You decide to protect her?"

"I can't commit to that," Freeman said. "I ain't her daddy," Freeman added.

"You don't have to be her daddy to want to protect her," the quiet warrior said.

Kaiyote having finished his speech and looked behind Freeman. Freeman looked back and there by his side was Kate, with her ring of braids above her ears and her clothes bag.

"What about me?"

Freeman blinked finding Kate so close.

Kate looked at the two men talking in a language she did not understand.

"We're leavin'," Freeman said to the little girl.

The quiet warrior walked to his horse and mounted it.

"What 'bout me?"

"We can drop you at that outpost I tol' you 'bout," Freeman said as he walked to his horse.

Kate was suddenly trying to keep step with Freeman. She was suddenly beside Freeman and his horse.

"Where's the outpost?" Kate asked, looking back at all the bodies covered in canvas.

"About a day's ride from here," Freeman said as he put his foot in the stirrup.

Kate thought and, in that moment, she pouted, and her eyebrows pushed toward each other, and a line appeared between them.

Freeman smiled and looked at Kaiyote. The quiet warrior, stoic generally, smiled at Freeman.

"First outpost?"

"Or we can leave you here," Freeman said.

"Hey," Kate said, putting a small hand on Freeman's boot to get his attention. "Weaver had a gun like the red man," she said.

"Why did she look at me?"

"She sed the waggun boss had a gun like yours," Freeman said.

The quiet warrior nodded.

"You gonna look for this boss with my gun?"

"No," Freeman said. "I figure we can drop her off at Stratton's before we head into the territories."

The quiet warrior nodded.

He shook his head. He reached down to the little girl with an open hand. "You coming? Or staying?"

# Chapter 8.

Kate
Nevada-Utah Territory, 1877


Kate smiled as the wagon bumped along on the trail. Missus Lawson was an oval faced woman wearing a scarf and two long braided pigtails that day. She was usually dressed in denim. On her feet were comfortable boots. By her side was Charlotte, the youngest. Charlotte, like Elisabeth, had their mother's oval face and almond shaped eyes.

"You okay?" Elisabeth Lawson asked.

Kate blinked and shook her head.

"I'm fine," Kate lied.

Elisabeth and Kate became quick friends as the wagon train pulled away and onto the trail again. They had left Oregon behind and were now on the edge of Utah. Nevada had been lumpy from the start and the undulating nature of the trail never let up. There were few moments in the trek across Nevada that did not offer a hill or upgrade.

"When we reach Utah things should be a little flatter," Elisabeth said to Kate and her brothers.

The trip was supposed to take no more than four months.

Kate did not pack much. She brought her clothes bag that she had brought west when she climbed on the wagon train with Thaddeus Monroe and the well-armed wagoners. She also brought the belly buster, and the gun and gun belt Freeman gave her for protection. She had two dresses and trousers in her bag.

Kate dressed in a fabric jacket, vest and skirt. On her feet were cowboy boots. Under her jacket she hid the Colt revolver.

The wagon train rolled along eastward. The boys were always entertaining. Ricky was always the one with the most energy in the morning. He was the youngest and seemed to wake up ready for anything. Randolph, the middle, was always a little slow in the morning but after lunch seemed to get his second wind and was a dynamo until the wagon stopped for the night. RJ,

Reginald Junior, the oldest, was friendly and polite but always pensive.

Generally, the wagon was a free for all in the mornings. Missus Lawson, to maintain her sanity, made them take a nap after lunch. Of course, the three boys by lunch were tired from all their rough housing. Their nap was a welcome relief for Elisabeth, Kate and the boy's mother.

After lunch one of the boys would ask for a story before their nap. Elisabeth or her mother usually offered to tell a short story to entertain and calm the boys down for their nap. Infrequently, Kate was asked to tell a naptime story.

This was the Lawson wagon routine.

Usually, Kate sat in the rear of the Lawson wagon and usually just watched as the boys rough housed and played games until they tuckered themselves out. She would listen to Elisabeth talking about all the things she would do when she arrived in Kansas and got to see her cousins and uncle.

Missus Lawson, always calm and collected in the rear of the wagon would braid Elisabeth's or Kate's hair. She had strong hands and nimble fingers. With Elisabeth's hair divided and combed out she was able to corn row braid half her head in a few hours. She was done, if she began after feeding the boys and little Charlotte before lunch.

"What you gonna do when you get to Kansas?" Elisabeth asked.

Kate did not answer. She had no real answer. She wanted to tell Elisabeth the truth, but she hesitated. She looked at the three young boys in the rear of the covered wagon sleeping in a pile of heads, legs and arms and then to Elisabeth's mother who was quietly sleeping now that her little Charlotte was sleeping. Kate looked to Elisabeth and shrugged her shoulders as an answer.

Elisabeth looked at Kate, curiously. The younger girl did not smile, instead she looked concerned. Elisabeth leaned forward and closer to Kate.

"You think you're gonna find this cowboy of yours?"

"I hope to," Kate said, quietly.

Dressed in her brother's blanket jacket, plaid collared shirt, T-shirt, jeans and cowboy boots Kate looked at Elisabeth Lawson. They had been on the Oregon trail and headed to Kansas for nearly a month. Kate wanted to tell Elisabeth that she was on the run from the law. She wanted to tell the talkative girl who seemed to have an endless amount of questions and thoughts about everything that she had shot a man who tried to manhandle her, but Kate remained silent.

She felt that opening that door might lead to opening another door and another. Kate took a deep breath and looked at Elisabeth with her hair in a distinct fishbone cornrow pattern that flowed back to the nape of her neck and fell into a dozen finger long braids touching the top of her shoulders. The younger girl sensing something was wrong looked at Kate.

"What is it?" Elisabeth asked.

Kate pressed her lips tightly together to suppress the urge to tell someone else what she was hiding.

"Kate," Elisabeth said, quietly, reaching out and placing a hand on Kate's. "You can tell me anything."

Kate looked at Elisabeth and weighed the girl's words on the scale inside of her head.

Could she trust Elisabeth? Could she believe that Elisabeth would not tell her mother what Kate said? Worse, Kate thought, what if Elisabeth told her father?

For a long moment Kate did not speak. It seemed, at that moment, as if Kate was having an internal struggle the likes of which Elisabeth had never seen. Kate wondered if she could tell Elisabeth a little bit of what was going on and that would be enough to ease her mind.

"Don't worry," Elisabeth said.

"Okay, you know that my family and our wagon train was ambushed?"

Elisabeth nodded.

"Well, I wanted to kill the men that ambushed us," Kate said, emotional.

"I understand that," Elisabeth said.

"Do you?"

"Well, I understand that you wanted to hurt the men that hurt and killed your family," Elisabeth said, slowly. Her words were measured. It seemed as if Elisabeth was walking on eggshells, suddenly. "I can't imagine. I mean, I cannot imagine how you felt for the loss of your family and all the people on the wagon train," Elisabeth said, correcting herself.

There was a long silence that built and Elisabeth fidgeted on the wagon bench but did not dare speak.

"Well, I looked fir the wagon master and," Kate said, only to pause. She looked away from Elisabeth, suddenly unsure if she should let the younger girl in on her secrets.

"Well?"

"I wanted to kill him," Kate said through gritted teeth.

Elisabeth nodded.

Kate fell silent.

"Did you ever find him?"

Kate chewed on her lower lip. She closed her eyes. Instantly, she saw the wagon master on the dirt in the middle of street, bleeding.

*Thomas Weaver, if she was to believe her own eyes, was the first man Kate killed. She was nine years old at the time. Freeman, the dark and dangerous cowboy, had said different, but Kate did not believe the cowboy. He had lied to her before. So, to tell her that she had not killed Thomas Weaver, even though he had handed her a pistol and urged her to kill the dying man, and she had pulled the trigger on the big horse pistol and felt the kickback of the gun as it bucked in her hand. The thunderous explosion, so close to her ear, deafened Kate. Suddenly, unexpectedly, all of her other senses went into overdrive after pulling the trigger of the pistol. The hint of gun powder wafted through the air, in her memories and her hand tingled like she had frostbite.*

*Yet, it had been the nine-year-old looking down at the place where Thomas Weaver had been lying bleeding, already shot by Freeman earlier. Before Kate had pulled the trigger, he was futilely reaching for a gun Freeman had placed just out of reach, like a cat toying with a mouse. After Kate pulled the trigger Thomas Weaver lay in the same general position but unmoving. He had been alive one second and suddenly he was no longer alive.*

*"Now, don't start thinkin' you killed Weaver," Freeman said. He had his own pistol out and in hand. He smiled and took the derringer from Kate. He smiled and later returned the small handgun to the nine-year-old.*

*"You ain't a killer Kate," Freeman said. "Don't let this life get ahold uv you. It will never let you go."*

*Kate looked at the dead man at her feet.*

*"Forget this," Freeman said. "Erase this. Don't look at this 'n let it haunt you. Believe me girl, this life ain't fir you."*

*Kate nodded.*

*"You got a pass today. No blood on your hands," Freeman said, holstering his pistol. The dark cowboy looked out into the seemingly unending plains. "The plains has a way uv balancin' things, by 'n by," Freeman said.*

Kate blinked and found Elisabeth looking at her, waiting for an answer.

"No," Kate lied to Elisabeth. "I never found him. I never killed him," Kate said, disheartened. "That's my burden."

# Chapter 9.

Kate

End of May, Nebraska territory, 1877

Weeks passed. The wagon train made its way across the Utah frontier and in the days that morphed into weeks saw a dozen wagons heading west. For a week straight Kate and the Lawsons and the following wagons watched as a dozen covered wagons past them.

Then one day, Ezekiel jostled Mister Lawson nodded. Ezekiel tapped RJ.

"What?" RJ said in a growl.

"Look," Mister Lawson said, lifting his chin to the wagons passing.

Ezekiel, the gunner, holding a rifle on his lap, looked in the direction Mister Lawson gestured. The boys were curious and leaned forward behind their father and cousin. Elisabeth leaned on RJ's shoulder and looked. She pulled Kate behind her and the family all looked.

It was as Kate got close to Elisabeth and she and RJ pointed to the covered wagon. Kate narrowed her focus and stared at the covered wagon passing with a flapping side loose enough to see inside. Kate was surprised to see the dark brown faces of three women dressed in blue checked tops. On their heads were scarves. They looked frightened, as if they had been spirited away from somewhere and only now awoke and realized their predicament.

Were these slaves? Were settlers taking slaves west? Was there some place between Nebraska and Oregon where slaves were still enslaved?

"Kate?" Elisabeth said, snapping Kate out of her reverie. The teen looked at the oval-faced girl with the small eyes and teeth and smiled, awkwardly. "I said are you coming? Or are you staying in the wagon? We jus' made it to Clem Deaver's."

Kate blinked and tried to shake the memories which seemed to be all around her suddenly. She rubbed at her eyes, tired. Kate looked out the rear of the wagon and took in the arid terrain that made up the seemingly endless space of Clem Deaver's ranch, which was located in Sands Hill.

If they were at Clem Deaver's ranch they were only ten miles from Brownlee, then this was the first place that Monroe and the wagon train stopped as they left Garrett and Kansas.

"Welcome," someone said and suddenly the wagon was in action.

"Clem, always a good sight to see after a long ride on the trail," Reginald Lawson said with his low growl. Ezekiel, the constant figure on the buckboard beside Elisabeth's father stood up and stretched before climbing down and disappearing.

The boys, excited for a stop and an opportunity to stretch their legs were already climbing out of the rear of the wagon against the protest of her mother and older sister. Kate smiled at the mass exit of the Lawson boys.

"There's no use in trying to stop 'em," Missus Lawson said with a smile, lifting Charlotte who was watching Kate and Elisabeth.

Elisabeth chuckled. Kate nodded.

"We're getting out here," Missus Lawson said. "Stretch your legs and get some food. Maybe we get a little rest before heading to Kansas."

Elisabeth stood and watched as her mother moved to the rear of the wagon. Ezekiel was there and helping his aunt and baby cousin from the wagon. Elisabeth moved to the rear of the wagon and looked back.

"You coming?"

Kate looked around the wagon and realized she had been with the Lawsons for months. The journey was never dull or boring. They rode the bumpy roads all day and until the sunset. At sunset the wagons would pull off the trail and make camp. They would eat a good dinner and talk through the night. The wagons were driven by freedmen with hopes and dreams of land ownership.

Kate got to know all the people in the wagon, but she did not go beyond their names. There were nearly thirty people making their way east. Six families were headed east.

There were the Carters, led by Mister George Carter. He was a bearded pot-bellied man that looked like a friendly type. There were the Adams, led by Fred and Mary Adams. Fred was a taciturn and reflective man, who did not speak much. The voice of the Adams was Mary Adams. She was an apple cheeked woman with her hair hidden beneath a scarf and conductor's cap and wearing a gun on her hip.

The other three families were the Sawyers, the Rices and the Hills. The leader of the Sawyers was Paul Sawyer. Sawyer was the wagon train cook. His dream was to start a cook house back in Kansas. The Rices were led by Dennis Rice. Dennis Rice had a gold tooth and was a man interested in business opportunities. The Hills were led by Thomas Hill. Thomas Hill was a giant of a man. He intended to start a stable when they returned to Kansas.

In the Lawson family were made up of four boys under the hand of Mister Lawson. The three young Lawson boys were made to stay in the rear of the wagon. From the time Kate climbed into the rear of the covered wagon until she finally climbed out in Coffeyville they were always playing, wrestling, or sometimes fighting.

Seated next to Mister Lawson was the dour and extremely serious Ezekiel. Ezekiel was Mister Lawson's nephew. He sat on the buckboard next to the stocky Mister Lawson riding shotgun. In the twenty-one days Ezekiel spoke a dozen words to Kate. He was a chocolate-colored boy of fifteen or sixteen with broad features, big, thoughtful eyes and a pinched, reflective look. The most distinctive characteristic of Ezekiel was a two-inch scar that creased his broad forehead.

Unlike the Lawson boys Ezekiel wore a gun belt and carried a shotgun. He was not talkative and seemed always in deep thought. Mister Lawson's nephew seemed devoted to watching the horizon for any trouble.

"We're in Nebraska," Elisabeth said.

Nebraska? It was in this state that Kate realized that Freeman would not be riding up and rescuing her and taking her back wherever he and Kaiyote were headed. The wagon train was bumping along the wide Oregon trail away from Kansas and toward the west.

# **Chapter 10.**

Freeman and Kaiyote
Day One, Kansas territory, 1869


Freeman and Kaiyote mounted their horses and prepared to ride away from the ruins of the wagon train with Kate and her clothes bag on the back on Freeman's horse. Kate's clothes bag was two feet high and a foot wide. Once on the horse, Kate tried to balance herself and her clothes bag.

Freeman waited patiently. He looked at the little girl adjusting herself and then to Kaiyote, who seemed silently amused. Freeman watched silently from the saddle.

Kate finally placed her bag between her and Freeman and reached out and grabbed the edge of the cowboy's wool coat.

"You ready to go?" Freeman asked.

Kate adjusted herself on the back of the black quarter horse and nodded.

"Is this your horse?"

Freeman looked back over his shoulder at the little girl with the circle of braids and big eyes.

"What's its name?"

"Shadow," Freeman said, climbing onto his horse's back.

The quiet warrior shook his head and tapped his horse, a painted palomino. The quiet warrior wheeled his horse around and moved down the trail in the opposite direction the wagon train was headed. Freeman kicked at his horse and turned it to follow Kaiyote.

Kate pouted. She looked at the back of the cowboy and then to the quiet, long-haired Rider.

"Where did that trail, we were on go?"

"Don't know," Freeman said.

"You never been that way?"

Freeman did not respond.

The trio rode on quietly as the hill prevented their easy exit to the right. If there was an emergency Kate imagined the only way out was through the brush and woods on the other side of the trail.

"Is this trail safe?"

Neither Freeman nor the other man spoke.

"How you know they'll help me at that outpost?" Kate asked.

Freeman did not respond. He and Kaiyote rode side by side. As they reached a bend in the trail the pair rode on. At the first fork in the trail Freeman spoke.

"We'll turn up ahead," Freeman said.

Kate nodded, looking back at the last two wagons now with just strips of canvas covering their interiors as the trio moved slowly past and away.

"Mister Freeman? Where you meet your Injun?"

"In the territories," Freeman said. "His people took me in. They wanted to make me..." Freeman shook his head. "We travel in the same direction."

Kate listened and nodded.

"My dad sed there's freedom in California. How far is that from here?"

"A lot farther than I'm willing to go," Freeman said.

"How far?"

"Don't know," Freeman said. Freeman did not answer.

The quiet warrior looked at Freeman and the little girl and smiled. Freeman lowered his head rather than speaking.

"How far is the outpost?"

Freeman rolled his eyes.

"You think we'll make it before the sun goes down?"

The three rode down the trail and after about ten minutes onto a wider trail. The trail was two wagons wide, by Kate's estimation. Behind them was the trail where the six wagons had turned off and onto a one wagon wide trail.

Freeman looked at Kaiyote and spoke in the language that only they knew.

"She asks a lot uv questions?"

"She asks too many questions," Freeman said.

The quiet warrior nodded.

"You know this was your idea," Freeman said.

"You didn't have to take her, Wearing Dead Man's Clothes," The quiet warrior said, with a smile.

"You made me take her," Freeman said. "And you know I like you to call me: Freeman."

"Freeman? We all freemen," The quiet warrior said.

"But," Freeman said, flustered by Kaiyote's logic.

"Deadman freeman," The quiet warrior said with a smile. "I think that is better."

Freeman shook his head.

"What you talkin' about?" Kate asked Freeman and Kaiyote.

Freeman did not respond.

"Mister Freeman that's not nice?" Kate asked, holding the cowboy's wool jacket for stability. "You should talk so I understand."

Freeman looked over his shoulder and exhaled.

"Listen," Freeman said. "We're takin' you to that outpost. The sun is workin' against us. We goin' to ride fir a few hours. We ridin' into the setting sun. We'll stop before the sun sets 'n then camp out. 'Til then I need you to be quiet," Freeman said.

Kate took in what Freeman said.

Freeman looked to Kaiyote. The quiet warrior smiled.

"I never talk that much about anything," Freeman said to Kaiyote in their unique language.

"Children ask lots uv questions," The quiet warrior said to Freeman is his native tongue.

"That's the reason I didn't have no kids," Freeman said.

"That's not the reason," Kaiyote said, knowing the truth. He spoke in his tribe's ancient language.

The two scarred and battle-weary warriors exchanged a quiet stare. Freeman had told Kaiyote of what little he remembered of his growing up in prison. Kaiyote and all of his tribe could not imagine a place as horrible as the prison Freeman had escaped.

"Why do I have to be quiet?" Kate asked.

"I need to think," Freeman said. "We don't know who's on these trails. We have to be careful," Freeman said.

"You were jus' talkin' with... the Injun," Kate said.

"Kaiyote," Freeman said, correcting Kate.

"Kai-Yotay?" Kate asked. "What does that mean?"

"Kaiyote" Freeman said, his annoyance growing.

"You were jus' talkin' to Kaiyote," Kate said.

"That's different," Freeman said.

"How?"

The cowboy gritted his teeth. He took a deep breath and looked left to Kaiyote who seemed silently amused.

"We were tryin' to figure out how to," Freeman said, thinking. "We need to figure who we can hand you off to so that you safe?"

"Safe?"

"Yep. Some riders aren't always... friendly," Freeman said. "Findin' you out on the trail would be somethin' they would kill for." The cowboy quieted. "So, we have to be careful."

"Careful?"

"And quiet," Freeman said.

"Quiet," Kate said and nodded.

The trio continued down the wider trail with the great plains to their right which extended as far as the horizon without deviation. There were trees scattered along the trail but not too many close to the wagon trails. The trail was relatively smooth and well maintained. The trail rose and fell ten minutes after the three emerged from the smaller path. For the next hour the trail rose and fell but nothing that seemed too taxing for the horses.

Exiting the rolling small hills, the three turned onto a more serpentine part of the trail which afforded more shade on the right side of the trail. For nearly two hours the trio rode on the two-wagon wide trail running into no one so late in the day.

"You sed people would kill fir me. Why?"

Freeman did not respond.

"Why?"

"This place is mostly hard legs 'n hard men," Freeman said, reluctantly. "There's all these settlements, but there ain't a lot uv women out here."

A few minutes later Kate asked another question.

"Where are all the women?"

"We're on the edge uv the territories," Freeman said in answer. "It's a tough place. Ain't too many women want to rough it. So, the hard legs come out first. Then the women."

"So, ain't too many soft legs," Kate said.

Freeman nodded.

"Where the fam'lees?"

"If we see anyone it'll be closer to the outpost. The men playin' like men buildin' 'n killin' 'n buildin' to take land. There's some tryin' to make it attractive fir women to come this way. But there ain't many women here. The ones here are protected 'n spoken fir.  So, you valuable." Freeman stopped talking.

He took a few moments to think and added, "We're easily half a day's ride from the outpost." Freeman paused. "We goin' to stop 'n camp. No one wants to be caught at night on the plains."

"Why?"

"Robbers, bandits 'n badmen," Freeman said. He paused. "Bears, buffaloes 'n whatnot."

The three rode down the trail and climbed a small rise to reveal a break in the plains. To the right of the three was the plains seemed to stretch out forever. To the left were the speckled outcropping of trees that thickened as they moved toward the hills that seemed to create a natural border.

"What's on the other side uv those hills?"

"Mountains," Freeman said.

Kaiyote looked toward the hills.

"That's where Kaiyote's people stay," Freeman said.

"In the mountains?"

"No, in the plains, on the other side uv the mountains," Freeman said.

"What's in the plains?"

"Ev'rything. Buffalo. Bear. Antelope. Wolves 'n ev'rythin' else," Freeman said.

"We headin' that way?"

"No," Freeman said.

The trail they were on seemed to go on westward into the rolling hills ahead. To the left of the trail trees thickened and formed a thick forest which led toward the foothills. The trail they were on seemed to go on westward into the rolling hills ahead. To the left of the trail trees thickened and formed a thick forest which led toward the foothills.

'Where's the outpost?"

Freeman looked at Kaiyote and his silent partner only smiled.

The trio rode on as Kate asked a hundred questions that Freeman sporadically answered.

"We need to make camp," Freeman said to Kaiyote.

The quiet warrior nodded.

With about an hour of sunlight left Freeman and Kaiyote pulled off the trail and into the thinning trees. The quiet warrior led the way as the pair weaved their horses away from the trail. About ten minutes later Kaiyote stopped and looked to Freeman.

"There's a stream not too far away," The quiet warrior said.

"Okay, we'll camp here," Freeman said.

The quiet warrior climbed off his horse and walked deeper into the thickening forest. The quiet warrior shook his head and walked toward the stream.

"Where's he going?"

Freeman slid Kate off his horse. He dismounted and led the two horses to a tree with low branches and tied them there.

Kate watched silently.

"How did you learn Injun?"

"Injun?"

"You know, talk like him?"

"I ran into Kaiyote 'n his scoutin' party when I was runnin' from some prisoner catchers. I rode into the plains 'n they took me in," Freeman said as he and the quiet and ever observant brave began to set up camp. "I thought they was tryin' to make me a prisoner, at first. They had two other freedmen in their tribe. Those two taught me how to talk."

Kate frowned, confused.

"Wait. There were other slaves in Kaiyote's tribe?"

"Yep," Freeman nodded. "They were accepted 'n seen as regular members." Freeman smiled at the idea. "Whistling Bird 'n Tall Wolf had run off 'n been found by Kaiyote's people before me. They liked livin' with Kaiyote's people. I did too, for a while, then decided I needed to wander." Freeman chuckled at the thought. "Kaiyote decided to come along."

The camp was near a stream. Freeman and the stoic brave had picked a spot that was off the trail and hidden enough to protect them while sleeping.

"So, do you know ev'rything he's sayin'?"

"Yep," Freeman said with a smile. He paused. He added, "Mostly."

"Can you teach me?"

Freeman chuckled.

"Okay, listen you are with us, for now. We all pull our weight. So, you feed the horses. You give them water and create the fire ring 'n then gather up some firewood. That's your job with us."

Kate looked at the cowboy curiously.

"What are you doin' while I do that?"

"Protectin' you 'n gettin' the fire started," Freeman said. "Got to make sure we ain't on an animal trail, since we close to water." Freeman paused. "I also watch out fir baddies hidin' 'n waitin' fir easy pickins." Freeman rubbed at his shoulder absently, having taken off his horse's saddle and brushed him down. Freeman placed his Dragoon and Springfield rifle on the side of the saddle. With just a pistol on his hip Freeman walked to his silent partner's palomino and stroked the horse's neck.

"Easy, fella," Freeman said.

He reached under the horse, unbuckled the saddle, and took it from his trail partner's horse. He walked the saddle to where he had placed his own and deposited it there. He walked back to the palomino and wiped the horse down. He took the blanket after he was done and placed the saddle blanket on top of his partner's saddle.

Kate watched Freeman as he cared for the horses. She placed her clothes bag near the two saddles. Kate gathered rocks and created half of the fire ring.

Freeman watched the trail. He checked his pistols and bullets. He also watched as Kate went about doing her chores.

"Hey?" Kate said, waving her hands. "What do I feed the horses?"

"There's some grain in the side saddle."

After feeding the horses Kate set to finishing the fire ring.

"Is this big 'nuff fir the fire ring?"

Freeman studied Kate's handiwork. The little girl's fire ring was a little smaller than Freeman wanted.

"When you build a fire ring the easiest thing to do is think in threes. Three steps across is a good fire ring," Freeman said.

"Three uv my steps? Or three uv your steps?"

"You decide," Freeman said with a reluctant smile.

"Think I could do your job?" Kate asked measuring out her fire ring.

Freeman smiled and laughed.

Just then the warrior returned from the stream with fish. He paused finding Freeman laughing.

"What you laughin' about?" The brooding warrior asked. He spoke in an ancient language, a language that sounded like singing.

"Girl thinks she can do my job," Freeman said checking his pistol. There was a comfortableness with Freeman and his pistols. In his hand, the Colt Model 1860 seemed an extension of Freeman. Freeman rolled the Colt's cylinder along his left sleeve, listening to the revolver's mechanics click from chamber to chamber with a contented smile. After allowing the revolver to complete its rotation Freeman released the cylinder and made sure all the bullets were in good shape.

Freeman holstered his Colt and drew out the Dragoon. He methodically inspected his second pistol. He rolled the Dragoon's cylinder as he had done with the Colt. Freeman holstered the heavier Dragoon and looked at his usually quiet trail partner.

Kaiyote looked around the camp. "Maybe she can."

"Funny," Freeman said.

Kaiyote smiled.

"She thinks I can teach her to speak to you," Freeman said.

The brave smiled at the idea. He looked at Kate finishing the fire ring and piling the dry kindling in the center. He looked back at Freeman and nodded.

"Are you?"

"What?"

"Gonna teach her," The curious brave asked as he began to gut and clean the fish.

"Teach her?"

Kaiyote smiled.

"I'm not a teacher," Freeman said.

"We all teach, Deadman," The dark-eyed brave said with a slanted smile as he cleaned the fish for the camper's dinner. "Some want to teach. Some teach wit'out knowin'."

With the camp set up and the quiet warrior back from foraging, Kate marveled at the seeming simplicity of the two men in the camp. They did not speak much. They signaled each other and made head gestures but little more. Kate imagined the pair had been friends for a long time.

The cowboy knelt and started a small campfire from the sticks gathered by Kate and surrounded by the rocks the little girl had found and used to create the fire ring.

While the quiet warrior cooked a camp stew of fish, vegetables and berries Kate went to change. She took her clothing bag and removed some of her clothes from inside the bag.

"This will be an in'trestin' night," The quiet warrior said.

"Yeah," Freeman said. "You take first watch?"

The quiet warrior smiled and nodded his head.

"When we get to the outpost things are goin' to get more in'trestin'," Freeman said.

"I know," The quiet warrior said. "You know they will want her. She's young 'n strong. Are you sure you want to drop her off there?"

"It's the only choice," Freeman said. "We can't take her wit us 'n we can't take her where she wants to go. We have to keep movin' west 'n away from Coffeyville 'n the Robinsons."

"They ain't followin' us no more. I think we lost them," The quiet warrior said.

"We can't take her with us, is my point," Freeman said. "We can't take her to where she wants to go," he added, looking back toward the trail.

"Where she want to go?"

"It don't matter," Freeman said, frustrated. "We can't take her there."

"The outpost is not good place," Kaiyote said. He spoke in the ancient language. "They don't like my kind there 'n they only accept you because they're scared uv you," the quiet warrior said.

"I tol' you before, only Stratton and Madison matter there. They won't bother you long as I'm 'round. Anyway, we jus' get in 'n find someone to take the girl off'n our hands 'n get out," Freeman said.

"But the banker tol' us not to come back," The quiet warrior said.

"The banker? The Suttons? Duncan 'n Harold Sutton? Blowhards. Drunks," Freeman said, reminding his trail partner. "They prob'bly won't even remember. Or they won't be there."

The quiet warrior smirked.

"You don't have to go. You can sit this one out," Freeman said. "Jus' plannin' to find Stratton 'n trade in some trinkets 'n try and find someone to take the girl off our hands. The toughest part is contactin' Madison to pick up those dead bodies." Freeman stopped and looked at his silent partner. "There might even be a reward. Problem is, if the sheriff is on the moneyman's side 'n they gets jumpy things can go bad real quick."

Kaiyote shook his head.

"But the Suttons won't be there. The moneyman won't notice us," Freeman said.

Kaiyote shook his head again.

"That's a night 'n a day, if that," Freeman said, with a slight smile.

"The problem is...," Kaiyote began.

Freeman raised a hand. The dark-eyed, bearded cowboy did not want to hear of the problems.

"We can't have bad luck all the time. No card deck is filled with aces or spades," Freeman said.

"We make our own luck," Kaiyote said.

"Sometimes that's our only choice," Freeman said.

The quiet warrior nodded at the idea.

# Chapter 11.

Freeman and Kaiyote
Day One, Kansas Territory, 1869

The sun had set. The darkness was all around them. The trees protected the horses and the trio from prying eyes. In the trees appeared eyes of nocturnal animals. The only light came from the small fire in the fire ring.

"You know white man don't like me?" The quiet warrior asked. He spoke in an ancient language, a language that sounded like singing.

"What you two talking about?" Kate asked.

"The outpost," Freeman said, realizing that Kate was nearby. "Doesn't matter," Freeman said, sitting on a tree limb that separated the fire ring from the sleeping part of the camp. The log also was used as a makeshift seat where Freeman and the quiet warrior sat and ate.

"How long you live wit Injuns?"

"What? Why?"

"I was curious," Kate said.

Freeman studied the little girl with the band of braids.

"Four years," Freeman said, looking at the little girl dressed in trousers. "Did your people hire someone to take you to California?"

"I think so," Kate said, surprised at the question. She paused, thinking. Kate looked at Kaiyote and then Freeman. "There was a man on the waggun train they called: Tom Weaver. He was in charge."

Freeman nodded.

"Do you have an Injun name?" Kate asked.

Freeman shrugged his shoulders.

Freeman looked at Kate, unsure. "What did Weaver look like?"

"Tall, yellow, curly hair, crooked teeth," Kate said. "Pointy nose, big eyes," she added. Kate paused.

"Okay," Freeman said, with a smile. "That's pretty good."

The night creeped in and suddenly it was dark and creatures comfortable in the darkness prowled.

"Are there lots uv wild animals out here?" Kate asked. Kate continued. "I think the strangest thing I ever saw on the trip was a porcupine."

Freeman did not answer, instead he looked at the campfire and the quiet warrior on the other side of the flames.

After eating the camp stew of fish and herbs and sitting around Kate started to get tired.

"Can you tell me a campfire story?"

Freeman looked across the fire and exhaled, knowing that if he didn't speak Kate would keep talking.

"Okay," Freeman said. "You may have heard this one, but it's the only campfire story I know."

"Tell me," Kate said. "I doubt that I've heard it. All the stories I've ever heard came from my mom or dad."

Freeman raised his hands in surrender.

"Okay, here's my campfire story. There was this prison 'n this prison was controlled by unhappy monsters playin' like men. The fake men were always angry 'n hated the prisoners they stole 'n forced to work fir them. So, the fakers killed the male prisoners everyday fir the littlest reason. The monsters beat 'n raped the prisoners, but the prisoners refused to die. The prisoners refused to become the monsters that controlled the prison. At least, most prisoners thought that way. Now, there were some prisoners the monsters, the fake men, picked 'n made believe they were special. Those weak-minded prisoners thought they were better than the other prisoners because the fakers didn't beat them as much. They were raped. They were killed. They were mistreated, but the weak-minded prisoners, who were in the same prison, thought they were better 'n luckier than the other prisoners.

"The fakers loved dividin' the prisoners. So, the prison, filled wit prisoners, was divided. There were the prisoners that thought they were better. There were the regular prisoners, 'n within the prisoners the fakers 'n their women divided them even more based on the shape of the prisoners' noses. The thin nosed prisoners were treated better than the broader nosed prisoners. So, the prisoners divided themselves 'n thought they were special because uv how the fakers treated them.

"Okay, so there was a prisoner who escaped. The prisoner, once away from the prison, found that outside the prison there was still a bigger prison. There were monsters still. Outside the prison where he had been all his life, there were still fakers trying to beat, steal, rape 'n kill. The thing that surprised the escaped prisoner was that outside the prison the monsters 'n fake men were unhappy even though they had ev'rything. The escaped prisoner could not understand why the fakers were so unhappy 'n mean. He thought the fakers unhappiness was because uv the prisoners, but out uv the prison the prisoner saw that the fakers were unhappy without prisoners.

"The prisoner found out that outside of prison the fakers beat, stole, raped 'n killed their own. Again, he had thought the monsters only hated the prisoners. The prisoner found that the fakers hated each other.

"So, the escaped prisoner found a horse 'n a gun 'n tried to live away from the unhappy fakers 'n their women. He rode 'round the prison in a prison on his horse 'n got good wit the gun. He rode 'n knew the fakers would one day come for him.

"He wasn't the fastest gunslinger. He wasn't the slowest either. The difference, fir the prisoner, was that he had lost ev'rything 'n when the monsters attacked, he did not get rattled. He expected them to attack. He simply was ready fir the attacks.

"So, the monsters 'n fakers disliked the prisoner. They plotted against him. One day they tried to kill him. The next they tried to be his friend. The prisoner did not 'n could not trust any of them.

"For a time, the fakers tried to make the escaped prisoner believe he was a special prisoner. They tried to make the escaped prisoner believe he was better than the other prisoners, like they did in the prison he grew up in. The escaped prisoner did not believe the monsters. They were liars. Nothin' they said could be believed. The monsters were always monsters, even when they smiled or acted nice.

"The monsters were not happy wit the escaped prisoner bein' around. The fake men were always looking fir a reason to kill the escaped prisoner 'n to be unhappy. They were always lookin' fir things to divide 'n things to be different. So, they plotted 'n planned a way to get rid uv the escaped prisoner.

"Gettin' rid of uv him was easier sed than done. Every town he stopped in he was attacked. Now, he wasn't afraid to shoot it out wit anyone. The escaped prisoner escaped death 'n ambush more times than he could remember. Every escape added to his story.

"The unhappies came together after the escaped prisoner had killed more than a dozen fake men. They decided to ambush 'n kill him. They knew that he picked up supplies in a small town near a creek. In that small town the fake men hid. When the escaped prisoner showed up, he found himself shootin' it out wit five fake men tryin' to kill him. That day the escaped prisoner killed five monsters on the streets uv that small town," Freeman said. "The escaped prisoner thought he was safe to leave that town. Leaving the town, the escaped prisoner found the sheriff 'n the deputy waitin'.

"The sheriff 'n deputy drew down on the escaped prisoner. The sheriff, like the escaped prisoner, was not a quickdraw. He was jus' calm. The deputy was the first to pull his gun, but the escaped prisoner pulled his pistol 'n fired a half second later 'n hit the deputy in the middle uv the chest. He killed the deputy without much thought. The sheriff pulled his pistol and fired 'n hit the escaped prisoner in the arm. The escaped prisoner fired 'n killed the sheriff. Wounded, the escaped prisoner rode away 'n was never seen again." Freeman shrugged at the end of his campfire story.

"I heard that story before," Kate said.

Kaiyote sat quietly. Freeman nodded. Kate studied Freeman, curiously.

"Was that a story 'bout you?"

"No," Freeman said. "I ain't killed no sheriff."

Kate yawned. The little girl smiled. She studied Freeman as she made herself comfortable on the bedroll and fell asleep a few minutes later.

"Seems like you like the little girl," The quiet warrior said in his tribal tongue.

"It's not like I hate her," Freeman said.

"It's not a bad thing," The quiet warrior said.

Freeman smiled.

"What?"

"I think you like her too," Freeman said in the tribal tongue of Kaiyote.

The quiet warrior looked shocked.

"I think you laughed fir the first time since I met you today," Freeman said.

"She says the most unexpected things," The quiet warrior said.

Freeman and Kaiyote talked through the night.

The quiet warrior took the first watch after Freeman walked the campsite. He checked on the horses before resting against his saddle. The last thing Freeman did was arrange his rifle and pistols so that they were close at hand in case there was any danger.

Kate laid on the blankets silently sleeping. She turned toward Freeman and the cowboy studied the sorrel-colored little girl with the oval shaped face and thick eyebrows. As she slept Freeman could not help but imagine his life as another man, not living on the plains and moving from town to town and being a cattle owner or a farmer on a ranch with some fat and loving wife and three or four kids.

Freeman rubbed the back of his neck and adjusted his bulk on the saddle roll and the saddle. He looked to the left and the darkness of the forest. Freeman peered into the darkness and the shadows of the trees. In the darkness Freeman thought he saw the shadow of three deer moving just one hundred feet from the camp.

The cowboy turned back to Kate and again found himself thinking of how his life might have been had he made different decisions. He looked to Kaiyote and though his partner was not always the most talkative, he seemed to understand Freeman. He laid back and closed his eyes to Kate sleeping silently and comfortably next to him and the quiet warrior sitting on the log with his Springfield rifle.

# Chapter 12.

Kate.
Day Two, Kansas territory, 1869

The night the trio camped out was uneventful. The only thing of note came during the end of the quiet warrior's watch when he watched half a dozen racoons appear from the trees and underbrush. The quiet warrior watched the curious creatures' edge to the camp and the fire and sniff about the camp. They nosed around the horses and Kaiyote had to climb to his feet and scare them off before spooking the horses.

Freeman slept and was plagued by his recurring dream. The dream, the nightmare that made his sleep fitful.

There were flashes, always just flashes, of a brown-skinned woman Freeman believed was his mother, running from a pale faced bearded menace with a belt. The pale faced bearded ghost swung the belt in the air and hit the brown woman and drove her to the ground. Once the woman was on the ground the bearded ghost leaped upon her.

The nightmare flashed forward and the brown-skinned woman, Freeman was sure was his mother, gathered Freeman and two other younger children that looked like Freeman in their prison cell. The woman was in tears. She showed her stomach to Freeman and the others and pulled a knife from beneath her dress.

She, crying and panicky, spoke in Freeman's dream.

"I can't let them take you from me," she said to Freeman, and she reached out and grabbed one of the two other children.

"I should have done this when he came the first time," the brown-skinned woman said.

The knife tore across the throat of the youngest of the small children.

The pale monster was suddenly at the door and snatching Freeman from the woman. The second child fell limp and bloody on the prison cell floor.

"You ain't gonna have no more uv me," the woman said, and Freeman watched as she dragged the knife across her own throat. The blood came gushing out like a fountain. In seconds, the woman slumped to the prison floor and was dead.

The cowboy woke and took his shift watching the camp while Kaiyote and Kate slept.

For Freeman the only visitor he had during his watch was an old gray owl. The gray owl landed on a branch just to Freeman's right and watched the cowboy watching it. The pair watched each other for a solid hour before the bird took wing and disappeared into the night.

In the morning, as the sun stretched its fingers over the hills Freeman stretched and walked the perimeter of the camp. He watched Kate and Kaiyote sleeping.

A few minutes after the sun had caught hold of the sky Kaiyote stirred. The native sat up and was fully awake in moments. The quiet warrior climbed to his feet. He rubbed at his dark eyes after the sun began to slant through the trees and tree leaves.

The frontiersmen spoke in whispers as they prepared for the day. The quiet warrior blinked, stretched, and stepped outside of the camp to relieve himself. When he returned Freeman stepped outside of the camp to do the same.

When Freeman returned Kaiyote had stoked the campfire and was making coffee. The unlikely partners sat and had a morning cup of coffee.

Freeman looked to the still sleeping Kate.

"We jus' leave her?"

"No," The quiet warrior said. He walked by Kate and tapped her foot gently.

Kate woke up and as she rubbed at her eyes saw Kaiyote first, near his horse, patting its neck. Looking back toward the campfire she saw Freeman sitting on the fallen log, sipping from his metal cup.

"Mornin'," Freeman said.

"Mornin'," Kate said.

The quiet warrior nodded to Kate as he walked back to the log and picked up his metal camp cup and sat and seemed in no real rush.

"How long I been asleep?"

Freeman sipped from his cup.

"Why you didn't wake me earlier?"

"You slept like you needed it," Freeman said, sitting on a tree limb. Freeman and Kaiyote sat and waited for Kate.

"You hungry?"

Kate looked around the campsite and noticed that the fire had been put out and the horses saddled. Freeman had a tin cup he was sipping from. Sitting in the fire ring on the smoldering remains of the fire was a coffee pot.

"What are you goin' to offer me? Coffee?"

"No, we saved you some berries 'n fish from last night," Freeman said. "That should tide you over until we reach the outpost. Then you can get you something to eat in the saloon."

"The saloon?"

"Yeah, it's decent 'n proper before sundown," Freeman said with a smile.

Kate climbed to her feet and stretched still dressed in her brother's jeans and collared shirt from the night before. Her hair was now wrapped in a bandana that hid her band of braids beneath the fabric. Kate rubbed at her big eyes and slipped on her shoes while Freeman and Kaiyote finished drinking their coffee and talking. She reached out and grabbed her clothes bag. After a brief search, Kate found a big jacket that had belonged to her brother and slipped it on. Immediately, the jacket cut the morning cold. The jacket had two pockets on the outside.

"Can I go 'n wash up? Before we leave?" Kate asked.

"Yeah," Freeman said. "Jus' be careful. Call out if you run into anythin'."

"Like what?"

Freeman shrugged his shoulders.

Kate twisted her lips, not sure what to ask.

"Hurry up," Freeman said, seeing Kate still standing where she was. "We're tryin' to get there before it gets too hot."

Kate walked down to the stream and washed her face and cleaned up as best she could, before returning to the campsite and her two protectors. The water was cold and refreshing after a good night's sleep. Kate was surprised that she had fallen asleep so quickly.

As the stream gurgled and bubbled Kate found herself drifting back to thoughts of her family and the ambush. For the first time, the memories the horrid images washed over her. The nine-year-old felt as if she was standing on the edge of a great chasm that one wrong step would cast her forever into the darkness and depths below. The idea chilled her. She stepped back instinctually and tried to gather herself.

The child closed her eyes to the great abyss and memories. Kate shaken and crying wiped at her big eyes. She tried to recover and think of something else. All her memories were dominated by her family's wagon trip. She closed her eyes tightly and searched for a moment a memory that moved her away from those darker moments.

In her head, there was the dark-eyed, bearded cowboy Freeman and the quiet, long-haired Rider arrived. Kate thought of the two strangers' arrival and their removal of the dead bodies. She liked Freeman's friendly but gruff nature. He seemed nice enough, Kate thought. He was quiet and prickly, like a porcupine. On the horse ride Freeman reluctantly talked. Kate tried to connect with the cowboy. When they stopped and began camping Freeman seemed nice. He was helpful. He was stern, like her father.

The Black cowboy and Indian talked in their strange language that they only understood sounded like singing to Kate at times. The nine-year-old liked listening to the pair even if she didn't know what they said. The sound of the two strangers was a refuge. In their voices, there was a confidence and safety that Kate needed.

Kate opened her eyes and found herself standing near the stream, where she had been earlier. The little girl listened to the stream and the morning noises. A few birds chirped on trees near Kate. In the stillness that surrounded her, Kate willed herself to turn around and head back to the camp where Freeman and Kaiyote were waiting.

The quiet warrior watched silently as Kate returned, her eyes big and taking in everything around her. Freeman had finished his coffee and was putting the coffee pot and cup in his saddlebag as Kate returned. Beside his saddlebag Freeman slid his rifle.

On the log sat Kate's breakfast. She sat and ate her berries and fish as the two men busied themselves trying to erase the last few hours of their presence in the trees less than ten minutes from the trail.

Freeman and Kaiyote mounted their saddled and rested horses and prepared to leave their campsite. Kate stepped to Freeman and the cowboy reached down and gently lifted the little girl up and onto the back of his horse.

Freeman waited patiently. He looked at the little girl adjusting herself and then to Kaiyote, who seemed silently amused. Kate clutching her clothes bag balanced herself and her bag. Freeman clicked his tongue and urged his horse forward.

"How far is the outpost?"

"Not that far," Freeman said. "We should get there a little before noon."

Kate nodded. Freeman knew for the length of the ride to the outpost the little girl would not be quiet. It was more likely that the sun would fall out of the sky than the little girl would be quiet.

"The people nice where we're going?"

"Nice?" Freeman asked. The dark-eyed, bearded cowboy frowned at the idea. Freeman didn't know too many people that he came in contact with who were nice. The closest had been Kaiyote's people and they were seen by the villains as savages. "I wouldn't say that. They jus' like most. They not all evil," Freeman said, with a shrug. "That's better than all evil."

"Not being evil is not better than not being all evil," Kate said, from the back of the horse. "That means that they still evil."

"Sometimes that's the only choice you got," Freeman said.

"Not much uv a choice," Kate said.

Freeman fell silent.

"You takin' me some place that is worse than yesterday?"

"It's not like that," Freeman said.

Kate fell silent. The little girl rode thinking. After a couple of minutes, she spoke.

"Are you takin' me some place where they're goin' to hurt me? Or kill me?"

Freeman stiffened at the question.

"No," Freeman said. "I wouldn't do that." He looked back over his shoulder at the little girl. Kate looked frightened. "I didn't save you to let someone hurt or kill you," Freeman said.

"But you are takin' me some place filled with evil people," Kate said. She wriggled on the back of the horse. "If that is where we're goin' you can stop and let me off," Kate said, pushing against Freeman.

"It's not like that," Freeman said. "I wouldn't let them hurt or kill or sell you," Freeman said. He reached back with his freehand and grabbed Kate by the shoulder. "I'm jus' takin' you some place where you can get back to Kansas."

"But I don't want to go to Kansas," Kate said.

Freeman looked to Kaiyote. The quiet warrior watched silently as Freeman and Kate squirmed on the horse.

"She thinks I am takin' her to be sold," Freeman said.

The quiet warrior shook his head.

Kate listened to Freeman and Kaiyote as they moved down the wagon trail and toward the outpost.

In the four hours it took to get to the outpost eight wagons passed going in the opposite direction. The eight wagons were steered by white men. Some were burly. Some thin. One wore a flat top brimmed straw hat. Most wore wide brimmed slouch hats. They all stared at Kate and Freeman and the Usually quiet rider as if they were in the wrong place.

"Why do they do that?"

"Do what?"

"Look at us like that?"

"Don't know. Maybe seeing us reminds them uv bad things they were runnin' away from," Freeman said. The cowboy stopped and Kate thought Freeman would not say anymore. After a minute he added, "All I know is a look don't amount to much. They ain't as evil by themselves. They have to get worked up 'n be wit someone else as crazy to do somethin'. If they get bold or a little jumpy 'n say somethin', then I know I need to be ready fir anythin'."

"What do you mean?"

"Well, they always lookin' fir an excuse," Freeman said.

"An excuse?"

"Yeah, they like to have a reason fir their killin' or whatever out here" Freeman said. "That's why I'm always with peace 'n quiet." Freeman tapped his pistol on his hip.

"You named your guns?"

Freeman chuckled 'n nodded.

"What's the name uv your rifle?"

Freeman tilted his head, thinking.

"Justice," Freeman said with a smile.

Kate laughed at the name.

"Why you name your guns?"

"Everything' that matters has a name," Freeman said.

As was his nature and that of Kaiyote the cowboy fell quiet. Kate seemed to just accept that the two did not speak much.

An opened back wagon slowly creaked along in front of Freeman, Kate and Kaiyote. It was still early, and the sun was still climbing into the sky. It had not reached its zenith yet as Freeman and Kaiyote looked ahead and to the left and right to pass the slow-moving wagon.

Kaiyote and Freeman looked at each other. There was a silent exchange between the two riders. Freeman was the first to nudge his horse from behind the open back wagon and into the wagon trail to the right of the wagon. The cowboy and little girl rode slowly around the wagon as Esdaowa followed.

As Freeman and Kate drew even with the wagon the little girl looked to the thick bearded man wearing a thick blue flannel coat, dirty blue canvas trousers and roughed up work boots, sitting on the buckboard guiding his two brown horses. Sitting next to him was a boy dressed in brown fringed coat and brown trousers who looked like a smaller version of the wagoner.

The bearded wagoner nodded. The younger version of the driver stared at Kate and frowned.

Kate touched Freeman's sleeve as he and Kaiyote pulled ahead of the wagon and took in the unobstructed view of the outpost.

"They were starin'," Kate said in a whisper, looking back at the wagoner and the boy beside him.

"Yeah, they ain't used to seein' us out here not under their control," Freeman said.

"Should we worry?"

Freeman looked back at Kaiyote. The quiet warrior was riding unconcerned. Freeman turned back to the trail leading to the outpost.

"If he ain't worried, then I ain't worried," Freeman said.

Kate looked at Kaiyote who seemed focused on the trail and nothing else. The usually quiet warrior rode easily in the saddle and Kate found herself looking at the gun strapped diagonally across Kaiyote's chest. Kate smiled at the sight. She had seen guns and men wearing guns most of her life, but no one wore their gun like Kaiyote. The nine-year-old wondered if Kaiyote could pull the gun as quickly as the normal hip slinging gunfighters.

The quiet warrior looked from the side of the trail and to Kate, seeing her looking at him. He looked at her evenly, with no visible emotion on his face. Kate smiled and looked away from Kaiyote.

"Mister Freeman," Kate said, looking away from Kaiyote. "Is your Injun dangerous?"

"Dangerous? How?" Freeman asked.

"I don't know. I mean, towards us," Kate said, struggling to put her thoughts into words.

"No. He ain't got a mean bone in his body, when it comes to us," Freeman said. "Why you askin'?"

"I don't know. I heard stories. My brother 'n others sed the biggest fear crossin' the territories to California was the Injuns. They were supposed to be scalpin' settlers," Kate said.

"Don't know about that," Freeman said. "I lived with them fir nearly four winters 'n they treated me better than any white man I been in contact with," Freeman said with a smirk. "The way I see it, if I had a choice in the territories I would go to the red man."

As the trio drew closer to the small outpost sitting on the plains just a few miles from the foothills of a mountain range in the distance Freeman slowed. The quiet warrior slowed as well. The pair made their way to the main entrance to the outpost. Kate could not help but be amazed. The outpost was a mix of a group of painted buildings, with only a handful taller than one story. The outpost was as big as some towns Kate and the others of the wagon train had rolled through leaving Kansas.

Freeman led the slow march through the wide main street made of dirt. Kate noticed that the sidewalks were elevated at least two feet from the dirt, in case of floods. She scanned the outpost as Freeman rode into the center of the busy place, for that time of day. There was a wagon parked in front of most of the buildings and horses hitched to hitching posts.

By a rough calculation Freeman decided there were maybe a dozen people walking around the outpost, at least. It, the outpost, was made up of a dozen free standing buildings that included one of the biggest general stores around, next to the store was a saloon. There was an assayer's office near the saloon and a barber and dentist there as well. At the far end of the outpost was also a big barn and a stable in the outpost. As Kate scanned the outpost, she noticed there were two buildings being built.

Freeman slowed at the Stratton Outpost where there was
a horse and wagon already waiting. He pulled up to the hitching
post and reined his horse to a stop. Freeman looked back and
lifted Kate off the back of his horse and placed her gently on the
ground below. He slipped off the horse and tied it to the hitching
post. Kate stood and watched as Kaiyote pulled up and
dismounted his horse.

"Stay here 'n watch the girl," Freeman said to Kaiyote.

"You sure you want to do this?"

"There's nothin' bad that's goin' to happen here. We here
fir a day 'n then back to the open spaces," Freeman said. "What's
the worst that can happen?"

"Remember, I warned you," The quiet warrior said.

Freeman chuckled.

"What you talkin' about?" Kate asked.

"You," Freeman said. "Stay wit Kaiyote. I need to go in
here 'n talk wit a man to talk to a man 'bout those bodies we left
back there," Freeman said.

Kate nodded and looked to Kaiyote.

Freeman walked into the outpost. Kate and Kaiyote
watched.

Kate smiled at Kaiyote and studied the weathered face of
the quiet warrior. He had thick black straight hair that fell to his
shoulders. It was braided into one long ponytail underneath his
curled sombrero. Kate noticed that Kaiyote had a rawhide necklace
around his neck. On his cheekbone was a scar from what Kate
could not tell. The buffalo coat Kaiyote was wearing was open and
showed off the diagonal rigged pistol. The Indian stood next to his
horse with his forearms resting on the saddle.

"You speak English?"

The quiet warrior looked at Kate, but there seemed to be
no understanding.

The nine-year-old girl twisted her lips, thinking.

"You know people think you're all savages?"

The quiet warrior looked at Kate and then to the people
milling around the small outpost.

Kate looked at Kaiyote and then back toward the building Freeman had entered. That afternoon there were at least a dozen or so people near the four buildings closest to the pair milling about.

There were two or three knots of soldiers dressed in blue wool coats like Freeman. They looked old to Kate, maybe twenty or thirty and bone thin, carrying rifles and smiling and laughing. Of the twenty plus people crossing to the store, or one of the other buildings, there were two women visible and no children.

"You know my name?"

The quiet warrior tied up his horse and walked around the horses. He went to the front of the store and leaned against the hitch post next to the rear of a wagon waiting in front of the store.

"You have kids?" Kate asked.

The quiet warrior looked at the little girl and smiled.

"You understand what I'm saying?"

The quiet warrior did not respond.

Kate looked back to the general store. The quiet warrior watched silently.

"You stay here," Kate said, gesturing to the spot where Kaiyote was standing. She pointed back to the outpost store and looked at Kaiyote. "I'm goin' to go 'n check on Freeman. He might need my help."

The quiet warrior watched as Kate bolted from her spot next to the horses and into the general store. The stoic Kaiyote watched as the little girl jumped to the door of the general store and looked back thinking he might follow or complain.

As she reached the door a white woman nearly knocked the little girl over. Kate halted and let the thin woman wearing a blue and white dress step out of the store in a huff. She looked flustered. Behind her followed a man, dressed in a blue shirt and gray pants and wearing a flat wide brimmed hat. He looked back into the store and in his hands held a wooden box containing a bag of coffee, flour, rice and potatoes.

Kate waited and watched as the pair exited the store. The thin woman looked at the little girl with surprise and open disgust.

"They're everywhere," the woman said with a shake of her head.

The man, carrying the box of supplies, stumbled behind the woman and toward the waiting wagon.

Kate giggled as she ran inside the incredibly large general store and right into back of a tall man wearing a long black coat that was split in the back.

All around her were barrels of things, heavy coats hanging from posts, a glass display case and a bar where there were rolls of fabric in various colors. In the corner of the store Kate saw a stuffed bear. Behind the bear hung two deer heads.

Bumping into the man resulted in Kate being caught by the long fingers and hand of the man wearing half glasses and a scraggly gray beard. Kate froze. The stranger turned and stared at the little girl with ice blue eyes. Kate recoiled. The white man had a bald head with a gray wreath of hair that made his head look like an egg in a gray nest. Kate did not smile at the odd-looking man but instead noticed that he had a bent nose and small teeth.

"Whose are you?"

Kate did not answer, instead, she looked around the vast store for Freeman. There were five other people, all white, in the space. A dark-haired woman with thin eyebrows and thin lips was standing behind the main counter of the store with some small items in front of her and suddenly watching Kate as a man, maybe a foot shorter than Freeman, stood with a box of shells and a bag of potatoes walked across the store to the counter.

An oily-faced boy was standing near a barrel, dressed in a rolled up collared shirt and overalls with a gun belt and gun on his hip.

The last two people in the store were a pair of older bearded men near the rear of the store. One was wearing thick jacket and canvas trousers. The other was wearing a slouch hat, thick shirt, gun belt and pistol against his dark gray wool trousers. The two bearded men stopped what they were doing and turned and stared at Kate in the hands of the tall, thin white man.

She tried to pull away from the white man, but he held her with an iron grip. Kate panicked and was about to scream when Freeman appeared, wearing a canvas duster with a brown fur collar that fell just below his knees.

"Freeman? Is this yours?" The tall white man asked.

Freeman's contented smile melted and changed to a frown seeing Kate being held by the white man. He narrowed his dark eyes to the man and the little girl.

"She's not mine," Freeman said. "I tol' you Stratton I was back here to trade some goods, try on this jacket 'n see Madison about that waggun train that was ambushed. She's the one I tol' you about."

"Yeah, I recall, but didn't think you were really interested in findin' someone for a moppet that you could make money fir, Freeman," Stratton said. The tall thin man held Kate firmly and though it was uncomfortable, seeing Freeman was in the store, Kate did not struggle. She expected Freeman to help her. "Now, I'm all sorts uv interested in your sudden change uv profession," the tall white man said. "She could bring a whole lot uv money to you 'n me."

"I ain't interested," Freeman said, frustrated. "I tol' you that already."

"Yeah, yeah, you did, but now that I have her in hand 'n I'm lookin' I think you might part with her for a hundred," Stratton said with an evil smile.

Freeman studied Kate and then Stratton.

"Like I tol' you Stratton, when I came in, I was lookin' fir someone to care fir the girl, not buy her."

Freeman shucked off the jacket he was wearing. He kept his eye on the man holding Kate.

"Now, let her go, Stratton," Freeman said.

Stratton smiled at Freeman's response. He looked at the little girl and then back at Freeman, no longer wearing the coat. The tall man smiled. "You ain't never been someone I would consider willin' to stick his neck out for others."

"Some men change," Freeman said.

"Some, that's fir certain, but you the same cowboy that shot one uv the Sutton boys for cheatin' at the card table," Stratton said.

Freeman nodded. He also placed his hand on his pistol heel.

Stratton looked at Freeman and then those in the store. The oily-faced boy had pushed away from the barrel and was circling away from the counter to get a better vantage point.

"Stratton, you know I don't like to repeat myself," Freeman said, looking at Stratton and placing a hand on the butt of his gun at the same time. "I sed, let her go."

With that the white man released Kate and the little girl stepped back from the man. She seeing Freeman standing in the middle of the store Kate instinctively moved toward him. Kate looked back and noticed that she was moving deeper into the store and away from the exit. It seemed counterintuitive but simultaneously the smart thing to do. The little girl distanced herself from the white man and closer to Freeman.

"No harm done," Stratton said, with a smile, raising his empty hands.

"Kate," Freeman said as the little girl stopped near Freeman, only to hesitate. He gestured to Kate. "This here is Tyler Stratton, the son uv Mister Lawrence Stratton, the owner uv all the buildin's and the land this here outpost sits on."

Kate looked at Freeman and then Stratton. In front of her was a table with tools and on it were brand new pots and pans. Behind it, Kate could see there were windows already built with glass panes. On a wall of the hung several ready-made doors, several scythes and three plow heads.

Tyler Stratton smiled at Freeman's words. Freeman watched the boy in overalls come to a stop with his hand hovering over his gun butt.

"Tell your boy to stop shadowin' me," Freeman said.

Stratton looked at Ned and smiled.

"Back off, Ned," Stratton said with a smile.

Ned took a few steps back but never took his eye off Freeman.

"What has come over you Freeman? You ain't the type to be stickin' your neck out for no one. You comin' back here is somethin' I would have never bet on," the white man said.

Kate looked at the white man in the black long coat and then to Freeman, dressed in his collared shirt and trousers. The girl rubbed at her wrist where the white man had held her tightly. She moved toward Freeman, only to pause near a table.

"So, this little moneymaker is all alone?" Stratton asked with a greasy smile. "Freeman, I have to admit that I thought you were tellin' tall tales, until I saw her." Stratton placed a hand on one of the displays. "I think I could find a good price fir your... excess baggage."

Kate looked at Freeman. Kate took a few steps and found herself next to Freeman. He had a spotty ducktail beard that covered his upper lip and chin.

Freeman did not answer. Instead, he stared at the boy wearing overalls and then Tyler Stratton like he was a deadly snake. Freeman looked down at Kate with his dark eyes.

"Thanks fir the offer," the bearded Freeman said. "We'll be goin'," Freeman said, retrieving his wool coat, as he looked at Kate and then Stratton. "I'll collect what I'm due," he said to the dark-haired woman.

She nodded and counted out a small stack of coins. Freeman thumbed the coins and slipped them into a leather purse, which he slipped inside of his jacket pocket. Freeman looked around and nodded to Stratton. Kate watched silently.

"I gotta catch up wit the sheriff 'n see if he can fetch back those bodies 'n give them people a decent burial," Freeman said.

"All right," Stratton said. "We'll have that jacket waitin', you been eyein', when you come back." Stratton smiled. "If you do come back, I will have a good offer fir your... moneymaker, as well."

"Thanks fir the trade," Freeman said. He buttoned his blue wool coat. The dark-haired woman studied Freeman and the little girl as he donned his coat.

The dark-haired woman smiled at the little girl. "How old is she, Freeman?"

Freeman looked at Kate, who was by his side and then to the dark-haired woman. Freeman did not answer. Instead, he put his Hardee hat back on his curly head and let the corner of his mouth jerk, for a second, into a small grin. The small smile appeared and disappeared.

'Don't matter," Freeman said. "She's not fir sale 'n we're jus' here to find someone to care fir her," Freeman said.

"Care fir her?" One of the bearded men at the table repeated.

"Yeah," Freeman said as he pushed Kate toward the store exit.

"How much?" The bearded men said, standing to his feet. "I'll take care uv her," he said behind his long scraggly beard.

"Did you get religion out there on the plains?" The woman asked.

Freeman chuckled and looked from the woman to Stratton, who was leaning against a beam.

"Freeman? Are you sure I can't convince you to part with your excess baggage?" The thin man asked by the beam.

"Suppose I'll be keepin' my...excess baggage, Stratton," Freeman said. "I'm many things but I ain't someone to sell off... someone."

Stratton nodded and smiled, looking at the retreating Freeman.

Freeman smoothed down the front of his wool coat as he stepped toward the exit of the store with Kate.

"See you, Freeman. Always a pleasure doin' business wit you," Stratton said with a smile.

Freeman tipped his hat and exited the general store with Kate. Once out of the general store, with Kate by his side, Freeman paused seeing Kaiyote on the dirt road by his horse.

"I thought you were supposed to watch her?"

The quiet warrior shrugged his shoulders.

Freeman looked back at the storefront and saw a sign that he could not read.

"Stratton sed his father did not want Injuns or one-time slaves in his store," Freeman said in their distinct language. "Now, because uv me, accordin' to Stratton, his father doesn't want me in the store wit him 'n absolutely there are No Injuns."

The quiet warrior stood beside his horse. The quiet warrior did not seem to care what Freeman was saying.

Freeman looked up at Kaiyote and nodded. He looked from the sign and to the jail. The jail sat between the saloon and the one of the barely framed structures. The jail was one story with shutters over the two windows. The main door looked sturdy and banded with three lengths of metal. The building itself was well made and crafted.

Freeman looked from the jail and to Kate by his side.

"Okay, listen, this time I mean it. You stay wit Kaiyote. Some places aren't safe fir you or me," Freeman said. "Usually, I ain't worried 'bout myself, but you add to the problems."

"Why?"

Freeman opened and closed his mouth, deciding not to answer.

"Would you have sold me?"

Freema shook his head.

"Would you sell me?"

Freeman pursed his lips, deciding not to speak.

"Were you?"

Freeman winced at Kate's words but did not speak. He instead, looked left and right at the buildings around him. The dark-eyed Freeman returned his gaze to Kate.

"Look," Freeman said. "I'm a lot uv things, but I ain't that. I ain't going be a monster jus' because I walk with monsters."

Kate frowned, unsure.

"Should I worry?"

"Always worry," Freeman said. "It's the thing that'll keep you alive out here."

Kate frowned. The little girl fell silent. She looked at the cowboy and then his silent partner.

"Are you a good guy?"

Freeman did not answer.

'Am I in danger?"

Kate looked around the outpost the three were in and noticed that of the dozen people on the walkways and in wagons there were no women or children there. Earlier she had seen two women and the white woman that looked like she wanted to spit on Kate, but now there was no women at all. It was a weird thing to find herself the only female out of doors in Stratton.

"Stay with Kaiyote," Freeman said. "I won't be long. Then we'll go to the saloon 'n eat."

Kate walked to Kaiyote as Freeman walked away from the store and toward the only brick building in the outpost.

Arriving beside Kaiyote, Kate smirked.

"What?"

The quiet warrior only shook his head.

# Chapter 13.

Kate.
Beginning of June, Kansas 1877

Kate woke from her nap thinking about Stratton and Kaiyote. The wagon bumped along the trail. There were wagons but no wagon trains as they got closer to the border of Kansas.

Kate napped when she could. In the chaos and mayhem that ensued daily in the interior of the Lawson covered wagon Kate found a routine. When the boys woke, usually Randolph first, then Ricky and lastly RJ the interior of the covered wagon became a place of whining and time to stop and let the boys go to the bathroom. Kate and Elisabeth and her mother would also step off the trail and go to the bathroom.

The wagon ritual was pretty regular. When there was quiet Kate found her thoughts returning to the days with Freeman and Kaiyote. Though the times were fearful, the times were vivid as if the mere thought alone recreated every moment, feeling, thought and sensation.

So, as the wagon bumped along on the trail from the outpost and toward Kansas, Kate looked around the interior of the covered wagon. Elisabeth was sleeping. Randolph and RJ were quiet and that could only mean that they were sleeping as well. Ricky had found a piece of charcoal and was attempting to draw on the boards of the wagon floor.

Charlotte and Missus Lawson watched Kate silently.

"How do you do it?"

"Do what, dear?"

"Watch out for everyone?"

Missus Lawson shrugged her shoulders.

"My momma was like you. She loved everybody," Kate said.

"Maybe, it is a part of bein' a mom," Missus Lawson said.

Kate nodded.

The wagon slowed and finally stopped. Kate knew the stop on the border of the Kansas territory and Nebraska territory had been an Army outpost.

Suddenly, the wagon was slowing. All around them were one and two-story buildings. It, where they were, was not the outpost but a town that Kate did not recognize.

"We need to get some water for the horses and check on some supplies before our last push to Kansas," Mister Lawson said to his wife in the rear of the covered wagon. "We shouldn't be here too long."

With that Mister Lawson handed the reigns of the wagon to Ezekiel and stepped off the buckboard. Along the side of the wagon there was a muffled conversation. Three male voices talked and grumbled. Then two men went into the storefront.

"Nobody move," Missus Lawson said, firmly as the wagon slowed and stopped. "We wait for your daddy to say we can climb out." Missus Lawson was holding Charlotte. The boys, always a bundle of energy, pushed and shoved each other as Elisabeth grabbed the railing of the wagon and tried to see out of the rear of the covered wagon.

A few minutes later, the two men came out with supplies. The wait ended as quickly as it began.

Kate silently waited. As she waited, Kate found herself thinking about Mister Monroe and her first trip past the Army outpost and the visit to Deaver's ranch.

Mister Monroe had stopped there after passing an Army outpost with a bunch of soldiers traipsing around. Monroe never explained why they did not stop at the outpost, but Kate seemed to understand. From the wagon Kate was surprised to see that the outpost was larger than Stratton or Garrett. The outpost looked like a fortress more than anything else. There was a wooden gate and men standing on the wall looking down.

The wagon train had not slowed but continued on to Deaver's ranch.

From what Kate remembered Deaver was a businessman. He had been a slave and bought his freedom. He had heard of land being available to purchase and bought his ranch some years ago. He had five sons and four daughters. The oldest, was preparing to take over the ranch from his father.

Mister Lawson appeared with a tight smile on his face. Kate climbed out of the wagon after Mister Lawson to be sure his wife had not left anything valuable behind. He helped Kate out of the wagon.

Once out of the wagon Kate found herself surprised at the vastness of the Deaver ranch. The ranch she had been to, nearly ten years ago, was a small but comfortable home for Deaver and his family. Now, it was as far as the eye could see a wheat farm.

Deaver, short, wiry, dressed in brown low brimmed hat, jacket, trousers and boots was wearing a gun belt and a pistol. He had a collarless white shirt on and his pants held up by suspenders.

"Deaver, thank you for the welcome, again," Reginald Lawson said with a smile. The two men smiled at each other.

Introductions were made. Kate did not imagine that she would be expeced to remember all the Deavers in attendance and the half a dozen men and women on hand that day. All she recalled was that Deaver had a pretty square headed wife by the name of Adeline. She had the round features and high cheekbones of Kaiyote, Kate thought upon meeting her.

"How long you here?"

"Just long enough to rest the horses before we head to Garrett and then Stratton and Coffeyville," Lawson said, sitting at the firepit where everyone gathered. Kate listened silently.

"Be careful," Deaver said to Lawson. "There are a bunch of Rebs that don't think the war is over," Deaver said just loud enough for Kate to hear. "They ain't happy with us out here. They ain't happy with us out of chains," the businessman said sitting and sipping something from a tin cup. "They usually are not too much of a problem until sundown," Deaver said.

"I know," Reginald Lawon said scratching the side of his face. "We try 'n avoid towns we don't know and sleep away from their places," Lawson said.

Kate listened and found the conversation intriguing. All around the wagons, children, from three to twelve, ran and played. In the middle of the area where three long tables sat men and women were preparing places for food. There were easily half a dozen riders trotting around the ranch.

That night, Deaver fed everyone to they could not move.

They ate green beans, mashed potatoes, candied yams, collared greens, boiled corn, steak, fried chicken, buttermilk biscuits, apple pie, blueberry cobbler and chocolate cake and strawberry lemonade. Kate could not remember a better meal or night. Everyone seemed so happy and comfortable to be around one another.

After dinner one of the ranch hands pulled out a mouth harp and another sang. There was a little dancing and a lot of laughing and smiles.

The next day Mister Monroe and the wagon train headed toward Nebraska. At the same time Mister Lawson's wagon train headed to Kansas.

A few days later the wagon pulled into Garrett.

Unlike Deaver's ranch, everyone was hyper-alert.

"Stay close," Mister Lawson said to everyone who was near the wagon train. "This is only a brief stop before we stop fir the night. These ain't our people."

Kate stood, with her clothes bag in hand, looking at the small town that had been just an Army outpost more than anything else when she was nine. Elisabeth smiled from ear-to-ear at the people, wagons, horses and business of a military outpost in Nebraska.

Mornings, as the wagon rolled from its night stop the boys were fed and cleaned up. They barked and groused at being washed up, but it was a necessary annoyance for the sanity of all in the covered wagon. For three or four hours the wagon bumped along the trail and the boys complained, argued with each other, and were generally pests to each other more than anyone else. Thankfully, the boys attention was usually aimed at each other and never at their mother, Elisabeth or Kate.

Elisabeth touched Kate's arm bringing her back to the Lawson wagon and Missus Lawson.

"Our story will be written by the monsters," Missus Lawson said.

"It could end another way," Elisabeth said.

"That's true," Missus Lawson said, agreeing. "At some point, maybe our story gets heard." She smiled. "My hero is right there," Elisabeth's mother said, pointing to the back of Reginald Lawson who was guiding the wagon from the buckboard.

Kate smiled.

In the two or three hours the three rested Missus Lawson, Elisabeth and Kate talked and rested.

"Mama, you know that Kate is looking for this Black cowboy," Elisabeth said.

Missus Lawson nodded.

"You know when she was rescued, she went to Stratton?"

Missus Lawson nodded again. While Elisabeth peppered her mother with questions Kate found herself drifting away from the interior of the Lawson and to the trampled down space between the two sides of Stratton where Freeman had brought them. Kaiyote stood silent and watching as Kate tried to decide what to do.

Now, there were moments on the journey from Sacramento to Coffeyville that stood out for everyone. Those moments usually came before the boy's midday nap.

The midday nap was instituted by Missus Lawson and every day, after lunch, the boys were expected to take a nap. The rule, if there was a rule, was that until all three woke they were to rest.

To get the three rambunctious boys to quiet and nap they always asked their mother or older sister for a story. Most of the times their mother offered to tell a story. Sometimes the boys asked their sister for a story. Her mother understanding the burden usually stepped up, despite having told the boys stories each day. Many times, surprisingly, Elisabeth decided to tell stories.

Kate, at first, did not pay any attention to Elisabeth's stories. Then one day, Kate caught the end of a story that Elisabeth decided to tell. It was oddly familiar. There was a girl running away from a failed love in search of a man she believed was her true love. Kate listened absently to Elisabeth's story of a girl who had been abandoned by her family and left for dead. It was an interesting story, Kate had to admit.

Perhaps, it was as a result of hearing her own story retold and romanticized by Elisabeth that Kate decided to tell a tale to the boys, even though she had passed each and every time before. So, the boys listened intently, hoping for something they had never heard before.

Kate told a story that Freeman had told her on the trail to Garrett.

"This is a story uv the black fighter who woke up locked up, beaten, mistreated 'n under the threat uv death. He was born into the abuse and knew until he died, he was gonna receive that abuse every day. One night he escaped the prison 'n if that had been all he had done the story would have ended there, 'n he would have been like so many others who escaped. But the fighter once free did more. The fighter once free went back 'n tried to help some escape, but he was surprised that the prisoners were too scared to escape. He escaped 'n found that the monsters that locked up everyone he knew 'n loved were not as united as they appeared.

"The day the fighter came upon the battle he watched as hundreds fought 'n hundreds died. Again, this is not what makes the fighter important. It's simply background.

"The fighter, fir the first time, since his escape, found a pistol. He held that pistol in his hand 'n felt the power uv it. That same day he found a rifle. He watched the brutal men shoot, stab, blow up 'n kill one another 'n that day he realized the only thing that mattered to the cruel men was power. The power to kill was incredibly important.

"So, the fighter learnt to use the pistol 'n the rifle as good as the heartless men. He found a horse on his journey and some coins to buy what he needed. He ate. He slept. He had no real home and in the back uv his mind he began to come up with a plan. That lesson he taught to hundreds. The escaped fighter tol' ev'ryone that would listen that he came upon a battle 'tween two armies, one in blue 'n the other in gray, fighting in a valley. There were all types uv guns the fighter tol' the prisoners. The loudest 'n most destructive thing was the short cannon, but there was more. "There a lot uv monsters but they ain't all fightin' us. They fightin' themselves too," the fighter tol the prisoners.

"But the fighter could not get the prisoners to leave the prisons no matter what he sed. So, he left, escaped again, the prison. He returned to the hills 'n plains where he found peace 'n quiet. In those hills he decided he would protect the weak if they needed help. He decided he would teach all those that wanted to know how to use a gun or a rifle too. He taught hundreds who somehow escaped how to protect themselves. He taught those willing to learn how to have real power," Kate said and stopped. She looked at the three boys lying on the bed of the covered wagon and smiled. Ricky and Randolph were asleep already. RJ was fighting the call of sleep but moments from giving in. Missus Lawson rocking a sleeping Charlotte smiled. Elisabeth smiled too.

"That was a good story," Elisabeth said.

Kate smiled. She rubbed the side of her face awkwardly. The action felt oddly familiar.

"Is that who you're looking for?" Missus Lawson asked, holding Charlotte in her arms. She too had fallen asleep.

"The fighter?" Kate asked, knowing the answer before asking the question. "I suppose I am."

"I have heard that story before," Missus Lawson said. "If you lookin' fir someone like that you need to be prepared for the end uv the story."

"What you mean, mama?"

"I mean that all our heroes found in unmarked graves all over this land, baby girl," Missus Lawson said.

Kate nodded understanding. Freeman had said the same thing, in his own way. The thought of Freeman drew Kate back seven years when she was nine years old and on the trail with Freeman and Kaiyote. They were making their way to Garrett with the hope of finding freedmen to take Kate to California, even though Kate did not want that to happen.

The wagon train rolled out of Garrett after picking up some essential supplies. Kate sat in her seat next to Elisabeth and shared a piece of licorice. The two girls had been close since the journey began. Elisabeth told Kate all of her secrets. She told the teenager about her love of a boy named: Tony Adams. He was the son of a preacher back in Sacramento. Elisabeth told Kate she had kissed him.

Kate did not blink. She did not comment. Elisabeth was thirteen and preparing for marriage, Kate knew. The push to marry and have children was intense in the unsettled territories. Marriage meant another man to help with the work.

Mister Lawson was heading to Kansas to be a farmer. He had hopes of being a bean or corn farmer, but his hopes depended on buying the right land for the right price. He had three sons and Ezekiel, but he would need more hands if he was to be successful. Marriage could help.

"You know that Tony is the son uv a preacher?"

Kate listened.

"He is really smart," Elisabeth continued talking about Tony.

Kate smiled and nodded. She wanted to tell Elisabeth that the thirteen-year-old's hopes and dreams of a relation with Tony were sadly over, but she could not build up the courage to dash Elisabeth's dreams. Kate knew as soon as Elisabeth's father decided to move to Kansas with his family his only daughter's hopes of anything other than a long-distance relationship with Tony was impossible. If Elisabeth was to find anyone, Kate knew, it would have to be someone in Kansas.

"You know anyone in Kansas?"

"Why you ask?"

"Your daddy's people in Kansas?"

Elisabeth nodded.

"Jus' trying to understand your family moving back to Kansas," Kate said.

"Well, my daddy sed that land is cheap in Kansas," Elisabeth said. "He plans on buyin' land 'n startin' a farm or a ranch," Elisabeth said. "I tol' you that already."

"I know," Kate said. She smiled.

The wagon bumped along the trail eastward.

"Like I sed, we got family there. The land is cheap. It's supposed to be better now," Elisabeth said.

*Better?* Kate tried to think how Elisabeth, or her father measured better. The last time Kate had been in Kansas it had not been *better*. It had been anything but *better*.

"What you goin' to do after you find your Black cowboy?"

Kate smiled at the question. She had never really considered what she would do after finding Freeman. Would she give him a hug? Would she sit and have a meal with him? Would Kaiyote be there?

"I don't know," Kate said, admittedly. "I just hope that seein' him answers some questions."

Elisabeth smiled and nodded.

Thankfully, just a few miles away from Garrett, was a smaller black town on the edge of the growing Garrett. The town was named: Curtis.

"You've been here before?"

Kate shook her head.

"I thought you sed you crossed the Oregon Trail before," Elisabeth said, curious.

"I did. But when I climbed in the wagon train there was no Curtis. I got picked up in Garrett. But that was seven years ago."

"I forgot," Elisabeth said. "Was it dangerous back then?"

"It is always dangerous," Kate said, recalling that Freeman had said that too.

"How did you survive?"

Kate smiled. Kate didn't tell Elisabeth how she survived. The teen didn't think it was her business.

When the wagon train pulled into Curtis the sun was melting on the mountains behind. Mister Lawson decided that it was best to stay in Curtis overnight. Mister Lawson had the wagons circle up. Paul Sawyer made food for the families.

The five fathers and sons took turns watching the wagons. Unlike Freeman and Kaiyote, the wagoners rested in the wagons. Some went to get supplies from the small-town store.

"How far are we from Stratton?"

"We should be there tomorrow," Mister Lawson said.

Mister Lawson and Elisabeth's brother Randolph were watching the wagons at the time.

Kate laid down and tried to rest.

Of course, as Kate fell asleep, she found herself back with Freeman and the silent dark-eyed warrior.

As the wagon rolled toward Stratton Elisabeth asked how Kate ended up at Stratton. At first, she didn't want to tell her. Kate had said that the wagon train had been ambushed, but little more. As the wagon train began to roll through the familiar environ, she felt memories all around her.

"You know that I tol' you 'bout Freeman 'n the Injun?"

"Yes," Elisabeth said, suddenly attentive.

"Well, we headed to Stratton because it was close. Freeman took me there wit the hope that someone would take care uv me. I think he wanted to leave me there," Kate recalled. "I didn't want to stay in Stratton. I didn't know anyone. Ev'ryone in Stratton was white 'n they seemed mean."

Elisabeth listened.

Kate studied Elisabeth. The teenager pressed on.

"Freeman wanted to hand me off," Kate said.

"Why?"

"I was jus' nine at the time," Kate said.

Elisabeth chuckled at the idea.

"I got in trouble in the general store. I met Stratton. Fir a long time, I thought Freeman would sell me to one uv the white men."

"Really?"

"Why not? He didn't know me. He was a thief 'n a robber as far as I knew," I said, rationally.

"But he protected you," Elisabeth said, pointing out the obvious.

"I know, but he seemed… I don't know, mean 'n angry. I don't know how to explain it. I was jus' nine 'n confused," Kate said, in answer.

Elisabeth nodded.

Kate told her how Freeman had decided to organize men to pick up her family and the dead of the wagon train and bury them. He went to the sheriff, but I had no idea what happened inside. Kate had nearly been sold in the general store. The nine-year-old Kate refused to go to the jail for fear of worse.

"We can't trust 'em. My parents left the south fir a better life. The people here hate us. They will never respect us." Elisabeth paused. "I think they would kill us if they could get away wit it."

Kate laughed at clarity of Elisabeth's logic. She laughed because, it wasn't until much later in Kate's journeys, that she came to the same conclusion.

"How old are you?"

"Fourteen. Why?"

"Seems like you're much older," Kate said.

"My mother said I have an old soul," Elisabeth said.

Kate nodded.

"You know that they hate we survived their torture," Elisabeth said, looking at Kate curiously.

"I know, but I think I thought," Kate began only to shake her head. "I don't know what I was thinkin'. I mean, I was nine," Kate said as if her age was an excuse.

"My mom tol' me we were brought here 'n the people brought us here, imprisoned us, beat us, mistreated us 'n then decided to free us 'gainst the wishes uv most," Elisabeth said. "But not ev'ryone wanted to free us. Those that didn't want to free us look at us as if what they did is our fault."

Kate agreed.

"This place is upside down. The people hate us. We are their constant memory uv their evilness," Elisabeth said.

So, as the wagon train slowly made its way to Stratton, Kate told Elisabeth what she recalled of her time in Stratton, once Freeman went inside the jail.

# Chapter 14.

Kate.
Day Two, Stratton, Kansas 1869

The jail sat at the end of Stratton and across from it was the white steepled building that was the only church in the outpost. Kate shook her head at the idea of a church in Stratton, on the edge of the territories. The church seemed impossible, like friendly and caring prairie men.

The nine-year-old turned from the jail and church and back to Kaiyote. The Indian still next to his horse and dressed in his buffalo coat looked to the jail and then Kate. Kate smiled.

Kate thought absently about following Freeman into the block-like building but hesitated. Unlike before Kate heeded Freeman's words. The little girl found Stratton an odd place without the sound of children or the sight of women or children on the sidewalks.

She searched her coat pockets and then buttoned and unbuttoned the two flat wooden buttons on the front of the coat. While she waited Kate pulled out a scarf and tied it around her neck. She seemed to never know what to do with her hands.

Kate walked to the horse trough and studied her reflection in the water. Very slowly Kate inspected her halo of braids that was more laurel than halo, made up of finger thin braids that swept up from her neck and were fashioned into the unique hairstyle.

Kaiyote standing between the two horses studied Kate silently. He allowed a slight smile to appear on his usually expressionless face.

Kate noticing the unusual reaction from Kaiyote stopped and studied the Indian as she adjusted her brother's blanket coat that was too large for her.

"Didn't think you smiled," Kate said to Kaiyote.

The Indian in his Indian way did not respond. Kate did not expect a response. In the entire time that she had known Kaiyote he had never spoken to her or for that matter seemed to understand what Kate was saying.

Kate reached up and adjusted her braids near Freeman's horse. The horse snorted and raised and dropped its majestic head as Kate drew near. Freeman's horse was high spirited and a bit like Freeman when he was not around. Kaiyote reached out and put a hand on the neck of Freeman's horse to calm it.

"Why does that horse get all jumpy when Mister Freeman ain't 'round?"

Kaiyote continued looking at Kate as he stroked the horse.

"When Freeman is 'round this horse don't make a peep," Kate said.

Freeman's horse calmed down slowly. Kate moved slowly toward Kaiyote and the two horses. She kept her hands close to her body as she approached the black horse Freeman rode. The horse studied Kate with its big horse eyes. The horse neighed and whinnied as Kate reached the horse's head.

Kate slowly lifted her hand and reached out to Freeman's horse. The horse whinnied and snorted. Kate reached out and placed a hand on the horse's nose. The horse pulled away, but Kate did not allow the horse to backed away from her.

"Don't be that way," Kate said to Freeman's horse. "You gave me a ride. You know me."

Kaiyote watched Kate and then the horse and when Freeman's horse calmed down, he turned to look at the general store. Kaiyote did not say a word, but on his face was a story of pain and fighting and choosing a tough life. Kate studied the Indian as she stroked the neck of Freeman's horse.

Kate, now by Freeman's horse, could not help but look at the first Indian she had ever been close to and wonder. Jonathan, her older brother, had said that Indians were savages and blood-thirsty creatures that loved killing and scalping, but Kaiyote did not seem that way. The nine-year-old realized that many things her older brother said, and she believed, were not true. At least, that was what Kate decided.

"Kai-Kai-yotay," Kate said next to Freeman's horse. "You ever kill someone?"

The Indian, standing between the two horses, looked at the nine-year-old girl in the blanket coat and looked away. He looked as if he was thinking about something, Kate decided but was not sure. Kaiyote looked toward the jail and then back to the general store. Kate twisted her lips thinking how Freeman had paired her with someone that refused to talk.

Freeman had a twisted sense of humor, the little girl decided. He rarely answered her questions and Kaiyote simply did not acknowledge or understand what Kate said.

"If I was in trouble, would you even know?"

Kaiyote hearing Kate speak turned to her for a moment. The Indian scanned her and turned back to his position he had maintained since Freeman walked to the jail. He stood waiting with his hands on the saddle horn of his saddle.

The little girl dressed in a blanket coat and the Indian wrapped in a buffalo coat stood on the wagon trail of Stratton and waited. Kate reached out and tapped the saddlebag of Freeman's horse. Kaiyote, ever watchful, studied Kate's movements.

"What's in here?" Kate asked, tapping the saddlebag on the opposite side of Kaiyote. The Indian did not respond.

"Doesn't Freeman need his rifle?" Kate asked as she reached up and touched the butt of the long gun holstered between the saddlebags and saddle.

Kaiyote watched the little girl from the other side of the horse. He did not speak. Instead, Kaiyote, in his quiet way, watched the little girl touching Freeman's saddle.

Kate watched the people, mostly men, going and coming of the people walking on the raised sidewalks of Stratton.

"What you think is happenin' in that jail?" Kate asked Kaiyote who was leaning against the hitching post and patting the neck of his horse.

Kate had watched as Freeman walked into the weathered building.

The outpost was busy. The people that Kate had nearly run into at the general store were in their horse drawn wagon and slowly moving down the trail. Five or six people were on the raised walkways.

"Is it always this busy?"

The quiet warrior did not speak. He instead, looked left and right at the people climbing in and out of wagons and walking up and down the raised sidewalks.

Outside of the sheriff's office, Freeman looked around for something. Kate seeing Freeman step out of the sheriff's office reached out to Kaiyote and pointed. The man dressed in a buffalo coat looked down and then back in the direction Kate was pointing. The quiet warrior nodded.

Freeman raised a hand to Kate and Kaiyote. He signaled he still had business to do.

The dark-eyed Freeman crossed the main thoroughfare and avoided two men on horseback who scowled at Freeman. Freeman smiled and paid them no mind. He walked to the storefront where a sign hung that read: Barber. Freeman did not pay attention to the sign.

The wooden building was painted white, and the sign was lettered in red. Freeman, looked at the sign and despite not knowing how to read entered.

"You read letters?" Kate asked Kaiyote.

The quiet warrior walked to the watering trough and took off his sombrero. He dipped it into the trough and let some of the water run through the fabric before putting it back on his head. He turned and walked back to the horses and Kate.

"Talkin' to you is like talkin' to a wall," Kate said.

The quiet warrior looked at Kate curiously.

A few minutes after Freeman had entered the white building the cowboy was standing on the raised sidewalk again. Outside of the barber shop Freeman stood for an instant trying to think of his next steps. He crossed the road and made his way back to Kate and Kaiyote.

"What you find out?"

Freeman did not answer Kate.

The dark and bearded cowboy shielded his eyes and looked into the sky. The sun was still high in the sky. "If they tryin' to fetch back those... people, they need to leave soon."

"How soon?"

Freeman looked down and smiled at Kate.

"I figure it'll take us half a day to get there if that 'n get the... 'n return to the outpost 'fore dark," Freeman said. "But I ain't in charge."

"So, what we goin' to do?"

Freeman rubbed at the back of his neck.

"Let's eat," Freeman said. "I think we have time 'n if they lookin' fir me, they got lots uv people know where I'm goin' to be."

Kate looked around for the outpost and realized that all the men walking around were watching the trio like a lion must when a lamb wanders into its eyesight. She looked back at Freeman and Kaiyote who were already moving toward the saloon.

The saloon was a two-story building. On the first floor was the double swinging doors in the middle of structure. On either side of the doors were six paned windows. On the second story was a balcony on the front, below the painted name, Saloon. As the three walked to the far side of the outpost and the saloon Kate looked up and concluded that there were rooms on the second floor. The saloon was on the opposite side of the double wagon trail that made up the main trail of Stratton. The saloon sat opposite the general store.

Kate tried to keep up with Freeman and Kaiyote as the two entered the empty saloon. Inside of the Copper Saloon were a dozen round tables with six wooden chairs spread throughout the interior of the main floor. A bar, more wood planks attached end-to-end, stretched halfway across the main floor. At the far end of the saloon were a set of stairs that led to the second floor of the saloon.

The bartender, behind the bar, looked up and at the trio curiously. The bartender was a long-faced man with curly gray hair, almond shaped eyes and straight nose. Beneath his nose sat a peppered gray mustache and beard. He was wearing a red and white checkered shirt.

"We're here fir food," Freeman said, pointing to a table.

"What you eatin'?"

"Jus' some eggs 'n bacon 'n," Freeman paused. He looked to Kate. He looked to Kaiyote. "How 'bout some flapjacks?"

"What you drinkin'?"

"Milk fir the girl. Whiskey fir me. Cider fir my partner," Freeman said, reaching into his jacket and pulling out a coin. He lifted the coin into the air so the bartender could see it.

The three sat in the quiet saloon and waited for their food.

"What happened in the jail?"

Freeman looked at Kate and reluctantly answered.

"We're goin' to get the bodies," Freeman said.

"When?"

"As soon as they come get me," Freeman said.

"Why did it take so long?"

"Had to make the Marshall remember who I was 'n how to talk to me," Freeman said with a sneer.

"What's that mean?"

Freeman did not reply.

Kate pouted.

Freeman scanned the saloon, looking for trouble.

"Remember, while I'm gone to protect the girl," Freeman said to Kaiyote in the unique language.

"What did you say about me?"

"How you know I was talkin' 'bout you?"

"I hear you sayin' little girl in that language you speak wit him," Kate said.

Freeman smiled. He nodded at the girl's intelligence.

"I sed to protect you while I'm gone," Freeman said.

"Am I in danger?"

"We're all in danger," Freeman said. "You? Maybe more than me or Kaiyote," Freeman said, reflectively. "We're grown men but dangerous. They see us 'n figure that any trouble they bring might be answered back. But we're still outnumbered 'n outgunned every which way we look. The only thing that is on our side is peace, justice 'n liberty."

Kate pouted.

"I don't have peace, justice or liberty," the little girl said.

Freeman smiled. He reached inside of his jacket and fished out the derringer he had found in the wagon train. He handed it to Kate.

"Now, you got a little peace," Freeman said.

Kate smiled from ear-to-ear. She held the derringer in her hand and aimed it to the left and the right. Freeman and Kaiyote redirected Kate's deadly aim.

"Listen," Freeman said to Kate, lowering the derringer. "This is not a toy. You aim that little puncher 'n pull that trigger 'n you will end up with peace 'n quiet." Freeman paused. "So, don't pull it 'less you plan on usin' it."

Kate nodded.

Freeman opened and showed Kate the inner workings of the derringer. He also pointed out how to load and unload the bullets.

"Jus' two shots?"

"Two shots is plenty in the right hands," Freeman said.

Kate weighed the small pistol in her hand. She smiled broadly. The little girl opened and closed the derringer as Freeman had instructed her. She smiled at her new weapon. She slipped the derringer in her clothes bag.

"Good choice," Freeman said. "Don't want ev'ryone to know you have a little peace wit you."

"Thanks, Mister Freeman," Kate said.

Freeman nodded.

Kate nodded again.

The food came out and the gray-haired bartender walked the food to the table.

"I'm doin' a little work fir the sheriff 'n will need a place to rest my horse 'n sleep, if that ain't a problem," Freeman said.

The bartender looked at Freeman and then at Kate and the Indian.

"For all uv you?"

Freeman grinned at the question. The three were going to be lucky to find any place in Stratton that would house one of them, let alone all of them. Freeman scratched his cheek before answering.

"Well, no sir, jus' need a room fir me 'n my girl," Freeman said. "The Injun will find his own place to bed down."

"Well, you're in luck," the bartender said. "We ain't too busy, right now, 'n we have a room on the other side uv this wall. It's nothin' special. Jus' a room with a bed." The bartender put the plates of food on the round table. "There's a stable, jus' on the edge uv the outpost. It's a great stable. Your horse will be fine there."

"How much?"

"Fir the night? Here?" The bartender paused. "Let's say three dollars fir the night," the bartender said.

Freeman studied the man evenly.

"It ain't quiet but it's indoors 'n dry 'n warm," the bartender said.

As the trio ate the bartender returned with a skeleton key. Freeman gave the bartender the gold coin for the food and a room above the saloon for Kate to stay for the night.

As the trio was finishing their cooked breakfast a thin man with thick black hair pushed into the saloon and paused in the dimness of the interior. He was dressed all in black and wearing a black bowler hat. Behind Adams, Fred Scott, the deputy, stepped into the saloon and squinted. He looked upset and annoyed. He was wearing a duster similar to Doc Adams. Scott walked a few paces into the saloon and stopped.

Freeman smiled seeing the deputy. He casually placed his hand on the butt of his pistol.

"That's far enough," Freeman said.

"All right Freeman," the deputy said easily. He raised his hands in surrender as he stood beside Doc Adams. "The sheriff tol' me to come get you," Scott said with a hiss. "We're headin' to fetch those bodies."

Before Freeman moved or climbed to his feet, he looked to Kate and Kaiyote.

"Should be back before dark," Freeman said. "If there's trouble, head to the territories. It's your best bet," he added.

Kate nodded.

"Get a move on," Scott said angrily.

"Ease up deputy. You ain't got your Marshall to protect you now," Freeman said. "I tol' you 'n ev'rybody thinkin' they can call me anythin' 'cept my name will get them deader than dead."

Freeman climbed to his feet and walked toward the exit.

Kate climbed to her feet as well. She followed the dark and bearded cowboy to the raised sidewalk outside.

Freeman slipped liberty, his rifle, back in his saddle holster and untied Shadow from the hitch. The horse whinnied. Freeman patted his horse and let it nuzzle against the cowboy's shoulder.

Freeman looked at his horse and for an instant it looked like the horse seemed to look at Freeman. The cowboy placed a hand on the nose of his horse and leaned forward to touch forehead to forehead with the horse.

"It's okay boy," Freeman said to his horse. "We just goin' to take a little ride."

Freeman looked back at Kate now on the raised sidewalk and Kaiyote, now beside her. The Indian stood just a few feet from his own horse. His horse stood quietly nodding his head before Kaiyote and Kate.

"Lis'sen to Kaiyote," Freeman said. "Don't do nothin' stupid while I'm gone."

Before Kate could think of something to say Freeman and Shadow slow walked across the wagon trail to a waiting freight wagon where a small white man sat on the buckboard dressed like he was going to a burial. The small man was dressed all in black, from his head to his pointy boots.

Freeman nodded to the man in black and then the dark and bearded cowboy tied his horse to the back of the wagon without much fanfare. Shadow, Freeman's horse, nuzzled against the gruff cowboy. Freeman stroked his horse's neck. Freeman lingered in the rear of the freight wagon with his horse.

"All right," Doc Adams said, getting Freeman and Scott, the deputy's, attention. Freeman grabbed his rifle from his saddle holster and slowly made his way to the side of the wagon.

Scott, the deputy, sitting on his horse, a gray mare with a white front leg looked at Doc Adams, curiously. "Hold on. We need to wait on my cousin. He said he would lend a hand."

"We need to get a move on," Doc Adams said.

Scott shook his head. Doc Adams pouted. Scott wheeled his horse around and looked down the wagon trail for his missing cousin. Kate, seeing the deputy wheel around on his horse, looked up and int he direction the man was looking. Kaiyote never broke his gaze or seemed to concern himself with the theatrics on the other side of the wagon trail.

A wagon with two bearded men lurched across the wagon trail and stopped in front of the general store. Both men were wearing boots, blue trousers, wool coats and slouch hats. The driver of the wagon pulled the handbrake on the wagon and his partner was the first to step down. On his hip, Kate saw, was a pistol.

"Let's get goin'," Adams said loudly, annoyed.

"Give me a minute," Scott said. "I got my cousin comin' to help out." The deputy, dressed in a thick overcoat, button front shirt, thick canvas trousers and square-toed boots said.

"Your cousin? This ain't no apple pickin'," Doc Adams said, angrily and looking up into the sky at the climbing sun.

"I know," Scott said. "That's why I got my cousin. He's got a strong back," the deputy said with a grin.

Kate looked at the white man on the gray horse and noted his gallon hat, pistol and cowboy boots. He looked a bit out of place like he should be somewhere else. He was not stocky or thickly built but whip thin, beady-eyed, snake-like and a bit jumpy. On his hip was a pistol. Like Freeman, Scott had brought his rifle.

"I'll give this cousin of yours a few more minutes 'n then we leave with or without him," Doc Adams said. "Remember I'm in charge. If what Freeman says is true the army is goin' to pay us ten to fifteen dollars a head," Doc Adams said.

Freeman slowly made his way to the side of the wagon and climbed aboard. Doc Adams turned to acknowledge Freeman's arrival on the buckboard next to him. The doctor did not smile but he did not frown either. Freeman sat on the buckboard and tried to get comfortable.

"Sorry I'm late," a wide mouthed boy said with a frown atop a brown horse. He was dressed in a blanket coat, a bandana, a green colored shirt, gray trousers and cowboy boots. On his hip was a big horse pistol. "Had to run a mission fir Pa."

The horse he sat on had a white shoulder and looked to be a mix of Mustang and Appaloosa. The horse had one white foot. When the boy pulled up short his horse lowered its head and shook it rebelliously.

"Glad you could make it," Scott said sarcastically. He hitched a thumb over his shoulder and looked to Adams and Freeman. "This here is Dale, my cousin, he's gonna help us wit the bodies," Scott said as they rode out toward the wagon trail.

"Did I hear right? The army is payin' fir dead bodies?"

"Not exactly," Doc Adams said. He looked at Scott incredulously. "You know this already. You sat 'n lis'ened to us talk 'bout the army payin' to keep the territory's image up."

"Yeah. Yeah. But 'xplain it ag'in. How come the army payin' fir the dead?" Dale, the cousin of the deputy, asked.

"Well, they ain't 'xactly payin' fir the dead. They payin' to make the territory feel safe," Doc Adams said. "They don't want settlers to think they can't settle here. So, the payin' fir us to clean up 'round settlements."

"How long you thinkin' this will take?" the deputy's cousin said as he slowed his horse to the pace of the deputy.

"Accordin' to the... accordin' to," Scott paused, looking at Freeman who had his rifle on his lap. Freeman studied the deputy and there was a palpable feeling of animosity between the two. Dale, the cousin, looked from Scott to Freeman. Scott regrouped. "The story I know come from the... Freeman that come on 'em.

Accordin' to... him it's less than a half day's ride east in an out uv the way trail," Scott said in earshot of Freeman, Kaiyote and Kate.

Freeman, who was seated next to Doc Adams, smiled at the two horsemen. Kate found herself smiling as well as the two bullies had to dance around the words that they usually said amongst their friends and everyone not Freeman or Kate. Freeman sitting on the buckboard holding his rifle in hand seemed to create a limited equality.

Freeman seemed amused at the fact that the two fakers stumbled over their words knowing the dark and bearded cowboy was on his best deadly and on his worst just dangerous.

"Okay, we ready to go?"

"Yeah," Scott said, turning his horse and ready to ride out. "We go out 'n grab the bodies 'n be back 'fore dinner."

Kate winced with the words. She looked at the man on the horse and then the other. Her eyes fell on Freeman. He was watching Kate evenly.

The little girl looked away from Freeman and wiped at her eyes as casually as possible. She looked around and then at Kaiyote. The Indian did not seem to be paying attention to Kate's weak moment. He seemed only focused on what was going on just on the other side of the wagon trail that separated Stratton.

Kate pouted, listening to the white men talking mater-of-fact about the retrieval of her family and the others who had been murdered and left for dead on a disused trail. Kate shook her head to shake the images of her family and trail family and friends wrapped in the canvas of the bullet riddled wagons.

"Sounds good," Dale said with a smile.

Doc Adams slapped the reins and urged the horses forward. Dale, the cousin, rode up to the deputy and his horse fell into an easy trot alongside the deputy and his horse.

The dark cowboy sat comfortably on the buckboard of the freight wagon. Freeman adjusted his hat and stretched his fingers in his gloves as Doc Adams coaxed the four horses forward.

The ill-tempered cowboy looked to the little girl and his partner as the man on the buckboard urged the four horses forward and toward the wagon trail heading back to Coffeyville.

Kate and Kaiyote watched as Freeman and the three fakers rode out of Stratton and down the wagon trail.

# Chapter 15.

Kate.
Day Two, Stratton, Kansas, 1869

Kate watched as Freeman rolled out of the Stratton outpost with Shadow, tied to the rear of the wagon. By her side was Kaiyote, the observant partner of the ill-tempered cowboy.

"So, we goin' to wait for Freeman to return," Kate said to Kaiyote.

The tall silent warrior dressed in a buffalo coat looked at the little girl silently.

"Okay, Mister Freeman left me in charge. We supposed to go to the stable 'n put your horse away 'n make sure Freeman has a stall for his horse," Kate said. "Then, we supposed to head to the room 'n wait fir Freeman to return," the little girl said. "He gave me the key to the room," she said, lifting the skeleton key Freeman had been given earlier.

The quiet warrior listened and scanned the outpost. It was still cool. The sun had not reached its zenith and people were milling about Stratton. As earlier, Kate found it odd that there were few women and no children walking around Stratton. There were easily a dozen men, dressed in shirt sleeves, jackets, cowboy hats walking back and forth from one small storefront to the other.

The little girl gestured to Kaiyote and his horse and waited for the silent rider to unhitch his horse. Kate pantomimed unhitching the horse and when Kaiyote did the nine-year-old pointed toward the end of the outpost. Kaiyote watched without saying a word. The little girl walked toward the end of the outpost with Kaiyote and his horse.

"We need to stable your horse," Kate said, knowing that Kaiyote would not respond. The pair walked the horse to the front of Daniels Stable. The quiet warrior watched and slowly, casually walked with Kate.

Kate stopped in front of the stable. The front of the building looked like a barn. It had two big barn doors opened. To the left of the two doors was a smaller door.

The stable entrance went from the dirt of the wagon trail to about three feet of gravel that acted as a barrier for mud to packed dirt and hay that made up the flooring of the stable. Inside the stable there was a wide aisle that separated the eight stalls. Two were already occupied. As Kate entered, she saw a white horse with a blonde mane poke its head out from one of the stalls. In the adjacent stall was a sorrel horse with a white patch on its forehead.

Kate and Kaiyote walked to the rear of the stable and met up with the gentle giant wearing overalls and toting a hammer.

In the rear of the stable were two more doors. Near those doors was a furnace and anvil. The doors were open onto two long pens. In one of the long pens were three horses. One of the horses was a speckled pony. With the pony was a slow-moving donkey. In the rear of the pen stood a brown and unmoving carthorse.

"You the blacksmith?"

The white bearded giant nodded.

"The man at the saloon sed to ask for a Mister Clement Daniels," Kate said. "To have two stables fir some horses."

"I'm Mister Clement Daniels, little lady," the blacksmith said with a smile. He was a thickly constructed man that looked as if he might be able to carry a horse on his shoulders without much effort. Kate found herself studying the man's bullish neck, thick chest and large upper arms. "How can I help you?"

"Well, Mister Daniels, we need to stable this horse 'n another fir the night," Kate said. She added, "I got money."

Clement Daniels smiled again and studied the little girl, her horse and the Indian by her side. The mountain of a man, who looked a foot taller and easily fifty pounds heavier than Kaiyote. He was wearing a thin soiled shirt underneath his overalls. He reached into his back pocket and pulled out a handkerchief to wipe his egg-shaped face. Daniels was a thin eyed and lipped man whose face was enhanced by a long beard and his short curly black hair.

"Usually, charge two dollars a night fir boardin' a horse," Clement Daniels said.

Kate lifted a gold coin Freeman had given her.

Clement Daniels smiled and nodded.

"That will do to board 'n feed your horses," the blacksmith said. He reached out his giant hand and Kate handed him the coin. She looked back and took the reins from Kaiyote. The silent warrior watched as Kate handed the reins to the blacksmith.

"Need to remove your saddle 'n personals," Clement Daniels said pointing to the rifle and the saddlebags.

The quiet warrior removed the saddle and pack from his horse. Kate watched as the blacksmith walked his horse to an open stall and led it inside.

The horse examined the stall. It walked around the interior and finally stuck its head out. Kaiyote and Kate moved toward it. The quiet man reached out and put a hand on his horse's neck. The horse whinnied, whinnied and nodded its head. Kate simply watched.

Kate and Kaiyote watched as the blacksmith closed the lower Dutch door stall door behind the horse.

"He'll be safe as houses," the blacksmith said, reassuringly.

Kate smiled at the odd phrase. Kaiyote leaned on the door to the stall and watched his horse move around the spacious stall. The horse turned and returned to the stall door where Kaiyote waited. The horse nuzzled Kaiyote.

With one hand Kaiyote stroked the neck of his horse while he looked at the saddle by his foot. In his freehand he lifted and placed his rifle inside the stall out of the sight of others. Kaiyote talked quietly to his horse. He spoke in an ancient language, a language that sounded like songs Kate's mother sang.

Kate smiled at Kaiyote and his horse and suddenly felt like an intruder. She turned and wandered to the front entrance of the stable. The blacksmith was in the rear of the stable near the anvil, much the way he had been when Kate and Kaiyote arrived.

The little girl stood in the doorway entrance to the stable and watched the handful of men standing on the raised walkway talking to each other. The sun had begun its inevitable slide from above and through the clouds to hide behind the hills.

Kate thought absently that like the sun, she and Kaiyote, needed to head to the saloon and the room in the rear that Freeman had paid for them that night. Simultaneously, the little girl thought that Freeman should be returning soon if his calculations were correct. The sun would be behind the hills in just a few hours.

Kate had all these thoughts in her head, along with the wish of waiting for the cowboy to return, so that she would have someone to talk to and understand her. Kate knew that Freeman had said to go to the room and wait, but the nine-year-old did not look forward to sitting in a room with someone that did not understand one word she uttered.

Kate was thinking about telling Kaiyote that they could wait until it got dark before going to the room when five men came riding into the outpost. Kate found herself frozen in the doorway, because behind the men trotted six horses. The number of riders and horses jarred the little girl.

She looked at the men as they passed her and there on a chestnut-colored horse, dressed in gray and slouch hat, was the briefest of possible resemblance to Thomas Weaver, but Kate could not be sure. The first two Kate did not see, but behind the possible Thomas Weaver was a pug-nosed bearded man, a mean looking tough wearing a bowler hat and a red checkered shirt, and a dull looking cowboy wearing a sombrero and pulling two horses.

Kate backed away from the stable door and into the blacksmith.

"Girl? What you doin'?" The blacksmith asked.

The quiet warrior looked at Kate and then toward the entrance to the stable and the sound of horses passing. The quiet warrior looked to Kate, who looked like she had seen a ghost.

"That's them," Kate said stunned.

"That's who?" Asked the blacksmith.

Kate shook her head. She could not stop looking out of the stable entrance. Kate had stopped talking but continued back into the stable.

"You all right?" The blacksmith asked, looking at the frightened girl.

Kate did not answer. She instead pushed back past the blacksmith and to the stall where Kaiyote stood, and his horse was held. The quiet warrior studied the girl, curiously.

A few minutes later, two gunmen appeared at the entrance to the stable. The gunmen climbed off their horses and walked into the stable with the six horses in tow.

Kate watched silently from inside the stall as the men approached.

"Hey, pard'ner, we was tol' you might be someone we could talk to about sellin' our horses," the bearded ruffian with squinty eyes and wearing a dusty bowler said. He was dressed in a thick jacket, buttoned only at the throat and opened to show off his red flannel shirt, silver belt buckle, gun belt and dark handled pistol on his hip.

His partner was an oval faced character with a pug nose and broom brush mustache and beard. He had a high forehead, dark eyebrows and a pug nose. He was wearing a wide brimmed cowboy hat with a feather in his hat band, a loose-fitting jacket, light blue stitched shirt, gun belt with a pistol on his hip, trousers and cowboy boots with spurs. He scanned the stable and saw Kaiyote near the stable stall.

The blacksmith turned from the rear of the stable and his anvil seeing the men and the horses. He met the two with their horses. The blacksmith stood studying the horses and the men.

"You got an Injun in here?" Asked the pug-nosed tough.

"What?" The blacksmith asked, slightly confused.

"I don't much like Injuns," the squinty eyed thief said, looking at Kaiyote.

The quiet warrior did not move. He had his rifle leaning against the stall with his horse. The quiet warrior leaned on the stall door and casually reached for his pistol under his buffalo coat.

"How you let a savage walk 'round in a decent place like this?" The pug-nosed tough said.

His friend reached out and touched the insulting gunmen.

"Maybe, that's why he let 'im in here? It's a stable," the other cowboy laughed.

"Don't you know they filthy animals?" The pug nose antagonist asked, then paused, thinking what his friend had said. He chuckled just a little. "Suppose this would be the place to have an Injun, come to think uv it."

The blacksmith shook his head.

"They will kill you sooner than look at you," the pug-nosed cowboy said.

"I ain't had no trouble from this here fella," the blacksmith said.

"Redman, you stay over there, away from us," the pug nose cowboy said, looking at the back of Kaiyote.

The two men were just at the mouth of the stable. The horses were spread out a bit but held by ropes around their necks. The bully eyed the Indian who was standing with his back to them. The blacksmith seeing the two gunmen focusing on the quiet Indian patted one of the horses on the neck to get the men's attention.

"Hey, how much you want fir your horses?"

The two gunmen looked at the blacksmith as soon as the topic changed.

"Thinkin' 'bout twenty dollars apiece," the squinty eyed stranger said.

"Twenty dollars?" The blacksmith asked, pushing past the two men and looking at the horses. The blacksmith did a superficial examination of the horses. He looked at the front hoof of one horse. He noticed the sway of one of the horse's backs. "I don't know 'bout that."

"That's a fair price," said the pug-nosed roughneck.

"Yeah, it is," the squinty eyed rowdy said.

"How you come by these horses?"

"What? We found 'em on the plains runnin' loose," the pug nose stranger said. "One man's loss is another man's treasure," the stranger said with a malicious grin.

"Yeah, we was on our way from Coffeyville and we saw these here horses on the plains. So, I sed to my friend, I sed, 'Let's go get 'em 'n sell 'em at Stratton.' I always try to look fir opportunities," the squinty eyed stranger said.

"Let me do a quick look see," the blacksmith said. "Twenty dollars seems a little high fir these nags. They ain't young 'n have seen a lot uv wear 'n tear."

"Come on," the squinty eyed goon said with a smile. "The lowest we'll go is fifteen a head."

"Let me give 'em a look see. If you lookin' fir fifteen, I can say that you ain't gonna see that from what I'm seein'," Clement Daniels said. He paused. "Let me look 'em over 'n think about it. If you want you can put them in the empty pen out back," the blacksmith said. "I'll charge you two dollars apiece fir the feed 'n pen. Then I'll see if I am in'trested."

"Sounds good," the squinty eyed stranger said.

"That's twelve dollars," the blacksmith said. "In advance."

The squinty eyed brute tapped his pockets and found the coins to pay for the food and pen for the night. He handed the coins to the blacksmith and grinned.

"We'll be back 'n 'spect to sell them horses," the squinty eyed man said. "It's only fair."

The pair walked the six horses through the stable to the rear pen. They looked at each other and nodded and smiled at the blacksmith as they walked back through the stable and past Kaiyote who had not moved from the stall, his horse or the hiding Kate.

"Thought Stratton didn't allow red skins in this spot?"

"Stratton's changin'," Clement Daniels said. "We know ain't all Injuns bad Injuns."

"You can say what you want but I don't trust 'em," the squinty eyed cowboy said with a scowl.

"I guess this'll be the last time we come here," the pug-nosed cowboy said.

The blacksmith shrugged his thick shoulders.

"How long you need to decide how much you goin' to give us for our horses?" The squinty-eyed gunman asked, looking from Kaiyote and to the blacksmith.

"Come back in an hour or two 'n I'll make a decision, good or bad," the blacksmith said.

"We'll be at the saloon 'n tryin' to knock some uv this trail dust out 'n our throats," the pug nose cowboy said.

"Yep," the squinty eyed rowdy said with a grin. "Hope there's some womenfolk to take the edge off."

"Stratton has a lot uv things," Clement Daniels said. "But this close to the territories women are few 'n far between."

"No women?"

"None not claimed or fir you," the blacksmith said.

"That's a shame," the plainsman said.

The pug-nosed bully stopped and thought over what the blacksmith had said.

"Ain't a woman available in this outpost?"

Clement Daniels shook his head.

"I heard there was a whore in Coffeyville that made fifty dollars a night," the frowning cowboy said. "This whore become one uv the richest people in the town," the squinty eyed tough said.

The pug-nosed brute nodded at the short tale.

"Don't know 'bout that," the blacksmith said. "I do know Stratton was talkin' 'bout shippin' in some women soon, but how soon is anyone's guess," Clement Daniels said.

"Ain't goin' to be anytime soon," the pug-nosed brute said with a smirk.

Clement Daniels looked at the two gunmen and narrowed his thin eyes, studying the men

"Until then, all the cows 'n goats on full alert," the pug-nosed bully said with a laugh.

"'N dogs 'n pigs 'n chickens too," the squinty eyed gunmen wearing the dusty bowler said with a chuckle.

"We'll be back to get our money, blacksmith," the pug-nosed tough said with a growl.

"Yeah, we'll be back," the squinty-eyed roughneck said, in agreement.

The two gunmen moved slowly to the exit. The blacksmith shook his head as the two men walked out of the stable.

# Chapter 16.

Kate.

Day Two, A night in Stratton, Kansas, 1869

After the two men left the stable Kaiyote looked at the little girl hiding in the stall with his horse. The dark eyed man did not give away anything as he looked at Kate. He looked at the girl evenly.

"Kate," Kaiyote said, slowly. He spoke in an ancient language.

Kate looked up. The little girl looked at the usually silent man standing at the stall door. She was completely shocked hearing her name from Kaiyote.

"They gone," Kaiyote said. He spoke in the ancient language of his people.

Kate climbed to her feet and tilted her head at the quiet warrior wearing a buffalo coat.

"You can speak like us?"

Kaiyote nodded.

Kate slipped out of the stall and looked at Kaiyote unbelieving.

'You understand me?"

The brave nodded.

"How come you didn't talk earlier?"

Kaiyote shrugged his shoulders.

"Those men stole my family's horses," Kate said.

Clement Daniels, the blacksmith, was standing at the stable entrance. The blacksmith watched as a wagon rolled by the stable. Kate looked toward the stable entrance and then back to where the two men had stood.

The little girl blinked, thinking. She looked back to the stable entrance and shook her head.

"Let's go," Kate said to Kaiyote and led the way. She exited out of the rear of the stable and as she did, she looked at the horses in the pen the men had brought. The horses were nothing special. They were carthorses and just six run-of-the-mill workhorses. Nothing stood out to Kate until she slowed and noticed one of the horses had a brand her father had shown her when he bought it.

Kate stopped and studied the horse to be sure. The brand sat on the horse's left rump. Her father had pointed the brand out to Kate and her brother when they were living in Kansas.

"You see that?" Kate asked, pointing to the horse with the brand on its rump. "That's one uv my dad's horses." She paused. "That means those two were part uv it."

The quiet warrior, with his rifle in one hand and his saddle over his shoulder stood and listened.

"You understand ev'rythin' I'm sayin'?" Kate asked. "I mean, I need someone to understand what I'm saying."

The quiet warrior looked at the little girl silently and nodded. He looked at the pen. He looked at the horses and back to the little girl.

"How come you didn't talk before?"

The silent man looked to the sky and noticed the sun was slowly sinking behind the hills and mountains on the other side of the territory. The quiet warrior pointed to the sky and Kate looked up. The little girl seeing the sun beginning to edge toward the hills nodded and twisted her lips.

"I know," Kate said.

Kaiyote looked left and right and pointed to the left.

"I know. We need to head to the saloon but let's go the back route. I don't want to run into those cowboys," Kate said.

The pair took a circuitous route to the saloon. They walked through the rear of the outpost and saw the dozen outhouses that sat on a berm that bordered the outpost proper. On the other side of the raised ground was a slight slope that fell maybe twenty feet to rocks and brush.

In the rear of the outpost, just beyond the outhouses, Kate noticed half a dozen wooden structures huddled together that looked like shacks more than anything else. She did not know the purpose of the wooden structures. They were not large enough for houses and too big for outhouses. Maybe, the little girl thought, they were storage sheds?

She looked at Kaiyote carrying his rifle and scanning the rear of the outpost which fell away to just plains for as far as the eye could see. For nearly a mile, in any direction, there was random clumps of trees but little else around the near dozen buildings that made up Stratton Outpost.

On the backside of the outpost in the dog trails she and Kaiyote watched three motley-colored dogs hiding in the shade of one of those wooden structures. The dogs were watching them as they approached. Kate seeing the dogs, stutter stepped. The dogs were hiding underneath a building and Kate seeing them jumped, surprised.

Kaiyote shook his head and continued walking. The stoic Kaiyote smiled just a little.

"You not like dogs?"

"I ain't scared uv them," Kate said. "I jus' ain't in love wit them."

Kaiyote nodded.

"How come you didn't talk earlier?"

"Didn't have anythin' to say," Kaiyote said.

Kate opened and closed her mouth, thinking.

She shook her head.

"Didn't have nothin' to say?" Kate said with a slight grin. "You understand what I'm sayin now?

Kaiyote did not speak. He simply walked, leisurely, his saddle over his shoulder. His rifle in his free hand.

"Those men," Kate said.

She replayed what had just happened.

The pair walked on.

Kate looked back toward the stable and past Kaiyote.

Kaiyote lifted his rifle to get Kate's attention. He tipped his chin in the direction they were walking on the dog run.

"Those men," Kate began. She shook her head, thinking. "Maybe we should've waited fir Freeman?"

Kaiyote slowed. Kaiyote looked at Kate and did not give any sign of his thoughts. The man carrying the saddle adjusted the saddle in his hand and stopped, barring Kate's view of the stable behind them.

The little girl frowned, confused.

"Do you think we should've waited?"

Kaiyote tipped his chin in the direction away from the stable.

Kate turned around, unhappily. She pouted. Kate began walking again toward the saloon.

"Turn here," Kate said, pointing to the corner of two buildings. "This way."

Kate paused and realized that she was on the nearest side of the saloon, closest to the stable. The room Freeman bought was on the opposite side of the building. She turned and pushed back against Kaiyote and toward the rear of the two-story building.

"Our room should be on the other side of the building," Kate said with a small smile. She pointed in the direction of the other corner of the building. Kate looked at Kaiyote and waited a beat, hoping the quiet warrior would speak. The quiet warrior did not react.

Kaiyote watched the little girl as she moved past him. He turned and nodded. The quiet warrior carrying his saddle and rifle simply followed silently.

After a moment, Kate exhaled, readjusted her grip on her clothes bag, and walked around to the rear of the saloon. The journey was short. The dog run had two outhouses. One outhouse was labeled with a sign of a woman. The other had a sign of a man. The outhouses sat on the dog run. Behind the outhouses for as far as the eye could see was the rolling plains of Kansas that eventually, inevitably led back to Lawrence, where Kate and her family he begun weeks ago.

Kate stopped at the entrance to the other side of the saloon. The odd little houses stuck out like a purple cow on a grass field. At the rear of the saloon Kate found herself looking at the half dozen small houses which lined the slight ridge of the dog run.

The little girl looked past the small houses and the plains and saw a plot of land behind a white building, where there was a short fence to separate it from the rest of the dog run. Kate focused on the white building and imagined it was a church.

The church steeple looked like an index finger pointed toward heaven. The church was painted white. It was a just a bit larger than the small buildings that dotted most of Stratton.

A church in Stratton seemed so improbable to the little girl. She had gone to a church gathering with her mom and brother in Lawrence. That gathering was fun, friendly, and full of singing and dancing. It was like a party. Kate remembered sadly that her mom told her: "God is here."

"How do you know?" Kate asked.

"God is love, baby. He is everywhere love is," her mother had told her that day in the gathering of smiling faces.

The idea of God in Stratton or anywhere in Kansas seemed far-fetched. She could not imagine a man of God coming to Stratton, not this Stratton, to pray or to start a church. Everyone Kate met seemed to be without the thing called neighborly love for others. The little girl decided, at once, that the church must have been built and then abandoned. There were too many evil men in Stratton for God to be here, Kate decided.

Kate looked back at the plot of land that held the dozen gravestones. The gravestones sat in a row. The nine-year-old was jarred by the sight of the fenced area and the gravestones in the rear of the small church.

Seeing the gravestones sticking up from the ground made Kate sad. The sadness washed over her as she thought in nine years of living, she had in one day seen the loss of nearly twenty people. She corrected herself. She had seen the loss of life of those individuals.

The nine-year-old wondered was that graveyard behind the church where her family and all the dead of the wagon train would be buried? She imagined it was probable and logical that the wagon train would be buried. Yet, as a child, she wasn't certain.

Kate turned from the church and to Kaiyote, who was standing a few feet away with his saddle and rifle, waiting patiently. He looked at Kate steadily and silently.

The little girl fished for the key she had been given to her. On the first floor of the building there was a small, weathered door on the weathered wall.

"You don't have nothin' to say?"

Kaiyote shook his head as Kate walked past him and climbed the three steps that led to a raised sidewalk that bordered the saloon. At the raised sidewalk Kate looked back to see Kaiyote standing at the foot of the stairs. He slowly mounted the stairs, following Kate at a distance.

She looked around at the three doors that stretched down the raised walkway. Each door had a number on it. Kate tried to decipher the numbers as she fished in her clothes bag for the key Freeman had given her earlier.

Finding the skeleton key Kate retrieved it from inside her bag and studied the number on the key. She looked at the door and then the key. The little girl walked to the first side door that had a turnkey lock.

Kate smiled at the idea of a door with a lock. In her short life she had never lived in a house with a locked door. At first the key caught and did not move. She unlocked the lock. Kate puckered her lips, twisted the key and unlocked the door. Kate entered the room. The key unlocked the door to the room the bartender had assured Freeman was nothing more than a room.

The room was a room in the back of the saloon, little used, but sufficient for Freeman, Kate and Kaiyote. There was only the one door for entrance and exit. The quiet warrior stepped into the small room and found himself shoulder to shoulder with Kate.

The room was just that a room with a single bed in it. There was a table, a kerosene lamp and wooden chair beside the table. There was a glass paned window that opened onto the alleyway of the saloon.

"This is it," Kate said, placing her clothes bag on the bed.

The quiet warrior studied the room. The Indian leaned his rifle against the wall of the room and sat his saddle on the floor before stepping out of the room. Once outside the room Kaiyote took a deep breath and leaned against the wall of the building.

"What?" Kate asked. "You don't like bein' inside?"

Kaiyote did not answer. Kate did not expect him to answer. He had said a handful of words to her, that she could understand, in the two days they had been together.

Kate decided that Kaiyote was a solitary individual. He rode with Freeman the way Kate rode with Freeman, not as a partner or friend but as someone riding along and not slowing him down. If he or anyone slowed him down, then they were expendable.

So, Kaiyote too, must have decided to look out for Kate, because it didn't interfere with his plans, the nine-year-old decided. He needed some place to rest and though he didn't like being indoors, the room happened to be some place he could keep his belongings safe while in Stratton and off the plains.

Kate pouted, thinking. Were her thoughts correct? Suddenly, there were a million questions the nine-year-old needed answered. She looked at the usually quiet and brooding Indian still standing in the doorway of the room like a wild animal thinking the room was the mouth of a trap and bit her lip before asking her first question.

"How come you wit Freeman?"

Kaiyote turned from the doorway and looked at Kate, curiously.

"I mean, Mister Freeman is a hard man to be around 'n doesn't seem to be too nice," Kate said, in explanation.

"Freeman? He like ev'ryone here," Kaiyote said.

"What you mean?"

"My people here fir long time. They here before others came," Kaiyote said.

Kate tilted her head, confused.

"My people watched 'n first thought the palefaces were like us," Kaiyote said. "My father 'n his father 'n his father tol' us all to honor the land. Honor ev'rythin that moves on or comes from the land. Honor it. My people tell uv a time long before the white man came the land was filled with all sorts uv animals' fir as far as the eye could see," Kaiyote said, thoughtfully. "Then the palefaces appeared 'n they thought the land was only... land. They fought 'n killed 'n took whatever they wanted. They took from the land 'n the land cried. The palefaces killed 'n didn't honor the land," the Indian said. "They do not honor anything," Kaiyote said in the doorjamb, holding his pistol.

"Honor the land?"

"Freeman is trapped, like ev'ryone here. My people trapped too."

"Trapped? Freeman said that he broke out of a prison once," Kate said.

"He still trapped. He just trapped in between. The palefaces trapped him 'n now he lost 'n on this walk."

"Walk?"

"He like wolf raised 'round rats," Kaiyote said, ignoring Kate's question. "The rats teach him, but he know he diff'rent. He have wolf mind. Most uv time he is growlin' wolf. He not loved. He not treated well." Kaiyote paused. "He on journey. He has the quiet wolf inside too. The good wolf," the warrior said. Kaiyote looked into the darkness and then back at Kate. "I wit Deadman to see his walk out of the in between."

"He in between? 'N on a walk?" Kate repeated, confused.

Kaiyote nodded in answer.

"Okay," the nine-year-old said. "Why you on his walk wit him?"

"Gray Hawk sent on a walk to learn my path. I am on spirit walk. Gray Hawk send me to see Deadman's Clothes journey 'n learn from it," Kaiyote said. Before Kate could ask her next question, Kaiyote answered. "I'm on spirit walk. I followin' to see 'n guide Deadman's Clothes journey."

"Who is Gray Hawk?"

"My chief," Kaiyote said.

"Wait," Kate said. "How long you been on this walk?"

"Two winters," Kaiyote said.

"How much longer you walkin'?"

"I return to Gray Hawk 'n my tribe...," Kaiyote lifted a hand and around his forearm was a wooden armlet made of rope and three-inch slats of wood and pointed to it. He paused trying to think of the appropriate word. "Three seasons to go on this journey."

Kate frowned at Kaiyote's words.

"Three years?"

"Some walks longer. Some shorter," Kaiyote said.

"What you 'n Gray Hawk 'spect to happen?"

Kaiyote hesitated. He looked at Kate without understanding.

"When will you know it's over?"

Kaiyote nodded, understanding. "Change," Kaiyote said with a gesture of his hand, like a fish moving in the water. "Deadman's change. My change. Change."

Kate nodded. The little girl felt satisfied with all the answers Kaiyote had offered.

The little girl thought about what Kaiyote said as she sat on the bed and watched the Indian guarding the open door.

"Why you call him... Deadman's Clothes?"

Kaiyote did not answer immediately.

"He first appear 'n we take him to Gray Hawk he was dressed in Deadman's Clothes," Kaiyote said. "Gray Hawk gave him that name."

"But he likes to be called: Freeman."

Kaiyote smiled at Kate's words.

"Why you laugh?"

Kaiyote smiled and did not answer for a moment.

"You, like him. You think the palefaces, the demons make you free," Kaiyote said. "They not make you free. You, me, we all free," Kaiyote said.

Kate did not know how to respond to Kaiyote. She shook her head.

"Is Freeman a good man?"

Kaiyote did not answer.

"Is he someone to trust?"

Kaiyote turned and looked at the little girl still dressed in her oversized coat, trousers and cowboy boots.

"He wolf," Kaiyote said as an answer.

Kate chuckled.

Kaiyote looked at the nine-year-old girl who was smiling at him.

"He money hungry wolf," Kate said.

Kate recalled that Freeman searching the bodies of the dead when he took her from the wagon train to Stratton.

"Do you think Mister Freeman will help me?"

Kaiyote did not answer.

Kate took a different approach.

"You on this spirit walk? Is that to help?"

The quiet warrior did not speak.

"What you walkin' fir?"

Kaiyote stared into the darkness.

"How you know you done?"

Kaiyote did not answer.

"I think I liked it better when I thought you couldn't speak or understand me," Kate said, suddenly annoyed.

Kate pouted. She sat and tried to understand what Kaiyote had said. He was a spirit walker. What was a spirit walker? Maybe, the little girl thought, she could ask Freeman and he would tell her.

The nine-year-old almost laughed out loud at the thought of Freeman telling her something she wanted to know. The man was mean, stubborn and ornery.

The saloon was just on the other side of the wall. Kate listened and tried to rest, but at that time of day, with the sky darkening, the saloon began to get busy.

Kate sat on the bed with her clothes bag in front of her. She sat in the room alone. Kaiyote, after depositing his saddle and rifle, stepped outside and guarded the room.

# Chapter 17.

Kate.
Stratton Saloon, 1877


The Lawson wagon bumped along toward Stratton. Kate looked out of the wagon and though they had been traveling for months through the green and yellow of the plains and most things looked similar, here, this place, seemed familiar. Kate smiled at the reality that she recognized this area. She couldn't be sure, but she was sure they were now on the trail toward Stratton. If she was right, they should be in the outpost in an hour.

She leaned back and tried to imagine what Stratton looked like now, nearly eight years since her last time there. She wondered if the sheriff in Stratton was the same sheriff when she was nine years old? She wondered if the blacksmith was still at his anvil hammering horseshoes and charging to stable horses? Now that she was older, Kate wondered if she was bold enough to go to the saloon where she, Freeman and Kaiyote stayed?

But none of that mattered in the Lawson wagon, at the moment. The only thing that mattered, according to Randolph Lawson was who could hold their breath the longest.

"Kate," Randolph said with his missing front tooth. "You gonna play?" The seven-year-old boy had the big brown eyes of his father, not as intense or intimidating as his father, but expressive. His high forehead, cheeks and big smile he had inherited from his mother. A round nose, thick lips and pointed chin seemed to be a combination of his mother and father.

The other boys were waiting. Missus Lawson, with the gentle and round features smiled at Randolph's question. Elisabeth looked at Kate and smiled. Little Ricky Lawson, the youngest boy, just five, leaned on his older brother with his dark eyes and slight grin.

"What you playin' now?"

"We tryin' to see who can hol' their breath the longest," Randolph said.

"The winner's gonna be me," RJ said confidently.

"No, it's gonna be me," said Ricky Lawson, pushing his big brother for emphasis.

So, as the Lawson wagon bumped along the uneven trail toward Stratton, Kate found herself looking at one of the Lawson boys who was trying to explain the newest contest.

"See, RJ thinks that we should all learn to hol' our breaths, in case we fall into the water," Randolph said with a toothy smile.

Kate frowned at the boy's logic.

"Can't none uv us swim," RJ said from the corner of the wagon where the boys usually played.

"Well, me 'n RJ is gonna learn," Randolph said with a smile, dressed in an undershirt, overalls and no shoes.

"I'm gonna learn too," said little Ricky.

"Well, 'til we learn we decided to see who can hol' their breath the longest. Makes sense," Randolph said, looking back at RJ and Ricky who were nodding in agreement.

"Okay," Kate said with a smile. "So, what do you want me to do?"

"You can play or judge or both," Randolph said. "Mama said she wasn't playin' 'n Elisabeth is bein' iffy. So, I decided to ask you," Randolph concluded.

"Thanks fir askin'," Kate smiled. She looked around the wagon and smiled.

The wagon was never without activity. Filled with three young boys, the covered wagon seemed to be the closest thing to what Kate imagined people to mean when they said, "family." There was laughter here. There was fighting, nothing malicious, and disagreement. Yet, at the end of the day, Ricky, Randolph and Reginald Junior always found themselves sleeping head-to-shoulder-to foot together, exhausted from a day of rough housing and laughing and trying to be the best.

"I think I'll play," Kate said and shocked everyone in the wagon, including Missus Lawson.

"Okay," Randolph said with a hoot. "The way we goin' to do it is wit a countdown. Whoever wins is the one that holds out the longest."

Kate nodded. Elisabeth did the countdown from five.

"Go," Elisabeth said, and the Lawson boys and Kate held their collective breaths. After a few seconds Ricky let out his breath and inhaled.

"Ricky you're out," said his older sister with a smile.

"Good job, baby," Missus Lawson said to her youngest son.

Kate, Randolph and RJ were locked in a contest for superiority. The contest was intense. The surprise of the contest was that it wasn't Kate or RJ who won but Randolph.

"I think Randolph cheated," RJ said, bitter.

"What? I didn't cheat 'n you know it," Randolph said, puffing up to his older brother.

"You know you cheated. I saw you smilin' 'n actin' like it wasn't hard to hol' your breath 'n it prob'bly wasn't 'cause you was cheatin'."

"Nobody was cheatin'," Elisabeth said to RJ. "We ain't no cheaters. Stop that talk."

"Okay, if he wasn't cheatin' let's do it a'gin. If he wins then I ain't goin' to call him no cheat," RJ said.

"Fine. Here's the new rules," Elisabeth said to the three boys, under the supervision of their mother. "No one can cheat. You hol' your breath 'n pinch your nose. If you let air out, then no air can come back in. Fair?"

The three boys agreed.

"One more time?"

The three boys did another contest of holding their breath. The results were the exact same.        By the end of the holding your breath contest Kate looked out of the wagon and saw the first signs of Stratton. Buildings had sprung up near the outpost. Wagons passed by in the opposite direction. Stratton seemed to be a bustling town now.

Things had changed dramatically in this new Stratton, but for Kate it was still the place where the men who had threatened to hurt Kaiyote floated in her memory. This Stratton was the same Stratton where Kate was shocked and surprised by Kaiyote.

"Were you scared?" Elisabeth Lawson asked. Through the front of the wagon, where the boys gathered, Kate could see the gentle undulations of grassy hills that led to Stratton. Elisabeth's mother was sitting with Charlotte next to her on a bench which was made comfortable with a half dozen blankets and quilts. There was always noise and screaming and complaining as Kate spoke exclusively to Elisabeth. The wagon was always a beehive of activity. In the Lawson wagon, there were three boys under the age of ten wrestling and fighting constantly. The youngest boy, Ricky, was six with a missing front tooth. The middle boy, Randolph, was seven and a stockier boy than the others. He had a constant grin on his fat face. The oldest boy, nine, was Reginald Junior. The youngest Lawson, Charlotte, was just turning two and clinging to Elisabeth's mother's skirt.

The wagon train was suddenly on the edge of Stratton. Reginald Lawson, driving the wagon Kate was in, looked back and inside the wagon. His look froze all the boys in mid-action. Kate could not help but smile at the boys stopping their continual punching, sticking out tongues, kicking and pointing.

"We should be in Stratton soon," Elisabeth's father said from the buckboard. "We goin' to rest in Bucktown while we here," he said.

Bucktown? Kate had never heard of Bucktown before.

Elisabeth's father turned back around and continued steering the wagon toward Stratton.

As soon as Reginald Lawson turned back to the wagon trail the chaos and play fighting resumed.

"So? Were you scared?"

"It's weird," Kate said, attempting to explain her thinking. "Freeman was horrible. He was mean. He didn't listen to me, but at the same time I knew if he or Kaiyote were around I was safe," Kate said.

Elisabeth chuckled. She chuckled because what Kate said did not make much sense.

"So, what did you tell the Injun?"

Elisabeth, never tired of hearing Kate's stories. When things quieted, usually when two of the boys tired and fell asleep, Elisabeth would question the serious Kate about parts of her story from the wagon train to Oregon where she had stopped or decided to skirt. The night in Stratton was one of those stories that Elisabeth wanted to know more about, for some reason.

"Were you afraid bein' wit the Injun? I mean, Injuns are dangerous," Elisabeth said.

"Kaiyote was diff'rent," Kate said.

Elisabeth looked at Kate, confused.

"I think if I met Freeman alone, he would've been diff'rent," Kate said, attempting to explain. "I don't know. I think he and Kaiyote watched each other and kind uv made each other betta."

"I don't know," Elisabeth said.

"They decided to protect me 'n that became... the reason I was always safe wit them. If that makes sense," Kate said.

"So, the Injun protected you when Freeman was gone, and Freeman protected you when it was jus' him?" Elisabeth asked, trying to understand what Kate said.

Kate smiled. Kate blinked and found herself back in Stratton the day she thought she had seen Weaver and almost had a run-in with two of the gunmen.

# Chapter 18.

Kate.
Day Two, Stratton, Kansas, 1869

She was sitting on the only bed in the room that Freeman had rented for the night. On the other side of the only door in the storage with a bed in it Kaiyote probably sat on the walkway and watched in the dark, guarding the room.

Kate looked around the room. It was not very big. It fit the cot that she sat on, a table and a chair in its space. There was nothing that gave it the feel of a real bedroom. Kate noticed there was a spittoon near the door. Perhaps, that was the only thing that suggested furnishing.

The little girl thought about Kaiyote. The cold of the night was not wintry. The night cooled off the warm of the day and was replaced with a chill. There was no hint of snow in the air, but it had not gotten cold enough yet.

Kate imagined if it got too cold Kaiyote would come inside the room out of the cold. The thought made her pause. She knew that Kaiyote was friends with Freeman, but for the first time she was concerned about the Indian.

It was just getting dark when Freeman entered the small room.

The little girl reached for her clothes bag.

Freeman smiled and raised his hands as he entered.

"How did you know where we were?"

"After... Well, one uv the bath house workers tol' me," Freeman said, standing in the doorway of the cramped room.

"Bath house... workers?"

Freeman did not respond.

"Did you get ev'ryone?"

"We got ev'ryone," Freeman said.

Kate smiled. She looked at Freeman and then Kaiyote who was still outside sitting on the raised sidewalk. The nine-year-old looked at Freeman and studied the ill-tempered cowboy.

"How come you didn't tell me that your Injun understood?"

Freeman looked at Kate and shrugged his shoulders.

"You don't think that was important?"

Freeman looked at the little girl and the room and sparse furnishings and then back at Kate.

"You... could have tol me," Kate said.

Freeman smiled.

"Anyone hungry?"

Kate nodded.

"I'll go to the saloon 'n get us some food," Freeman said.

"Can I come?"

Freeman frowned. He knew immediately refusing the little girl would only end with her slipping out and finding her way to the saloon. Freeman exhaled and leaned his rifle against the inner wall of the room. He looked to Kaiyote. The quiet warrior holstered his pistol and sat in the chair and grinned.

Freeman turned on his heels and walked out of the room with Kate in tow. The little girl, carrying her clothes bag, followed along reaching out for the cowboy's hand and then pulling back her own hand at the idea. She looked up and down the raised walk which ran along the side of the saloon and past three more side doors.

Freeman stepped off the raised sidewalk and to his horse. Kate followed. Freeman did not speak but walked in between the two buildings with the reins of his horse in his hand. His horse, whinnied, and walked effortlessly behind the bearded cowboy and little girl.

The cowboy turned onto the main street of Stratton Outpost and walked his horse past the saloon and toward the stable.

"Looks like he's closed," Kate said.

"Jus' because the door is closed don't mean no one inside," Freeman said, stopping in front of the stable. Freeman knocked on the stable door.

Kate peered through the slats of the stable and saw a dim light inside of the building. A few minutes later the smaller door of the stable, to the right of the main double doors, opened.

In the doorway was the giant blacksmith.

"Need to stable my horse fir the night," Freeman said. "Think the girl paid fir my horse already."

The blacksmith nodded, closed the small door, unbarred the double doors and opened one of them.

Freeman and the blacksmith talked, and Freeman walked the stable looking for a clean stall. Kate visited Kaiyote's horse and found the horse standing by the stall. She patted the horse's neck, and it nuzzled the little girl.

She looked around the stable for apples or carrots to feed the horse. In a wooden bin just a few stalls over were six carrots. Kate took a carrot from the bin and returned to Kaiyote's horse. It nibbled the carrot.

By the time Freeman removed the saddle from his horse and was ready to leave Kate was finishing feeding Kaiyote's horse.

"Let's go," Freeman said, and headed to the saloon.

Kate followed and found herself half walking, half running to keep up with the long legs of Freeman. The cowboy did not slow down or change his pace.

"You was gone a long time with those men," Kate said.

"Had a lot to do," Freeman said as he stepped up the two short steps to the second raised sidewalk in front of the general store. Kate nodded at his answer and climbed up to the sidewalk as Freeman continued walking toward the saloon.

The cowboy scanned the darkening spaces between the saloon and the general store and the jail across the wagon trail and noted that in an hour it would be pitch black outside. There were some streetlamps, but they were not lit.

"So, what now?"

"Food 'n hope to find someone that might take you in 'n then rest up fir tomorrow," Freeman said.

"You think someone in that saloon is gonna take care uv me?"

Freeman didn't speak. He smiled.

"There's less surprisin' things to happen," Freeman said.

"You might as well have left me at the waggun train," Kate said. "I might have better luck there than thinkin' these people goin' to take care uv me." She paused. "As soon as you leave, they goin' to sell me to the highest bidder."

Kate looked up and at the streetlamps that were in front of the main buildings only. There were two per building. The lamps sat on poles and inside the glass container was a glass door and candle.

"Slavery is over," Freeman said. "I ain't gonna let them sell you."

"You ain't in control ev'rywhere, Mister Freeman," Kate said. "My dad tol' us that out west things was goin' to be diff'rent, but only because there were less people out there," Kate said.

"Well, I ain't been out west. All I know is that there was fightin' over us, and some fakers made it 'gainst the law to own us," Freeman said.

"Don't know 'bout that," Kate said. "All I know is if you leave me, I won't be safe or free fir long."

Freeman smirked. He didn't look at Kate. He looked at the darkness surrounding him and the little girl.

"Don't that mean nothin' to you?"

Freeman did not respond. Instead, the cowboy stood in front of the pane glass of the saloon bathed in the light from inside.

"You supposed to care," Kate said, reaching out and grabbing Freeman's hand. His hand was calloused and rough.

The touch drew the attention of Freeman.

"We'll deal wit that when the time comes," Freeman said, decidedly.

Kate looked at the cowboy and smirked.

"Come on," Freeman said and entered the saloon through the swinging doors. Inside, the cowboy was greeted by a dozen men sitting at tables, standing at the bar and all of them suddenly watching him and Kate.

Kate slowed.

"Stay close," Freeman said, and started his slow walk across the suddenly tense saloon headed for the bar.

Sitting at a table were three men playing cards and drinking. They were dressed in loose fitting jackets, slouch hats, bandanas and cowboy boots. One of the cowboys sitting at the table had a dull look on his face and his sombrero dangling from strings around his neck. The dull faced cowboy smiled and showed off his jagged smile.

"You see that, Conway?" The dull looking cowboy asked, cutting his blue eyes in Kate's direction.

Conway, the cowboy with an eye patch, looked at the little girl.

"Got damn," someone said.

"Hey, boy," Conway said to Freeman, but the bad-tempered cowboy ignored the call. "How much fir the girl?"

The third man at the table, who had buck teeth and was looking at his cards, looked up at Conway and then Kate as she followed Freeman to the bar.

Kate watched the men at the table as Freeman reached the bar where four men were leaning and drinking and talking.

The man closest to Freeman was dressed in a dark sombrero, duster and cowboy boots with spurs. He had blue eyes and a long nose. The cowboy was shorter and a little broader than Freeman, Kate noticed.

The bartender walked up to Freeman.

"What can I do fir you?"

Freeman ordered some food. It was while Freeman ordered that Kate saw a familiar face just two men away from the cowboy in spurs. There on the far side of the man closest to Freeman leaned the tall, yellow, pointy nose of a man wearing a beat-up bowler hat, dressed in a gray wool jacket, gray trousers and cowboy boots. Kate found herself staring at the man wearing a bowler hat in the gray coat. She knew she should look away but was unable to stop herself from staring.

Weaver, the wagon master, was under that bowler hat. He looked in the little girl's direction and showed no recognition of Kate. Instead, he smirked, like he might spit and then leaned back toward the bar. Kate continued to stare in the direction of where Weaver stood.

"Can you 'n the girl wait outside?"

"What?"

"It's for... her safety," the bartender said, looking at the little girl. "She's drawin' a lot of... attention."

Freeman scanned the saloon and the dozen or so men and noted the men looking at him and Kate. He looked down at Kate and then back to the men looking at him and the girl.

"Suppose you're right," Freeman said. "It might be better to get some air between us 'n the Looky Lous," the grouchy cowboy said. He placed a coin on the bar and waited for the bartender to collect the payment.

Freeman placed a hand on Kate's shoulder and directed her toward the saloon's exit. The pair weaved through the tables toward the saloon's double doors.

Walking past one table with two men sitting and drinking Kate watched them as they passed. One of the men, with a gray beard smiled at Kate like he knew her. Kate looked at the man confused. She instinctively reached out and grabbed Freeman's hand. The cowboy flinched with the touch. Kate held on a little longer. Freeman did not pull his hand away.

The last table before the exit had another three men. One of the men had a mustache. The man sitting closest to the swinging doors had a diamond-shaped face and almond-shaped eyes and a trimmed beard. There was a bottle of brown liquid on the table. The third man looked up and puckered his lips as if he was going to spit.

Kate recoiled at the puckering man and veered away from him and parallel to the swinging doors. Freeman reached out and redirected the little girl toward the exit and passed the table.

Once outside Freeman directed Kate to the corner of the saloon on the far side of the building. The dark-eyed cowboy positioned himself so that he was at the corner of the saloon, just in the shadows. Kate noticed that Freeman had his hand on the butt of his pistol.

"Why we over here?"

"In case we have to do somethin'. We don't want to bring it back to where we lay our heads," Freeman said. Kate listened and tried to decipher the words.

Kate blinked and reached out to Freeman. She touched his brown, scarred and veined hand.

Freeman looked at Kate silently.

"Weaver was inside," Kate said.

"Where?"

"At the bar," Kate said. "He was wearin' a gray coat," Kate said, trembling.

"You sure?"

Kate nodded.

Freeman looked back at the saloon and then to Kate. The cowboy nodded.

"Are you goin' to do somethin'?"

Freeman looked at the little girl in the dark and smirked. He rubbed the side of his bearded face. He shook his head in answer.

"Why not?"

Freeman looked at the little girl and twisted his lips, thinking what to say.

"Not sure what you want me to do," Freeman said. "That man ain't done nothin' 'cept leave your waggun train on a trail. That ain't reason to go draw down on him..." Freeman trailed off. "I ain't got nothin' 'gainst that man."

"But he," Kate said, her voice a whisper. "He killed my family."

"Did he?" Freeman asked. "Or did he jus' leave the waggun train?" Freeman studied Kate. "Maybe, your fam'lee or the fam'lees didn't pay him? So, he left."

Kate stood silently in the dark next to the bearish cowboy with the guns on his hips and tried to understand.

"I thought you was diff'rent," Kate said, finally.

Freeman looked down and smirked. He did not reply. He looked back up and toward the saloon.

"I am diff'rent," Freeman said, more to himself than to Kate. "If'n I was like them in there you wouldn't be safe. They would beat you 'n mistreat you 'n when they got tired uv passin' you 'round 'n 'round like a wet rag," he trailed off. He stopped himself. "They'd sell you. They'd take you to some camp 'n use you 'til you died." Freeman shook his head.

Kate listened stunned. The gruesomeness Freeman suggested was frightening.

"You ain't safe here. You ain't gonna ever be safe here as long as there's more hard legs than soft." Freeman looked through the saloon window and pointed. "They act like they men but they ain't. They're monsters." Freeman shook his head. "Kaiyote 'n his people think they're ghosts or demons. Not me. I know they can die." Freeman paused, thinking. "I think they cursed. They evil 'n dangerous. I walk among 'em 'cause they fear me. They fear me 'cause I ain't afraid to kill 'em. They know I ain't one uv them." The ill-tempered cowboy stopped again. He seemed to have a different thought. "You sed that you thought I was diff'rent. I ain't one uv the monsters. I jus' walk among 'em. The way I see it they jus' waitin' fir the day I get slower or get hurt 'n they know they can gun me down wit'out too much trouble."

"But--," Kate said.

The steely cowboy wearing his Hardee hat shook his head.

"It's the way they think,"

"How you know so much?"

"I been on the run fir a long time," Freeman said. "I listened 'n learned."

"'Nuff talk," Freeman said.

Before Kate could speak out stepped a fat, short man with a basket.

Freeman took the basket and he and Kate walked away from the saloon and to the side of the building with the doors.

They re-entered the small room and found Kaiyote waiting where
they had left him earlier.

Freeman placed the basket on the small table and doled
out food for himself, Kaiyote and Kate.

"I thought you would help me," Kate said eating a piece of
chicken.

"Girl," Freeman said, eating a piece of fried chicken. "I am
helpin' you." He shook his head and wiped his mouth with the back
of his hand. "I brought you here. I ain't let no one to touch you. I
ain't let no harm come to you. In the mornin' we'll find a waggun
train or someone to take you back to Kansas and that will be the
end of it."

The quiet warrior ate silently, listening. He sensed the
tension. He did not ask. It was not his way.

Kate sulked. She clutched her clothes bag sitting on her
lap. The little girl pouted.

"You better eat," Freeman said. "Eat when you can. Never
know when you ain't gonna have somethin' until you need it."

Kate reluctantly grabbed a piece of chicken.

Kaiyote watched Kate eat.

"It ain't right," Kate said, finally.

Freeman did not look up from his piece of chicken.

"My family didn't do nothin' wrong. They paid that man to
get us to California. They didn't talk about money. They didn't have
no trouble. There weren't no problems. Then we got ambushed."
Kate stopped; tears filled her eyes. She looked at Freeman and
then Kaiyote. "That man killed my family. He killed 'em."

Freeman finished his piece of chicken and sat in the chair
and breathed, thinking.

Kaiyote, sitting on the floor closest to the door, stopped
eating and watched the room.

Kate, tears streaming down her cheeks, lowered her head,
despondent.

"I know you think that man killed your family," Freeman
said, slowly. "I know you believe it in your heart, but jus' because
you believe it don't make it so."

148

Kate continued to cry.

"If'n I was to believe that man I don't know bushwhacked your family 'n that waggun train I might be inclined to seek justice too. But all you got is a hurt heart 'n desire to hurt someone for what you believe happened."

"How can I prove it?"

Freeman shrugged his shoulders. "I don't know."

Kate wiped at her reddened eyes.

Freeman grabbed another piece of chicken and before he put it in his mouth stopped.

"Listen, we ain't like them. We here to find you someone to take care uv you or take you back to Kansas," Freeman said, raising his voice.

"I don't want to go back to Kansas," Kate said, meekly.

"It ain't like you got much choice," Freeman said.

"There's nothin' back in Kansas for me," Kate said.

Freeman did not respond. Kaiyote shook his head. Kate sat and stared at Freeman.

The three ate and when they were finished Freeman stepped out of the room with the basket and disappeared. A few minutes later Freeman returned.

"Get some rest," Freeman said. "We're leaving in the morning."

"Did you find someone to take care uv me?"

"No," Freeman said.

"So, what's gonna happen?"

"I'm not sure," Freeman said, sitting on the floor with his saddle roll. He leaned back and tried to get comfortable. The rugged cowboy looked at his trail partner and nodded.

"How come you didn't tell me that your Injun understood us?"

"Because--," Freeman said, stopping himself. "What difference does it make?" The cowboy seemed suddenly annoyed.

Kaiyote placed his pistol on his lap as he leaned against the door.

That night, before giving into to sleep Kate overheard a loud conversation through the wall that separated her from the saloon.

"You get the money fir the horses?" A squeaky voice asked through the wall.

"We went by, but it was locked up fir the night," someone said.

"You only had to sell the horses. How hard was that?"

"We'll get the money in the mornin', after we wake up," another voice said.

"Tomorrow?"

"All right, Conway, go and get us two rooms. We'll bunk here fir the night," a gruff voice said.

A chair dragged against the floor on the other side of the wall.

"In the mornin' we get our money 'n horses 'n head to the territories," a voice said.

"We're still headed to Bellevue?"

"Yeah, it's our next stop," a voice said.

"Three days ride," a voice said through the wall.

"Rulo, you still got people on the other side uv the river?" The voice that had asked about Bellevue asked.

"Yes," the squeaky voice said.

Kate listened and tried to discern the distinct voices, but as hard as she tried to figure out who was who there was another fight going on for the nine-year-old. While Kate was attempting to determine who was who on the other side of the wall the grip of sleep dulled her senses. Gradually, inevitably, Kate found herself embraced by sleep and the embrace pulled her into the arms of darkness known as sleep.

# Chapter 19.

Kate.
Middle of June, Leaving Stratton, 1877


The wagon train, led by Elisabeth's father, rolled into a much-changed Stratton than Kate recalled. The teenager looked through the canvas coverings and was shocked at the growth of the one-time outpost of just a dozen buildings. The boys peered out and Missus Lawson held Charlotte and warned Elisabeth with her eyes not to stick her head out of the wagon. Kate was under no such restrictions and looked out at Stratton Outpost now transformed into Stratton, a small town with a population of nearly two hundred.

Things had changed, Kate noted, but in the change, there were still things she recognized. The general store was still on the left side of the trail, but the trail was level now. There were no ruts in the ground Kate smiled. The wagon rolled over even ground with nearly no bumps. The barber shop was still where it had been when Kate had come to Stratton but there was a fresh coat of paint on the building. It looked quite respectable.

Kate craned her neck looking for the saloon. To her surprise there were two saloons in Stratton that day. One sat on the left side of the trail. The other sat on the right side of the trail.

"The night you stayed in Stratton," Elisabeth began having separated the boys from a wrestling match that had become serious. "Did you ever think about jus' runnin' away?" Elisabeth asked. "I mean, I get that the cowboy brought you to Stratton 'n all, but wasn't there nobody else?"

"The problem was that when I was nine there was not a lot of us here," Kate said. "There were a bunch of hardened men, what Freeman called monsters, pretending to be men, here 'n none uv them could be trusted."

Elisabeth quieted.

"You couldn't have left wit'out sayin' goodbye to your family," Missus Lawson said.

Kate nodded.

"I was nine 'n I was hurt 'n I knew I was in a bad place, but Freeman was bringin' my family back 'n I didn't know what to do."

Elisabeth nodded.

"Were you scared?"

"Elisabeth," Missus Lawson said, admonishingly. "Let her breathe."

Kate smiled to Elisabeth's mother.

"Scared? I don't know how to answer that," Kate said. "I know what you're askin', but I don't know if I was always scared. I was scared at times. I was scared when I realized all I had lost."

Kate paused.

Elisabeth reached out and placed a hand on Kate's arm.

"This place is hell," Kate said. "I left Kansas wit my family 'n came away empty-handed." She paused, suddenly emotional. Tears welled up in her dark eyes. "I left here 'n at first, I was mad. Things didn't go the way I thought." Kate shook her head. She wiped at her eyes. Her thin braids had an intricate pattern that was divided into two sides and made into two braided ponytails. "I remember going to the sheriff and hearin' that they were goin' to bury my family 'n all the others in the land beyond the dog run." The girl took a deep breath. "I never saw them buried. I suppose I thought leavin' here I would get away from all the pain 'n memories," Kate said.

"But it didn't," Missus Lawson said. The mother of the children in the covered wagon seemed to understand. "You can't run from memories. They follow you, like a shadow."

Kate nodded. She fell silent and seemed lost in her thoughts. Kate wiped away an unwanted tear.

"You lost so much," Elisabeth said.

"I did, but so did so many others," Kate said. "They're fine. They moved on, got married, had babies 'n have great lives."

Elisabeth did not speak.

"I jus' feel that fir all that I been through things should've been a little better."

"I think you bein' too hard on yourself," Elisabeth said.

Kate shook her head.

"Ain't nobody's life perfect," Elisabeth said. "Ev'ryone got somethin' they didn't do or want to change."

"Maybe, but I really screwed things up," Kate said with a shake of her head.

"You can't have done nothin' too bad. I mean, you ain't a killer?"

Kate did not respond. Elisabeth studied Kate and smiled. Her smile turned into a question.

"You ain't a killer, are you?"

"I ain't a killer," Kate lied.

"Yeah, I didn't think so," Elisabeth said.

As the wagon rolled through Stratton Kate's eyes fell upon the Stratton Stables where Clement Daniels, the blacksmith had cared for Freeman and Kaiyote's horses. The stable seemed to be able to withstand time itself as Kate noted the small door within the bigger doors that were open to customers. In the distance Kate was certain she heard to distinct sound of hammer banging against an anvil as blacksmiths were inclined to do.

Kate smiled, seeing women in Stratton. Elisabeth nudged Kate.

"A lot changed since you were last here," the girl said.

Kate nodded. Kate smiled seeing couples walking on the raised sidewalks of Stratton.

"What you smilin' at?"

"Couples," Kate said. "Last time I was here I think there were just two couples here," Kate said. "I don't think there were any girls or women walkin' outside by themselves."

Elisabeth smiled at Kate's answer.

"You know men and women, if they like each other, like to be together," Elisabeth said.

Kate chuckled at Elisabeth's attempted explanation of attraction.

"Don't you want to be married?"

"I was married," Kate said to the younger girl.

Elisabeth looked at Kate puzzled.

"All marriages don't last forever," Kate said.

"Why not?"

"There's a bunch uv reasons," Kate said.

Elisabeth frowned, thinking.

"Okay, men get bored," Kate said.

"Did your man get bored?"

"No," Kate said. She raised her hand, thinking. "Some men don't know what they want. They think they want to be with you 'n then that changes."

"Did that happen to you?"

"No," Kate said. "Well, sort uv. My husband thought he wanted to be with me 'n then thought that I was his punching bag."

Elisabeth did not speak. She lowered her eyes, shocked by Kate's words. The younger girl looked at Kate sympathetically.

Kate nodded.

"I'm glad you left him," Elisabeth said.

"It wasn't easy," Kate said.

Elisabeth nodded. She looked at Kate, curiously.

"You have any good memories uv bein' married?"

Kate twisted her lips, thinking.

"Was the weddin' nice?"

"No, not really," Kate said. "Jus' a preacher, his parents 'n me."

"Did you love him?"

Kate bit at her lower lip.

"Why did you get married?"

Kate exhaled. "I thought he was nice lookin' 'n funny. He made me smile, at first."

Kate seemed pained by the conversation. Elisabeth did not continue. She instead reached out and place a hand on Kate's shoulder.

"Well, I'm glad you left him," Elisabeth said with a shrug of her small shoulders.

"So am I," Kate said.

The wagon train rolled through the center of Stratton and out of the main artery to where the dog run had been. When Kate was nine the dog trail was the edge of Stratton. Now, it was the edge of where two dozen houses, mostly shacks, stood to make up Bucktown. The Lawson wagon train pulled up on the edge of the shacks and as the men climbed off the wagons were greeted by smiling black and brown faces.

"Glad you made it," one bearded black man the color of a clay pot said with a big toothy smile. He hugged Mister Lawson. Mister Lawson embraced the man and the two held onto each other for a long moment.

"Ev'ryone, this is my brother Caleb," Mister Lawson said. "He's the reason I made this journey."

"That's my uncle," Elisabeth said.

"We'll be here fir a day or two 'fore heading to Coffeyville. Coffeyville is the last stop fir this waggun train."

Elisabeth and Kate listened next to the wagon. The pair watched as older men and women made their introductions. There were hugs, kisses and tears. Some seemed incredibly emotional.

"They have been waiting for us for nearly a month," Elisabeth said to Kate out of the corner of her full lips. "You know that crossing the territories is never easy and...," Elisabeth trailed off.

Kate nodded. She knew that crossing the territories was never easy as Elisabeth said. There were robbers, bandits, highwaymen, killers and Indians in the territories. When Kate and her family left Kansas, her brother tried to tell her that the Indians were the most dangerous things in the territories. He had been absolutely wrong. The territories had Indians, but according to Freeman, the Indians rarely attacked freedmen.

"So, tell me 'bout Bucktown," Elisabeth said as they walked around the small section of houses on the edge of Stratton.

"I don't know nothin' 'bout this place. It wasn't here when I came through," Kate said.

Elisabeth seemed disappointed.

"Well, all I can tell you is this part uv Stratton was where the outhouses 'n bath houses were when I was here. This was part uv the dog run," Kate said, attempting to appease Elisabeth.

Elisabeth giggled. "Uv course, it was," the tall and slender girl said. She shook her head at the thought. The pair had walked to the eastern end of Bucktown and before them stretched the unending waves of golden grass.

Kate looked up and calculated the time to sunset. It would not be long.

"So, how long did you stay in Stratton before you headed to Garrett?"

"Jus' a day," Kate said.

The stand-offish Kate recalled the fateful day that she woke up in the Stratton Saloon room, after falling asleep.

# Chapter 20.

Kate.
Day Three, Stratton, Kansas, 1869

Kate Rawlins woke up in the rented room alone. Her clothes bag was where she had left it, but the cowboy and Indian were gone. She sat and scanned the room for the rifles and the saddles and saw them still in the room. Seeing the rifles eased her mind just a little, but it was seeing the saddles that calmed her. The cowboy would not leave without his saddle.

Kate climbed out of the lumpy bed and pulled on her boots. She grabbed the shapeless coat her brother had worn and her clothes bag. She opened the bag and searched it for the small coin purse inside. It was still there. She smiled and walked to the only door of the room.

As she reached for the door handle the door opened and there was Freeman, dressed in his wool coat, blue shirt, belt, canvas trousers and cowboy boots. On his hip was his gun belt. Instantly, Freeman had his hand on his pistol. Seeing Kate, Freeman relaxed and took his hand from his pistol. Freeman pushed into the room as Kate awkwardly stepped out and onto the raised sidewalk.

Kate studied Freeman.

"Were you goin' to shoot me?"

"No. Jus' habit," Freeman said. He stepped into the small room and retrieved his cowboy hat. He promptly put it on his curly haired head.

Kate watched as Freeman walked back out of the room. She noticed that Kaiyote was sitting on the raised sidewalk, wearing his sombrero and buffalo coat.

"We pullin' up stakes soon," Freeman said on the raised walkway. He was combing his beard with a thick wooden fork. Kate stepped out into the cold of the morning.

"There's a bath house out back, I plan on usin', before puttin' this place behind me," Freeman said. "Goin' to try and

knock some uv the trail off'n me before breakfast 'n findin'
someone to take you back to Kansas."

"I don't want to go back to Kansas," Kate said.

Freeman studied the little girl with the circlet of braids and
did not speak. Freeman sat on the raised walkway beside Kaiyote.
He shook his head at Kate. He reached inside of his coat and
removed a small leather pouch which jingled when he pulled it
out. Freeman smiled at Kate.

"I can't protect you forever 'n more important than that, I
don't want to," Freeman said.

Kate winced with Freeman's words. It felt like he had
spilled something hot on her in that moment. It took Kate a
moment to recover.

"You can't jus' leave me here," Kate said.

"Why not?"

"I don't know any uv these people," Kate said.

"So, you want to go back to Kansas?"

Kate did not respond.

"It's Kansas or here," Freeman said.

"Take me wit you," Kate said.

Freeman shook his head.

"Why not?"

Freeman studied the little girl.

"You wouldn't last a week on the trail."

"I wouldn't be no trouble," Kate said.

Freeman finished combing his beard and began a slow
combing of his head of hair with the wooden fork. He was working
the right side of his head when he stopped and looked at Kate,
seriously.

"I tol' you I'm diff'rent, but I ain't special," Freeman said.
"I'm mean 'n set in my ways 'n more likely than not to disappoint.
The plains 'n the wilderness, that's home to me. Sleepin' in this
room last night was diff'rent but not somethin' I want to do all the
time. I like the harshness uv the plains. I like the honestness uv
nature 'n the space out there 'n the cruelness." Freeman paused.
"I'm like the plains 'n that ain't fir ev'ryone," Freeman said. "I ain't

a monster, girl. I ain't a fakir playin' like I'm one uv 'em either, but I walk among the monsters 'n fakers not afraid. Because I know they're monsters, killers 'n worse underneath their painted-on smiles 'n kind words."

With that Freeman climbed to his feet and seeing the thin man gesture to the middle bath house began to move that way.

A thin white man dressed in black trousers and a white shirt, carrying a washtub stepped out of the small building and walked directly to Freeman. He was average in every way, Kate noted. He had dark hair, brown eyes, a straight nose and a thin mustache above his thin lips. He smiled as he drew closer to the three outside of the room.

"This mornin' I'm goin' to try 'n scrub off a little uv the trail 'n feel clean 'fore hittin' the trail," Freeman said and walked toward the dog trail. Kate stood on the walkway watching Freeman.

"That'll be three dollars," the thin man said, sticking out his bony hand. "You get the first bath uv the day. The water is hot 'n clean."

Freeman nodded and handed the man three dollars in coins.

"There's soap 'n a brush inside each bath house. There's a towel inside too. Just one to a customer," the nameless man said with a slight bow. The man nodded and pointed toward the six small bath houses.

"You really goin' to take a bath?" Kate asked, suddenly near Freeman.

"I might get a shave too," Freeman said, with a crooked smile.

"But what 'bout me?"

Freeman didn't respond. Instead, he looked at Kate, curiously.

"What about you?"

Kate opened and closed her mouth.

"Scat," Freeman said to Kate and walked to the bath house the thin man had walked from.

Kate watched Freeman open and enter the bath house.

She turned and found Kaiyote watching her.

"What?"

The quiet warrior looked from Kate and toward the bath house Freeman entered.

Kate crossed her arms in front of her, thinking. She looked at Kaiyote who silently watched her. Kate spun on her heels and followed Freeman to the small building. She hesitated. Then she set her jaw and barged into the small bath house where Freeman was removing his canvas shirt. The bath house was just a trough filled with water that was three feet tall. There was a table and chair in the small wooden shed.

After walking in Kate was surprised to see that Freeman was cashew-colored below his darker face and neck. His dark face was three shades darker than the rest of his body. He was strongly built. He was not thick of muscle, but across his shoulders and arms were thick ropy muscles. What shocked Kate was the sight of scarring on Freeman's arms, side and back. Across the pecan-colored skin of Freeman's left forearm was a raised puckering of skin. Similarly, below his chest, on his right side there were two scars about an inch apart that looked like claw marks. On his back was a crisscross of welts and raised scars that were discolored and began at his shoulders and stretched to his waist.

Kate stepped back seeing the scars. His gun belt and coat hung near the tub. His shirt and under shirt lay folded near the door. Freeman spun around as Kate entered and again was aiming his pistol at the little girl. The weathered cowboy shook his head at the little girl.

"What you doin' here, girl?"

"I can't stay here," Kate said.

"Well, it's here or Kansas," Freeman said, turning and showing more scars on his chest and burn marks on his arms.

"Why can't I go with you?"

Freeman gritted his teeth instead of answering.

"So, you jus' goin' to leave me?" Kate asked.

Freeman did not respond.

"Are you?"

"I ain't got much choice," Freeman said.

"But I don't know no one here," Kate said.

Freeman looked at Kate evenly. The nine-year-old looked at him, holding her clothes bag in her arms. The little girl pouted. Freeman shook his head.

"Get out 'n give me some space," Freeman said, ushering Kate out of his bath house. "We can talk 'bout this when I finish my bath." He pushed her out of the flimsy door. "Ain't nothing gonna change between now 'n then."

With a forceful shove Kate found herself on the dog trail in front of the six sheds that were the saloon's bath houses. She spun around and looked at the bath house and then toward the plain. She turned around and looked at Kaiyote who was still sitting on the raised walkway.

Kate turned on her heels with her clothes bag and considered returning to the room, but there was nothing there to help her. At nine, Kate had little choice. She walked toward Kaiyote, frustrated.

The quiet Kaiyote watched as Kate tried to decide what she was doing. He did not move. Instead, he waited for Kate to approach.

Angry and upset at Freeman Kate stomped past Kaiyote and without a word she looked back at the brave in his buffalo coat silently. Once past Kaiyote Kate picked up her pace.

"I'll be back," Kate said to Kaiyote. The quiet and observant Kaiyote lowered his head.

She ran to the main wagon trail in the center of the outpost and searched the buildings for direction. The general store was still closed. The saloon's front door, at that hour, was barred and closed. The stable, if anything in the outpost was open, had to be opened. The blacksmith had to feed and water the horses.

Weaver and the others would be coming to get their horses. All she had to do was wait for them to return and end the nightmare that was her life. The little girl set her jaw and found the raised sidewalk and began her walk to the stable.

It was early and the outpost was just waking up. There were a few people moving about but nothing like the day before. Kate looked around and saw the half dozen people moving from one building to the other. Most, looked like the owners of the stores and buildings. Kate did not slow down or hesitate. She walked swiftly to the stable and pushed at the small door where the blacksmith had appeared the night before. The door did not open.

Kate pouted. She looked at the two-story building and twisted her lips, thinking.

Moving to the rear of the stable Kate found a slat missing from the back of the building. Kate paused and pulled on the board below the missing one and found it loose. She stuck her head in the hole and found a horse looking at her.

"Hey, you," Kate said as she squeezed into the opening. The horse snorted and backed up as the little girl entered on her hands and knees. She reached out and pulled in her clothes bag. She stood inside the stable and stall and noticed that in the dim light of the stable she had nearly stepped into a pile of manure. Kate holding her clothes bag pushed back and away from one pile of poop and hop scotched her way to the entry of the stall.

The horse, an Appaloosa, backed away from Kate as she found the stall entry.

"Easy," Kate said. She unlocked the stall door and exited.

Once in the stable proper she locked the stall door and scanned the dark interior of the building. She looked at Kaiyote's and Freeman's horses and then looked for a place to hide and wait for Weaver and his men. Of course, she considered hiding in the stall of the two horses she knew but knew that Freeman and Kaiyote were planning on leaving soon. Add to that, the blacksmith would be there to open the stable. Kate spun around and looked to be sure he was not already there. He was not in the stable. So, the nine-year-old set out to find her hiding place in one of the empty stalls.

Hiding in the stall Kate saw the blacksmith arrive a little after her arrival and hiding. Almost immediately, the blacksmith opened the two stable doors that led to the two pens behind the structure. The blacksmith fed the animals and mucked out the occupied stalls. Thankfully, for Kate, he only concentrated on the stalls that had horses in it.

A few minutes after the blacksmith had mucked the stalls and watered and fed the horses in walked Weaver and two of the gunmen, she had seen in the saloon the night before. Weaver was wearing his gray coat, slouch hat, gray shirt and trousers. On his hip was a pistol.

The other two cowboys were dressed in loose fitting jackets, bandanas around their necks, canvas trousers and cowboy boots. The dull-faced cowboy was wearing his sombrero. The dull faced cowboy smiled a greasy smile.

"You buyin' our horses?" The dull-faced cowboy asked, cutting his eyes at the blacksmith, who was carrying a box of vegetables.

Conway, the cowboy with an eye patch, lurked in the shadows as Weaver and the dull faced cowboy talked with the blacksmith.

"I think I'm willin' to buy three uv the horses. The other two ain't worth the bullets it would take to shoot 'em," the blacksmith said, with a chuckle. "So, I'll give you forty fir the three and forty-five fir all five if you don't want to be bothered with the rest."

"I think you cheatin' us, smithy, but we ain't got time fir a back 'n forth," Weaver said, taking the money and looking at the dull faced cowboy wearing the sombrero and leaning on an empty stall.

"Cheatin' us, smithy?" The dull-faced gunman asked, leaning forward.

"They said you would be fair," the cowboy wearing an eye patch said with an attitude.

"It's a fair price," the blacksmith said.

Kate stepped out of the stall with the derringer in one hand and her clothes bag in the other. She walked through the shadows of the stable. When she stepped into the light that slanted through the upper windows and stable boards Kate looked ready to pull the derringer's trigger.

"Whoa," Weaver said, seeing Kate with the derringer in hand. "What you doin' wit that belly buster little... girl?"

"You killed my family," Kate said, in a whisper trying not to shake and stay focused. She took a step forward with the two-shot gun in her hand.

Weaver raised his hands and smiled. Conway, the eye patch wearing cowboy, stepped out of the shadows with his pistol aimed at Kate. The dull-faced boy wearing the bowler reached and pulled his pistol, as well. The dull faced cowboy leveled his pistol on the little girl. He looked at Weaver.

"You killed my family," Kate said again, raising her voice from a whisper.

Weaver raised his hands higher and smiled. The blacksmith seeing the little girl with the derringer stepped to the side trying to figure out what was going on in his stable. Conway reached out and stopped the blacksmith's retreat. The eye patch wearing cowboy put his arm around the blacksmith's shoulder and smiled a smile that had no emotion behind it.

"Now, girl, I don't know what you gone 'n made up in that little head uv yours, but I ain't killed nobody's family," Weaver said, looking from the little girl and to his partners with his hand on his gun. Weaver smirked at his partners. The brute shook his head, and his partners holstered their guns.

Kate took another step.

"Now, if you plannin' on killin' anyone wit that," Weaver said with an easy smile. "Let me point out some failin's uv that belly buster. I know many used that very same belly buster 'n not been unhappy wit it," Weaver said. "Problem with a belly buster is that if you ain't close you ain't gonna do much damage." Weaver paused and motioned to Kate to come closer. "You plannin' on killin' me you need to be a little closer."

Weaver beckoned Kate closer. The little girl stepped forward and stopped, unsure. She looked at the man wearing a slouch hat dressed in gray.

She stepped cautiously forward. Weaver waved at Kate to come closer.

"You killed my family," Kate said again. Kate took a few steps forward. She was suddenly within arm's reach of Weaver.

Weaver leaned to the left and then the right. Kate's derringer moved left and then right, following the wagon train master. The thin man bobbed to the left again and as Kate tried to track his action, Weaver closed the distance on the little girl. He was close enough to touch Kate. The cowboy smiled. In a blink of an eye the brute reached out and twisted the derringer from the girl's grip.

With his free hand Weaver grabbed ahold of Kate's buttoned front and leered at her.

"The good uv the belly buster is that if you close enough, you can do some real damage. The bad uv the belly buster is that if you don't know what you doin' someone can take it from you," Weaver said with a cruel smile.

"Let me go!" Kate screamed. Kate struggled and fought against the foul-smelling Weaver. Weaver pulled the little girl close to him and smiled evilly.

"Let me go," Kate screamed.

"Rulo, shut her up," Conway said looking back toward the stable entrance.

Rulo, the buck toothed tough clamped his rough and calloused hand over Kate's mouth.

"Hey, ain't no harm here," the dull looking cowboy said, stepping beside Weaver. He smiled evilly at the little girl. The dull looking gunmen reached out and grabbed Kate by her face.

"She young 'n full uv fight," Rulo said with a chuckle.

Kate struggled against Weaver and Rulo.

"What's that mean?"

"It means she'll get better wit time," Rulo said.

The dull cowboy reached out with his free hand and grabbed Kate by the waist. "She got nice hips."

"Easy Rulo," Conway said, cautiously.

The blacksmith seeing what was suddenly going on looked around and took a step back.

Conway stepped to the blacksmith and placed a heavy hand on the smithy's thick shoulder.

"Easy," Conway said. The one-eyed gunman had his hand on his pistol.

"Back off, Rulo," Weaver said to the handsy cowboy.  He looked at Kate. "If I did kill anyone, they prob'bly deserved it," Weaver whispered. "The waggun trail 'n the wilderness ain't no place fir tenderfoots. And it is def'nitely no place for a bunch uv uppity slaves wit'out masters," Weaver said, as he shook the girl in his hands for silence.

Kate blinked and blinked trying to gain back her rattled senses. She reached out feebly and grabbed at Weaver. He brushed the little girl's hand away.

"What we goin' to do wit her?"

Weaver looked at Rulo and Conway and smiled.

"You take this out my place," Daniels managed.

"Looks like the cheap smithy got a voice," the ruffian with the eye patch said. Conway pulled his pistol again.

"This ain't a place fir no rough housing," Daniels said, a little more firmly next to the gray bearded gunman Conway.

"Relax," Conway said. "We leavin'. First, we have to figure out what we're doin'." The one-eyed gunman smiled at the blacksmith. Conway looked to Weaver. "I say we take her to Garrett 'n sell her to the highest bidder," Conway said.

"Maybe we sell her after we all take a bite," Rulo said.

Weaver shook his head. "We take her to Barton."

"Yeah, that makes sense," Conway said.

"Barton? Okay," Rulo said, a little disappointed. He had found a strip of cloth to gag Kate and quickly tie it around her mouth. "When we take her to Barton I hope he sees that we can make some money from this one," Rulo said.

Weaver nodded. He looked at Rulo and Conway. He got serious. "People walk 'round wit guns 'n think you killed someone ain't people that live too long out here," Weaver said with a thin smile.

Kate recovered and kicked out at Weaver.

Weaver frowned and smacked Kate as hard as he could with the back of his hand. The little girl fell back and into the shapeless dark of unconsciousness.

# Chapter 21.

Kate.
Middle of June, Bucktown, 1877

Elisabeth and Kate returned to the wagon train and the evening festivities. They sat at a wooden table and watched as some of the Curtis residents brought out musical instruments and began to play music. There was food, music and dancing. Kate and Elisabeth watched as young boys asked girls to dance. The two giggled.

There was a man dressed in a green wool jacket and bowler who sang like an angel.

"He's good," Elisabeth said out loud.

"That's George," one of the girls sitting at the wooden table said to Elisabeth. Kate nodded.

"He's got a good voice," Elisabeth said.

"He's a pig farmer. No one knows where he picked up singin'. Or how he learned to sing like that. They say he sings all the time on the farm," the girl with her hair in a natural puff on the top of her head said. "I'm Natalie."

Natalie was pretty, with big eyes, even brown skin, big lips and a high forehead. She was dressed that night in a blue and green checked dress that fell below her knees. On her feet were pointy cowboy boots.

A gaggle of boys walked past the table and a few boys smiled at the three girls there. Elisabeth was all of fourteen and curious about boys. Elisabeth and the girl Kate and she had just met giggled at the boy's attention.

Kate shook her head, uninterested in the boys. She had been married and widowed, but at the ripe old age of seventeen was not dead. She was still interested in the idea of love, but not puppy love or love with young boys any longer.

"You gonna dance?"

"Maybe," Kate said. "I have to be interested or I can be a little hard to deal wit."

A few moments later three boys came by to ask the girls to dance. Kate refused politely. Elisabeth and her new friend refused politely as well.

"No, you two don't let me stop your fun," Kate said.

The two boys stood trying to think of a way to walk away from the table and not look like they had struck out.

Elisabeth smiled at a round faced boy wearing overalls and boots. Next to the boy in the overalls was a dark boy wearing a fabric jacket, button front shirt and canvas trousers above his brogans. Elisabeth and Natalie looked at each other and smiled. Natallie, the girl with a big forehead, thin eyebrows, full lips and a pointed chin stood up and grabbed a tall, thin boy with ears that stood out from his blockish head and pulled him into the dance area.

The boy in overalls and Elisabeth walked to the area where there was dancing. The two girls and two boys began to dance. Elisabeth looked at Kate. Kate waved and smiled. Elisabeth and the boy danced a couple of times.

As the darkness fell and light evaporated all around the dancers and party goers Bucktown was illuminated by a string of lanterns the residents brought out and placed strategically around the main area to continue the party.

Kate sat and did not dance. She watched the men, women, boys and girls dancing and frolicking and though she knew she should be enjoying herself, she did not. There was a somberness about Kate that night. Arriving in Stratton had been an achievement and instead of celebrating Kate felt a sense of dread being so close to the place where she had nearly been taken. There was no threat of Kate being abducted now with the Lawsons and the others around her, but she could not muster any excitement at being in Stratton. The last time she had been in Stratton and left things had not gone as planned.

While Elisabeth was dancing Kate walked to Mister Lawson's brother, Caleb, who was watching the dancing near a tree. He was shorter than Mister Lawson, but more muscled. That night he was dressed in a brown jacket, white button front shirt, belt, matching brown pants and pointy cowboy boots. Kate noted that Caleb Lawson had no gun.

"Mister Lawson, maybe you can help me," Kate said.

"Shouldn't you be dancing?"

Kate laughed and shook her head.

"I'm not much uv a dancer," Kate said.

"You too young not to dance," Mister Lawson said.

Kate again shook her head. She looked at the man that in another life could have been her uncle.

"Not ev'ryone dances," Kate said in answer.

Mister Lawson shook his head.

"I'm an old man, girl, 'n when my Carol was alive, we danced all the time," Mister Lawson said.

Kate giggled. The bearded man winked and looked at the couples dancing just a few feet from the small table by the tree. Kate looked and saw that someone had brought a homemade bass, made of a wooden box, a string and a pole. The man was bearded and wearing a green blanket jacket with canvas trousers and brogans. He was a thin man with long limbs, plucking and playing the homemade bass expertly. The sound of the melodic wheeze of a harmonica sounded and Kate looked in the crowd for the man or woman playing. Seated in a chair was a young girl strumming a guitar. Beside her was a ma n wearing a slouch hat and with his hands cupped in front of his bearded mouth.

"You sure you ain't int'rested in capturin' some uv your youth?"

Kate shook her head.

Lawson sat at the table and smiled as the dancing and music played. He took a few deep breaths before turning to the serious girl across the table from him. He smirked at Kate.

"How can I help you?"

"A few years back, I came here wit a cowboy named: Freeman 'n an Injun named: Kaiyote," Kate said beginning her story. She winnowed down the story to suggest that she was looking for Freeman. "I owe him a lot."

"Can't say I know a Freeman," Caleb Lawson said, with a frown. "I think if I had seen or heard uv  a Black cowboy wit an Injun, I would remember." He paused and thought. "Maybe, you need to ask someone who's been around here longer than me." Caleb Lawson paused, thinking. "I figure if anyone seen or knows about a Black cowboy 'n an Injun, 'round here, it's Miss Mary."

"Miss Mary?"

"She was here a couple uv years afore me," Lawson said, pointing to the ground.

"How long Bucktown been here?"

"Not too sure. Seven or eight years, maybe," Caleb Lawson said.

Behind Caleb Lawson and Kate there was the sound of a fiddle being played. Kate instinctively turned at the sound. She smiled at the sight of a dozen couples whirling around and dancing and singing.

"Where would I find Miss Mary?"

Caleb Lawson studied the girl across from him with his brown eyes. He did not answer immediately. Instead, Lawson tilted his head and paused, thinking.

"She don't talk to ev'ryone," Lawson said.

"I jus' want to know if she knows Freeman, the cowboy. Nothin' more," Kate said.

Lawson fell silent.

At that moment Elisabeth reappeared with Natalie. They were all smiles.

"Did you enjoy the dance?"

"I think so," Elisabeth said with a giddy smile to her uncle and Kate, never clarifying the answer. "What have you been up to?"

Kate smiled sheepishly. Caleb Lawson rubbed the back of his neck and looked to the dancing couples, just one hundred feet away.

"Did you enjoy him?" Her uncle asked with a devilish grin.

"Uncle," Elisabeth said, smiling awkwardly. She looked to Kate for assistance.

"He tol' me that Miss Mary might know about Freeman," Kate said, unsure.

"Miss Mary," Natalie said, shocked. "She ain't good people."

"Why you say that?"

"She runs a...," Natalie said only to stop herself.

"She runs a cathouse on the edge uv Stratton," Lawson said.

"A cathouse?"

Elisabeth looked at Kate and Natalie and then her uncle, confused.

"A house where men go to be wit women," Natalie said.

"Fir money," Kate added.

Elisabeth frowned.

Kate wanted to go to the cathouse the night that Mister Lawson's brother told her where Miss Mary stayed. Of course, it was late, and Kate knew that she could not go alone or just with Elisabeth. So, Kate enlisted the help of Elisabeth.

Kate pulled Elisabeth and Natalie to the side.

"What is goin' on?"

"I need your help," Kate said.

Elisabeth looked to Natalie, the girl she had only met an hour ago. "You know where Miss Mary lives?"

Natalie shook her head in answer.

"Will you ask your uncle to take us to see Miss Mary?"

"What? Why me?"

"He's your uncle," Kate said. "He will do it for you."

Elisabeth made a pained expression.

"I think it won't be long," Kate said.

"If he says no?"

"If he says no then that's it 'n that's all," Kate said.

"Okay," Elisabeth said.

The three girls went to Caleb Lawson and found him sitting at a table drinking something and listening to the music.

"Uncle," Elisabeth said, with a small smile.

"Yes," Caleb Lawson said, putting his cup down.

"Can you help me?"

"What do you need?"

The two girls enlisted the service of Elisabeth's uncle Caleb.

"I'm goin' too," Natalie said.

"Okay," Lawson said. He pressed his hands on the table in front of him and stood up. "I ain't goin' to drag this out. I'll take you. If she's anywhere, she's there." He paused and looked at Elisabeth.

Kate thought about what Mister Lawson said. The idea of visiting a cat house struck a chord in Kate's memories of her adventures in Stratton with Freeman and Kaiyote.

# Chapter 22.

Kate.
Day Three, Kansas territories, 1869

Kate came to in stages, in the arms of Weaver. Conway and another tough, the pug-nosed bully from the day before, were suddenly on the dog run. Kate tried to break the grip of Weaver only to find her hands bound by a length of leather. She could taste blood in her mouth. The little girl ran her tongue inside of her mouth and found a sore spot on the left side of her jaw.

"Let me go," Kate mumbled under her gag which had loosened while she was unconscious. Her words surprised the gunmen as she tried to break the grip of the brute.

Weaver tightened his grip on Kate as she attempted to break away.

"Knock her out again," the thin-faced and dark-eyed plainsman wearing a slouch hat said.

Kate struggled and felt a gag tighten over her mouth. Kate looked back and the thin-faced roughneck stood smiling as a cheeky-faced rowdy with mutton chops and a potbelly danced away from her.

"She got a little kick in her," the square-faced gunman said with a sneer.

Looking around nervously, the thin-faced goon smiled.

Kate struggled still. She tried to get her bearing. They were on the dog run in the back of the outpost. Kate recognized the bath houses. The church, painted white, stood just a couple of hundred feet away.

"We need to tame this little Mustang," the thin-faced, dark-eyed goon said.

Kate despite being bound and now gagged tried to break free and run for safety. For her attempt to break free Weaver shook the little girl until it felt as if she might black out again. Woozy and rubber legged Kate tried to stand beside the curly haired wagon master.

"Let's move away from here," Weaver said.

The thin faced weathered goon wearing the bowler sneered.

Kate took a deep breath and tried to break Weaver's grip again.

Weaver drew back his hand to hit her.

Kate seeing Weaver's reaction froze. She recoiled instinctively and didn't dare move.

"She learnin'," Conway said with a laugh.

"They learn to fear the hand," Weaver said with a smirk.

Conway laughed.

"You make a noise 'n you're goin' to feel the back uv my hand," Weaver said to Kate.

The pug-nosed tough sneered.

The curly haired ruffian adjusted his grip on the little girl's bicep and pushed her toward the church. Kate looked up and around at the four men that controlled her. Weaver was the only one Kate knew by name. He looked down at the little girl as if she was nothing.

The look from Weaver stopped Kate's struggling. She knew that Weaver was heartless and dangerous. He had hit her once. Kate did not put it past Weaver to hit her again. Her mother had told her that there were men who tried to control women by being mean and physical. Kate could not believe her mother, even though she knew her mother did not tell her things that weren't true, but the idea of a man hurting a woman seemed unthinkable. Then, she came in contact with Weaver and all the warnings her mother had made about those men made sense.

That moment Kate looked up and saw another man dressed in a duster and gallon hat appear. The man was distinctive in that he had a long scar across his cheek that looked like it might extend from his mouth to his ear.

As soon as the scarred man appeared Weaver and Conway gave them their undivided attention.

"So, what Barton plannin'?"

"Barton sent me to tell you to go 'head 'n head fir Garrett 'fore anyone catches you wit our new moneymaker," the stranger said annoyed.

"How you goin' to find us, Morris?" Rulo asked.

"It ain't goin' to be that hard. We should catch you at the ghost town. Barton makin' 'rangement. He just thinks it's better to get out 'fore anyone comes lookin' fir her."

"Sounds right," Conway said, standing next to Weaver.

Weaver nodded.

At that moment Fitz, the beady-eyed thief, appeared with four horses.

"We ridin' out now, maybe we see you 'fore we get to that ghost town north uv here near the dry gulch?"

"Maybe. If you get there 'fore us, wait," Morris said. "We should be leavin' soon. Barton talkin' with the deputy."

"'Bout what?"

"Hell, if I know," Morris said.

"Barton always thinkin' ahead," Conway said.

"Well, we got the money fir the horses," Weaver said, tapping his jacket.

Morris stuck out his hand.

"Think I'll hol' onto it 'til I see Barton," Weaver said.

"Fine," Morris said.

"We'll plan on headin' to the ghost town 'n holdin' up there 'fore headin' to Garrett," Weaver said.

"Sounds good?"

"Think we're headed to Garrett after that dead ghost town," Rulo said.

"Think when we catch up, we might head north 'n see if we can sell this little piece uv ass up 'n down the territories," Morris said.

"Okay," Morris said with a growl. "Get some distance 'tween you 'n this outpost."

Morris took hold of Kate as the four climbed on their horses. After Weaver was on his horse Morris rough handled the squirming Kate and boosted her up to Weaver.

Unlike riding with Freeman, Kate sat in front of Weaver with the saddle horn pressed into her midsection.

"How old she?"

"Not sure," Weaver said to Morris. "Why?"

"Old enough," Fitz sneered.

Fitz's comment got the other gunmen to laugh.

"All right now go," Morris said, with a reluctant smile.

"Okay, let's go boys," Weaver said and kicked at his horse.

Weaver, Conway, Jefferson and Fitz rode quickly from the dog run to the main wagon trail and toward the far end of Stratton and the open plains with Kate on Weaver's horse.

The little girl knew she was in a predicament, but she didn't know what to do. Everything she owned, her clothes bag, was back at the stable. Freeman and Kaiyote did not even know what had happened. As far as Kate knew Freeman was still in the bath house washing the trail off himself. Where Kaiyote was, at the time of Kate's attempt to get revenge, was beyond the little girl's calculations.

# Chapter 23.

Kate.
Middle of June, Bucktown, Kansas, 1877

"I will take you, but I'm goin' to say it before we go. I ain't too comfortable 'round Miss Mary," Caleb Lawson said.

"Why?"

Kate listened and did not care what Mister Lawson said as long as he took her to meet Miss Mary.

Kate was suddenly filled with the hope that this mysterious Miss Mary held the keys to the mystery of where Freeman and Kaiyote were. The prickly teen realized that Kaiyote was probably back with his tribe in the plains somewhere.

The three girls and Caleb Lawson weaved their way through the dog trails of Bucktown and then found themselves on the border of Curtis. Curtis was a step up from Bucktown, which didn't say much.

"You know, Elisabeth, your friend don't seem to care 'bout the niceties uv this life," Mister Lawson said as the three walked to the edge of Stratton and stood in front of a two-story building that might have been a store a long time ago and was now the home and business of Miss Mary Walker.        "She driven," Elisabeth said.

"You want to go to a cathouse?" Natalie asked Kate.

"I didn't say that," Kate said to Natalie with a little grin. "But I think I have to if I want to find Freeman."

Natalie shook her head.

"You think Miss Mary goin' to help you?"

Kate did not answer.

"She's goin' to help," Elisabeth said to Kate, patting her friend on the shoulder encouragingly.

Lawson twisted his lips, thinking.

"Miss Mary don't help no one but herself," Caleb Lawson said.

"Then why we goin' here?" Elisabeth asked her uncle.

"She asked 'n maybe she got somethin' Miss Mary wants," Lawson said.

"Well, Miss Mary sounds like somebody I ain't lookin' to meet," Elisabeth said.

Lawson stroked his beard as he walked. He slowed and raised a hand. Kate looked into the darkness they found themselves in now, away from Bucktown.

The three girls stopped behind Caleb Lawson as he stood looking at a two-story building that looked odd on the edge of Curtis. In the front of the building stood two men, one wearing a mustache and beard, a black coat, khaki pants and boots. The other man, shorter than the first, was wearing a gallon hat, scarf, button front shirt, gray pants and cowboy boots. They were both armed.

"Wait here," Lawson said to Elisabeth and the girls. Caleb Lawson approached the two men with his hands raised, in surrender. The three girls watched and listened.

"Hey, boys, it's me, Caleb, I come to see Miss Mary," the bearded man said with a slanted smile.

The shorter of the two put his hand on his pistol and peeked at Caleb and the girls behind him.

"Thought you said you were done wit us?"

"I am, in a way," Caleb Lawson said.

"What you doin' nosin' 'round here, Caleb?"

"Well," Caleb said, rubbing the back of his neck. "I need to talk to Mary."

"Mary?"

"Yeah, Mary," Caleb said, standing in the middle of the trail.

The shorter man again looked behind Caleb and at the three girls behind him trying to hide in the shadows.

"You bringin' us talent?"

"No, nothin' like that. I jus' need to talk to Miss Mary," Caleb Lawson said, stopping about ten feet away from the two men. The taller of the two seemed uninterested in the conversation. The shorter man, wearing the gallon hat, smiled.

"Miss Mary's time is precious," the guard said. "How much you got to see her?"

Caleb removed a coin. He handed it to the talkative man. The guard examined the coin and nodded.

"Wait here," he said. "I'll go see if she's here."

Caleb looked to the three girls and gestured to them. They immediately crossed the space and stood beside Caleb Lawson. The younger Lawson looked back to the one bearded man standing guard.

"You sure 'bout this?"

# Chapter 24.

Kate.
Day Three, Kansas territories, 1869


Kate nodded and peered into the dark. The girl that had been snatched by Weaver and his rough crew blinked and found herself again with Weaver, Conway, Jefferson and the short and round Fitz. They had ridden from Stratton Outpost westward.

The four silent horsemen crossed the plains and rode to the nearly invisible foot trail that led to the nameless ghost town. Jefferson was tall and stringy. Fitz was round and pot-bellied and had mutton chops sticking out beneath his slouch hat. The ghost town was just about a two-hour ride from the outpost. It was hidden in a low bit of land that might have had a stream nearby, long ago, but unfortunately for those in the ghost town the stream had dried up.

From the main wagon trail the ghost town was a ten-minute lope down an unspectacular trail that slowly wound its way to the less than spectacular dozen or so rundown buildings near a dry gulch. All of the buildings had been abandoned and most had yet to fall over of their own accord. That dozen or so buildings were all that was left of a badly planned town no one wanted to live in.

There was the typical dry foods store, jail, feed store, land assayer, stable and several other buildings making up the ghost town. There was a bank sandwiched between a weathered nameless structure and the dry foods store. The jail, little more than a shack, looked ready to fall over. The roof was missing and there was no door. The land assayer office sat on the same side of the ghost town as the bank, with three non-descript buildings on either side.

The four riders rode up the main stretch of the ghost town and slowed in front of the feed store.

"Let's wait here," Weaver said. He pulled up on his horse's reins and slowly turned to the others. They slowed and pulled up their horses as well. The gunman climbed off his horse and pulled Kate from the saddle.

The other outlaws all climbed off their horses and stretched a little from the ride. Jefferson was the first to notice the lack of water for the horses. He gestured to Fitz.

"What we goin' to do fir water?" Fitz asked, scratching his stomach as he stretched.

The roughnecks looked around and noticed the ghost town was eerily quiet.

"No water?"

"All right, Fitz you 'n Jefferson go 'n find some water," Weaver said.

"What?"

"Why us?"

"Shut up 'n lis'sen. Me 'n Conway will try 'n find some place fir the horses. We can scrounge 'round 'n look fir some food. While you're gone, we'll set up camp 'n wait fir Morris 'n Barton."

"Take all the canteens you can," Weaver said.

"Got to figure that there's water somewhere close," Conway said. "I bet if you go on the opposite side uv the trail you'll find it."

Fitz and Jefferson climbed on their horses and trotted out of the ghost town in search of water.

While the pair were gone Conway and Weaver, with Kate in hand, walked around the ghost town. The pair settled on the building next to the feed store. The building was just four walls and a counter where the store keep handed people supplies.

Conway found a couple of boxes that seemed sturdy enough to sit on and he and Weaver used them as chairs. There were half a dozen burlap sacks lying in the store in a corner.

"You know that we should probably head to Garrett after high noon, if we're going to try to get there today," Conway said.

"Yeah, I know,"

"What you thinkin' 'bout the girl?"

"Think we make more off'n her than the horses we took," Weaver said.

"What you thinkin' 'bout Fitz 'n Jefferson?"

"I'm thinkin' that they got to know who's in charge," Weaver said.

"But Fitz has a quickdraw," Conway said, scratching at his salt and pepper beard.

"Everybody sleeps," Weaver said.

Conway nodded at Weaver's point.

Fitz and Jefferson returned and watered the horses.

"Where's the water?"

"On the other side uv the trail," Jefferson said. "Stupid hicks built a town with no water 'n wondered why it failed?"

"Yeah, the water was just on the other side uv the trail," the pot-bellied Fitz said with a greasy smile.

Fitz tossed a canteen to Weaver. The bully nodded and took a sip.

"All right, we planned on waitin' here fir Bart and Morris," Weaver said, sitting on what looked to be an old ammo box. "They can't be too far back," Weaver said.

"You know, I think I should be the first to get a taste uv the little nigger," Fitz, the square-faced brute, said.

"No one puts hands on her 'til Barton gets here," Weaver said.

"Why?"

"Yeah, why?

Weaver narrowed his dark eyes. He shook his head.

"You shouldn't care, Weave. You bein' what you is," the thin and tall Jefferson said with a crooked smile.

"Yeah," Fitz said, in agreement. "You didn't come by that rosy color naturally."

Weaver balled his fist to the comments. Conway watched.

"Bet you want to be the first to taste that chocolate tart," Fitz said with a devilish grin.

"Hell, Weave, you might know her," Jefferson said with a chuckle. "She might be your sister."

Weaver fumed. The gunman placed his hand on his pistol easily. Conway watched the back and forth and stepped to the side of Weaver.

"Easy, Weave," Conway said, raising a hand and placing it on the gunman's shoulder. "They jus' foolin'. They idiots. They don't know you or your history."

"Is that why you hate 'em so much?"

"Prob'ly tryin' to get back at 'em," Fitz said.

"Leave it," said Conway and the two gunmen noticed Weaver had his hand on his gun. He had not pulled it from the holster, but his hand rested on the heel.

There was a long pause.

"Barton tol' us to keep our hands off'n the girl 'til he got here, 'n that's what we're goin' to do," Weaver said seriously.

Fitz looked at Jefferson and then back to Weaver. Jefferson raised his hands in surrender to Weaver. The two toughs fell silent until Weaver looked away.

"We got a couple uv hours I figure 'til Barton 'n the others get here," Weaver said. "Go 'n do somethin'. Don't jus' sit in here lettin' your mind get you in trouble."

The two gunmen looked at Weaver and then Conway but did not move.

"Check your packs," Weaver said. "If we're leavin' I want to leave right away."

"I get the hint," Jefferson said, pushing off the wall and walking toward the door of the abandoned food store.

Fitz climbed up off the box he was sitting on and followed Jefferson.

After an hour Weaver looked to Conway who was closest to the door.

"What those two doing out there?"

"Nothing much," Conway said.

"Well, I think I should go 'n look fir Barton 'n Morris before Fitz or Jefferson get themselves in trouble," Weaver said.

"You can't stop stupid," Conway said.

"I know," Weaver said.

"I figure to ride out 'n find them comin' back this way," Weaver said. The curly-haired gunman seemed annoyed. "If they ain't there or I don't see them then I'll ride back 'n we can jus' ride on to Garrett."

Conway nodded.

Weaver pushed himself from the box he was sitting on and stretched his body to its full height. He seemed cat-like as he stood there near the counter of the feed store.

Conway slowly climbed to his feet as Weaver walked to the corner of the store where Kate was cowering. Weaver reached down and grabbed the little girl by her wrists and pulled her to her feet.

"Come on," Weaver said, more a growl than words.

Conway stepped out of the dimness into the brightness of the day. The one-eyed gunman shielded his eyes to the glare.

Standing near his horse was Fitz. Jefferson was sitting on what might have been the remains of a horse trough.

Weaver dragged Kate out of the feed store and stopped shielding his eyes to the bright sun that made everything immediately impossible to discern. Weaver paused and allowed his eyes to adjust to the sun's brightness. Kate too blinked and squinted against the glare of the morning sun trying to allow her eyes to adjust to the distinct difference of inside the feed store and out in the blazing sun.

After a minute or two Weaver proceeded to drag Kate to the side of his horse.

"Don't move," Weaver said to Kate. Weaver checked on his horse.

Conway walked to Weaver and chuckled.

"What ticklin' you?"

"Those bumpkins jus' poppin' off," Conway said. "Don't mind them."

Weaver smiled.

"I think they all have it wrong. I mean, if anyone should have first dibs on anyone it should be me uv all us," Weaver said.

"Seein' she tried to kill me. 'N that it was me that disarmed her 'n took her."

"Weave, you got a point," Conway, the one-eyed gunman said.

"Yeah, I might, but right now that don't matter," he said. He scanned the quiet ghost town that had been abandoned for some time. He imagined no one had been there for years. "Don't let them lay a hand on little chocolate," Weaver said.

Kate, gagged and bound, could only listen. She was encouraged by Weaver telling Conway to make sure that Jefferson and Fitz did not touch her. The little girl knew that if the clods decided to hurt her there was nothing the older Conway, the one-eyed gunman, could do.

Weaver climbed on his horse and wheeled around to head back toward the outpost.

"The sun will be at its hottest in a couple of hours," Jefferson said. "We got to head to Garrett, like we planned."

"Yeah," said Fitz.

"Okay, I'm going to give 'em a little bit of time then head back 'n see how far back they is," Weaver said. "If I don't see them, we head to Garrett."

"How long that goin' to take?"

"Not too long," Weaver said.

"What about us takin' a little sample uv the little bitch?"

"Hands off 'til Bart gets here," Weaver said. He looked at the two gunmen from atop his horse and stared at them menacingly. "Barton said keep your hands off her." He looked at Conway and Kate. "I shouldn't be too long," Weaver said.

Weaver rode back toward the outpost hoping to track down Morris and Barton.

"Don't take too long," Conway said.

Jefferson and Fitz stepped closer to Conway as Weaver rode slowly out of the small ghost town.

"How far is Garrett?" Jefferson asked, waving goodbye to Weaver who did not turn around as his horse picked up its pace and trotted down the trail back toward the main wagon trail.

"At least half a day," Fitz said to Jefferson. "That right?" Fitz asked Conway.

Conway did not answer. He walked Kate back into the feed store. Jefferson and Fitz followed behind.

The three gunmen sat in the shade of the store and studied each other and Kate.

As soon as Weaver left Jefferson and Fitz restarted the argument of who should be the first to sample Kate.

"Come on Conway," Jefferson said. "This is a perfect time to try out the girl."

"Hell, man, she might not even be good," Fitz said.

"Yeah, we try her out 'n then we can tell ev'rybody how tight 'n sweet she is," Jefferson said.

"Besides, it ain't gonna take too long to do what I want to do," Fitz said.

"Weave sed not to touch her 'til Barton says so," Conway said.

"He meant not to beat her up or break her," Jefferson said.

"We goin' to be as gentle as little lambs," Fitz said with a sinister smile.

Kate, gagged and bound, listened to the three grown men talking about her like she was a bone being picked over by three ravenous dogs. She cried and cried and wished for Freeman or anyone to save her.

"There will be no drawin' straws," Conway said, attempting to shut down the conversation about Kate.

"I think it should be me that gets first crack at her," Jefferson said.

"I don't want sloppy seconds," Fitz said, angrily.

"You would be happy with sloppy hundreds," Jefferson said leaning against the rickety wall.

That comment made everyone laugh except Kate.

"Okay, I think there's an easy way to figure this out," Jefferson said.

"What you thinkin'?" Fitz asked, curious.

"We can shoot fir her," Jefferson said.

"Shoot fir her?" Fitz said, leaning forward on the skeleton of a wooden chair he had found.

"Don't know if that would be too fair," Fitz said after a beat.

"Why you say that?"

"You know I'm the best shot between the three uv us," Fitz said.

"You think so?" Jefferson asked.

Conway listened but did not contribute to the conversation.

"Well, you look at the three uv us," Fitz said. "You ever draw down on anybody?" Fitz asked Jefferson.

Jefferson shook his head in answer.

"How 'bout you Conway?"

"How 'bout me, what?"

"You ever drawn down on anyone?"

"I have drawn down on a body 'n been drawn down on," Conway said, reluctantly.

"How many times?" Jefferson asked.

"Two times 'n survived them all," Conway said.

Fitz nodded and smiled at the one-eyed gunman.

"Well, I done been drawn down on 'n drawn down on three men that ain't alive to tell about it," Fitz said. "I like my chances over an old, one-eyed gunman," Fitz said with a slight shrug of his round shoulders.

"That ain't fair," Conway said. "I may be older than you Fitz, but that don't make me unable to outdraw 'n outshoot you."

"Why?"

"Drawin' down on someone don't mean much fir accuracy," Conway said. "When someone draws down on you it ain't ever about hittin' a target. It is about figurin' how to stop the other person from shootin' 'n killin' you."

Fitz rolled his eyes.

"Well, based on all your excuses, it seems that you already know I'm the best shot," Fitz said, with a crooked smile.

"Thinkin' we need to do a shootin' contest to see who's the best," Jefferson said, with an evil smile.

Kate listening to the three men felt that there was something wrong with the words coming from Fitz and Jefferson. Fitz seemed to have another thought asking Conway about shooting.

"Come on Conway," Jefferson said. "Three shots 'n the best three shots shuts Fitz up or you up forever," Jefferson said.

Conway looked to Kate.

"Leave her here. If we're all out shootin' you ain't got to worry 'bout either uv us trying to get a taste uv your precious chocolate while Weave is gone," Fitz said.

"Fine," Conway said. He seemed to hope that a shooting contest would shut up the two gunmen.

The three gunmen walked out of the feed store. Fitz smiled menacingly as he was the last to step out of the feed store. Kate watched the goings on from the feed store window, which was just an opening in the wall where a window would have been long ago.

"Okay, let's make this int'restin'," Jefferson said, scanning the area for targets to hit. There were few items to use for target practice, but Jefferson found three small and beaten-up cans. They were already peppered with bullet holes.

"Looks like someone else had the same idea," Jefferson said placing the cans on the ground about fifty feet from Fitz and Conway.

"Okay, here's the plan. I'll go first. If I miss, I'm out. Then you Conway. Then Fitz," Jefferson said once he was next to the other two gunmen.

"You miss you out," Conway said.

"Right," Fitz said.

"Now, I ain't the best shot," Fitz said with a slanted smile.

"Okay, I go first," Jefferson said. He took a deep breath, squared his shoulders and stared at the two cans just fifty feet away. The gunman took another breath and pulled his pistol and fired. Neither can had moved after Jefferson pulled the trigger of his gun.

"That was bad," Fitz said.

Conway did not comment.

Jefferson smiled.

"Conway. You up," Jefferson said.

Conway tilted his head to the left and then the right. He flexed his hands and took a deep breath. He drew his pistol in one smooth motion and lowered his right hip just an inch as he fired.

The can on the left jumped into the air. The can lifted up about three or four feet and spun in the air before hitting the ground on its side.

"That was good," Jefferson said. "I'm impressed."

Conway smirked at Jefferson's comments.

"Okay, Fitz. You up," Jefferson said.

The square-faced gunman who looked like he should be someone's uncle instead of a gunman stared down the two cans and focused. He took a deep breath and exhaled. In a smooth motion Fitz pulled his pistol and fired. Like Conway, the can jumped into the air. The can spun in the air and fell to the ground near the other can.

Jefferson and Kate, from the quiet of the feed store, watched Fitz and Conway shoot two more times.

Neither gunman missed.

"It's a draw," Jefferson said with a chuckle. "I can't believe it." He shook his head in disbelief. "I thought fir sure Fitz was better."

"I am better," Fitz said. "We in a gunfight you can bet on me," the square-faced gunman said with a curling smile.

"Okay, now that we done proved our worth," Jefferson said, with a slight smile. "What do you say Conway?"

"Say about what?"

"About lettin' me get a taste of that little choc'late treat over there," Fitz said with an evil smirk.  "I say between the three uv us we should jus' draw lots fir who goes first," Jefferson, the pointy chinned gunman with a broom brush mustache hiding his upper lip said.

"I think it should be either you, old man, or me that gets first crack at her," Fitz said. "If you can still get it up."

Conway looked at Fitz annoyed.

"How old you think I am?"

"I don't know, but you ain't twenty," Fitz said.

"That's right," Conway said. "I saw twenty about nine or ten years ago," the one-eyed gunman said.

"So, you what? Forty?"

"Naw he's," Jefferson said only to stop and do the math on his fingers. "He's thirty-two."

"Close," Conway said. "I'm thirty-one."

"I was close," Jefferson said.

"Don't care how old you are," Fitz said. "You 'n me we're the same. You understan' me. I go out 'n take what I want," Fitz said, easily.

"Yeah, 'n we want a taste uv that chocolate chip," Jefferson said leaning against the rickety wall. He had his hand resting on the heel of his pistol.

Conway looked at Jefferson leaning against the wall with his hand on his pistol.

"You ain't threatenin' me now? Is you?" Conway asked, studying Fitz who was sitting on the box Weaver had sat on earlier.

Fitz raised his hands in answer.

"Easy, Conway," Fitz said. "It don't make sense to threaten you," Fitz said with a grin. "I seen what you can do with that pistol." He motioned to Jefferson. "You know he can't hit the broadside uv a barn. We jus' talkin' is all," Fitz said with his jovial smile.

"Okay, I think this is easy," Jefferson said taking his hand off his pistol grip, easily.

"What you thinkin'?" Fitz asked, curious.

"You let Conway get his taste first 'n then you go 'n then me," Jefferson said. He paused. He looked at Conway and then Fitz. "Then we all happy."

"Okay, but these are the rules. No punchin' or bitin' or kickin'. "N I ain't goin' first," Conway said.

Fitz clapped his hand on Conway's shoulder.

"You good people Conway," Fitz said with a big smile. "It's me, then you, then Jefferson," he said climbing to his feet and looking at Kate in the corner.

"Fine, jus' do it somewhere else," Conway said, conceding to the two.

Fitz grabbed Kate and dragged her out of the feed store with a hungry look in his eyes. The transition from the dimness to the brightness of the day took Fitz and Kate a little off guard, but the pot-bellied gunman recovered quickly stumbling toward the building that had been an old bank, just a few doors down from where Jefferson and Conway were waiting.

Fitz threw the little girl into the shell of a building ahead of him and gave the frightened and abused little girl a big Chesire cat smile. He stood in front of the only door to the building and watched as Kate backed into a corner. The smug goon peeled off his jacket and smirked smugly.

Kate cornered and up against the flimsy counter that cut the interior of the building roughly in half looked at the wild man in front of her peeling off his gun and gun belt and undoing his buttons that held his trousers closed.

# Chapter.25.

Kate.
Middle of June, Bucktown, 1877

The shorter of the two guards returned and led them into the cathouse. The house was a great lobby with a bar and a bunch of couches and just visible a kitchen hidden in its darkness of the rear of the house. There were men, bearded and clean-shaven, drinking liquor from the bar, tended by a baldheaded black man.

"Caleb Lawson? What brings you back here? You sed that you were done wit Miss Mary 'n all uv us, the last time you was here," said a curly-haired woman the color of sand, wearing a long thin shirt over her nakedness. She had a diamond-shaped face and thin painted eyelids.

"I ain't here fir none uv that," Caleb Lawson said. "I'm jus' here to talk to Miss Mary, nothin' more."

"You sure?" The ageless woman asked.

"I'm sure," Caleb said.

A few minutes later a pear-shaped woman the color of cashews appeared dressed in a green and yellow dress that did little to hide her shapeliness. She had thick eyebrows, almond shaped eyes, a round nose and full lips. On her head was a thick and full head of curly brown hair that fell to her small round shoulders. She was not a big chested woman. Her wide hips and big butt held her shape. On her feet were golden slippers. The pear-shaped woman was Miss Mary.

"Caleb Lawson? I thought you were done wit us," Miss Mary said behind her almond shaped eyes. She smiled and a deep dimple appeared in her right cheek.

Lawson spent the next few minutes explaining why he had returned to the cathouse he had sworn off.

Miss Mary smiled at Kate and studied her behind her brown eyes.

"What can I help you wit?"

"I jus' want to know if you know Freeman, the Black cowboy?"

Miss Mary smiled at the question.

"I knew him," Miss Mary said. "He would come by here every time he came through Stratton."

Kate frowned. She looked confused.

"What child? That ain't the Freeman you know?" Miss Mary smiled, and her dimple appeared. "The Freeman I know was mean, tough. He didn't take no shit from anyone white, black, brown or purple."

"Freeman tol' me he wasn't gonna come back to Stratton," Kate said.

"Don't know 'bout that, but if we talkin' 'bout the same Black cowboy that carried two pistols 'n trucked wit an Injun, then that's the Freeman I'm talkin' 'bout," Miss Mary said.

Kate wracked her brains trying to be sure Miss Mary's Freeman was her Freeman.

"What kind uv horse did he ride?"

"He loved that horse," Miss Mary said. "He sed he found it, or it found him when he was on the run," she said. "Think he named it Midnight or Shadow or somethin spooky."

Kate smiled at the idea. Miss Mary knew Freeman. She also knew that the Freeman Miss Mary was talking about was her Freeman.

Kate knew that Freeman was not one thing but many. He was cantankerous at times, but at others caring and compassionate. On the way to Garrett Freeman had tried to change Kate's mind about revenge.

*"You been 'round too much killin' 'n mistreatin'," Freeman said on the way to Garrett. He was on Shadow, leading the way from the nameless ghost town. "This life can play tricks on you." Freeman paused, thinking. "You can see ev'rybody as monsters 'n that'll poison you to ev'rything good 'round you." He looked at Kate and bit his lower lip before proceeding. "Don't be like me girl. The monsters are ev'rywhere fir me. My story is already written."*

*"How you stop the killin' from poisonin' you?"*

*Freeman laughed, but the laugh was not one of joy or humor. It was a laugh of pain.*

*"When I figure that out, I'll tell you," Freeman said.*

*Kate rode on beside Freeman with Kaiyote watching the rear. The three found the wagon trail and headed west toward Garrett and away from the ghost town and Stratton.*

*"You need to live 'n love 'n find someone to be happy wit. When you get to California forget 'bout all this. Just live. None uv this should trail you."*

*"But--," Kate said.*

*"I think that you find somebody to love 'n all this killin' will jus' stop," Freeman said, answering the question Kate asked earlier. "Think that's why I'm still poisoned 'n hair triggered. I jus' got Shadow 'n Kaiyote. That ain't no life."*

*Kate had listened to Freeman and tried to understand in her nine-year-old brain what the gruff and dangerous man was trying to say to her. At the time it seemed just a bunch of noise from a man who threatened and killed men without much regret.*

"Everyone puckered up when Freeman showed up," Miss Mary said with a smirk. "They knew he had a temper." Miss Mary said drawing on her pipe. "That Black cowboy was so gentle here," Miss Mary said, remembering Freeman. "He liked to jus' sit 'n listen to me talk 'bout life outside uv the territories." She paused. "He liked to hear 'bout me coming west." Miss Mary seemed caught up in the memory. "He was an unusual man in this place. Gentle. Strong. Fair. But like I sed, mean 'n tough 'n feared."

Kate listened to Miss Mary and recalled the day that the gentle, strong and fair Freeman was not the Freeman she needed. She needed the mean, tough and feared Freeman to save her.

# Chapter 26.

Kate.
Day Three, Kansas territories, 1869

Kate was in tears. She was tied and gagged in a corner of a building with a man who was stripping down to his underclothes. The little girl closed her eyes and prayed that this nightmare end and that she wakes up safe and sound somewhere, anywhere, else.

The potbellied man with the mutton chops and smell of sweat approached.

"All right, little girl, this is goin' to be sweet like--" Fitz said, but never finished.

In the dimness of the building Kate saw the image of a dark figure appear in the doorway for just a second in between her hysterics. Freeman miraculously appeared out of the glare of the sun and grabbed Fitz by his scruff of the neck and slammed his head through the planking that made up the counter in the building where he decided to abuse Kate. The attack by Freeman was so quick and intense that Fitz barely had time to react. Fitz did not scream. He did not fight back. Before Fitz could react, he found himself dazed and stunned as Freeman punched him again and again in the face. In response, the goon, flailed as if he was falling from a great height and trying to regain his balance before landing.

Kate watched stunned into silence by Freman's violence. Fitz was suddenly bleeding from his nose and mouth. His left eye was watering. He reached out to attempt to defend himself.

Freeman slapped the dazed Fitz and allowed him to fall on the wooden floor with a thud. The hardened cowboy smirked. He placed his boot on Fitz's neck and held him down without much effort.

"You know you shouldn't snatch up someone out here," Freeman said in the shadowy darkness of the clapboard building as he held down Fitz.

Fitz groggily wiggled and squirmed under Freeman's boot.

"It ain't right what you was plannin' here," Freeman said standing there and looking Kate who was huddled in the corner, still tied up and gagged. "Kate? You, okay?"

Kate nodded, shakily.

"None uv you get to walk away from this clean," Freeman said. "I ain't come here fir killin'. I come here fir savin'. But sometimes the two come together 'n that's where I'm at."

Kate climbed shakily to her feet. The movement caught Freeman's attention.

Kate moved robotic-like toward Freeman, her hands still tied, and her mouth gagged. She bumped into the doorjamb as she reached the exit of shell of a building. Her face was streaked with tears.

"Kate," Freeman said, snapping the little girl out of her thoughts. "I need you to stand there 'n as soon as I give the signal, you run 'n hide in one of the buildings 'n wait fir me."

Kate listened. She nodded. She walked to the door and looked back as Freeman lowered his pistol closer to Fitz's head. The little girl turned back to the ghost town Weaver and the other roughnecks had brought her to against her will.

"Now, Kate," Freeman said. "Jus' go hide. If'n this ends the way I 'spect I'll come fir you." Freeman paused. "If it don't. You get back to Kansas 'n try 'n forget 'bout all this."

Kate opened and closed her mouth. She did not think it mattered at the moment to correct Freeman.

"Now, go," Freeman said, sternly. Simultaneously Freeman brushed Fitz's hand off his trousers' leg. Kate watched as Freeman drew his pistol and aimed it at the head of the struggling gunman.

Kate looked back one last time at Freeman with his pistol out and aimed at the head of the man that had nearly abused her. Fitz, still under Freeman's boot reached up and grabbed the cowboy's trouser leg. The sight of Fitz under Freeman's boot was hideous and beautiful to the nine-year-old. In that moment, Kate knew what Freeman was capable of and for the first time she felt that she understood why Freeman pushed back on the idea of being different.

Freeman was as violent as the fakers and monsters, but he had a line that he wouldn't cross. He had said it time and time again, but it had taken the sight of Fitz gurgling and spitting under Freeman's boot to really understand why he was different than the others.

Freeman looked at Fitz with his round belly and exhaled. "Ain't no laws here," Freeman said. "So, a man has to take the law into his own hands. Today that's me. Today, I'm judge, jury 'n executioner."

The thunderous boom of the pistol's report made Kate flinch as the sound bounced off the interior of the shack and washed over Kate. The nine-year-old jumped with the crack of the sound. She ran from the shell of a shack where Fitz had dragged her. There were two dilapidated buildings that stood on the opposite side of the building. Kate ran to the small nearly collapsed jail. She slipped inside of the small structure and found a broken chair, a desk that had only one leg intact. The floor was made of dirt. The boards that had been nailed together had spaces between them that Kate could see the main trail between the other buildings.

Kate, still with her hands tied, turned back briefly to see Freeman darken the doorway of the shack she escaped. The ghost town was brilliantly lit as the sun's rays danced above Kate's head and painted the top of the hills miles away. Freeman looked changed in the glare of the sun of the ghost town. He purposely put the sun at his back and looked menacing with his two pistols in his hands.

From the far end of the ghost town, in the shell of the feed store, two figures emerged. The gun shot drew the attention of Jefferson and Conway. Jefferson had his pistol in hand. Conway stormed out of the store and was the first to speak.

"I hope that fool ain't shot that girl," Conway said.

"He stupid 'n crazy but he ain't that stupid," Jefferson said his pistol in front of him stiff armed. He waved his pistol left and right trying to find a target.

"Stop wavin' that pistol 'round 'fore you shoot me," Conway said as he looked at Jefferson out of his unpatched right eye.

Freeman raised his pistols to Jefferson and Conway.

"Boy you don't want none uv--" Conway said, only to be silenced by Freeman shooting him in the shoulder. Instantly, Conway fell from the bullet. On the ground the one-eyed gunman lay wailing holding his shoulder as if he had just seen death.

Conway sat on the ground writhing in pain. His gun was behind him and useless. Freeman casually stood in the middle of the ghost town with one hand on the butt of his pistol.

Jefferson, waving his gun to the left and right in a panic sighted Freeman and fired.

The shot caused Freeman to instinctively shrink down, just a little.

Jefferson fired another shot before the steely cowboy stood and unrushed took a breath, in the middle of the ghost town, aimed and fired.

Kate closed her eyes as the gunfire filled the air.

The quiet and stillness made Kate open her eyes. In the ensuing quiet Kate found Freeman standing in the middle of the ghost town with his guns holstered on his hips. The dark-eyed and bearded cowboy surveyed the wreckage he had caused.

"Kate? You come out now," Freeman said.

Kate slowly stepped out of the barely standing jail she had sought and found for safety.

Freeman cut Kate's bounds and Kate dared to look at the two men lying on the ground bleeding. Conway, held his shoulder, trying to stop the bleeding. Conway, the one-eyed gunman, was not dead, but grimacing from the pain in his shoulder.

Kate stared at the older gunman and seemed transfixed by the blood pouring through his fingers. His gun was on the ground and just out of reach from the bleeding wrangler. Conway, who had been so tough and mean earlier, looked as if he was trying to not cry. Kate wanted to laugh at the now humbled and sniveling gun man.

The thin gunman, who was just a few feet from Conway, was making odd wheezing noises like he could not keep air in himself. Kate stared at the cowhand holding his chest with both hands and the blood seeping through his fingers. The blood pushed over his clutched fingers despite the cowhand's best effort to stop the bleeding. Kate watched as the thin outlaw squeezed his chest as hard as he could and then there was a twisting and kick of his leg as he let his jacket front go.

"Kate," Freeman said, placing a hand on the little girl's shoulder and breaking her focus on the sight of Jefferson's futile attempt to fight off death. "You got to get out uv here. You drawin' all sorts uv bad attention."

Kate looked from the dead body of Jefferson to Freeman and then back to Jefferson. The little girl looked and noticed that Conway was silent. He looked as if he had fallen asleep.

"What happened to him? Is he dead?"

Freeman looked at Conway and smirked.

"Think he passed out," Freeman said. "Seen it happen when they can't deal wit pain."

Kate blinked at Freeman's off handed response. The little girl paused and shielded her eyes to the sun's intensity. She blinked again and recalled something the gunmen said.

"They sed that the others would come here to meet them," Kate said finally. She cast her eyes back on the one-eyed man just a few feet away from her.

"Hmmm," Freeman hummed. The dark cowboy looked up and into the bright skies and seemed to calculate something. Slowly, Freeman turned and looked at Kate with his dark eyes.

"What do we do?"

"We?" Freeman said again.

"Suppose we could run," Freeman said, more to himself. "Or we could jus' hunker down here 'n wait fir the fakers 'n monsters to come," Freeman said, but he was not talking to Kate. The little girl looked at the intimidating cowboy curiously.

Out of the shadows stepped Kaiyote with his rifle in one hand and Kate's clothes bag in the other. Kate upon seeing Kaiyote smiled widely even though the Indian seemed more serious than ever. She giggled at the sight of her clothes bag.

Kaiyote handed Kate her bag. Kate greedily took her one possession in her arms and hugged it like she might have her best friend. Kate wanted to open the bag, but she would do that later.

"They come," Kaiyote said, looking back toward Stratton.

Freeman listened but did not respond immediately. The sun was sitting at its highest above their heads and the heat of the day pressed in. Freeman nodded. Kate waited uncertain.

"Okay, we need to move these bodies 'n prepare fir a fight," Freeman said, pointing toward a section of the ghost town that had a pile of lumber and boards near one of the structures.

"You sure 'bout this?" Kate asked. The little girl shook her head. "This place is scary," Kate said. "Why don't we jus' go?"

Freeman smiled. "You sed it yourself. This place is scary. It's a ghost town." Freeman paused. "We'll make a stand there," Freeman said.

Kate was surprised by Freeman's answer, but she did not say anything. Instead, Kate looked back in the direction where Weaver had gone.

Freeman dragged the dead body of Jefferson to what was the skeleton of the frame of the horse trough. Kaiyote dragged the unconscious Conway to the trough and propped him up against the side of the structure. Freeman tied up Conway and gagged him.

Kate smiled at the sight of Conway tied and gagged next to the dead body of Jefferson. The little girl liked seeing Freeman's rough handling of the monsters that had kidnapped and hurt her. She secretly hoped that Freeman and Kaiyote would kill everyone involved in her kidnapping.

Kaiyote tapped Freeman and pointed back toward the east, where the outpost had been. Freeman looked out onto the horizon. Kate looked in the direction Freeman and Kaiyote were looking.

"What you see?"

Freeman and Kaiyote looked toward the horizon and looked back. Freeman nodded. Kaiyote nodded and walked toward the far end of the ghost town. He slipped into the furthest building.

"They comin'," Freeman said.

"What should I do?" Kate asked, reaching out to Freeman and grabbing his coat sleeve.

Freeman scowled. The rugged cowboy's frown softened, and he looked down at Kate. His dark eyes took in the little girl.

"You need to hide. If things end 'n we're all alive then we head to Garrett 'n figure out things," Freeman said. He pulled his pistol and pulled the empty shells from the weapon. He methodically reloaded his pistol.

"What if things don't end well?"

"Well, you take that little bag you got wit you 'n make your way west 'n hope you find freedmen wit women folk to protect you," Freeman said, without any emotion.

Freeman looked at Kate again.

202

# Chapter 27.

Kate.
Middle of June, Bucktown, 1877


The room that Miss Mary and Kate sat in with Natalie, Elisabeth and Caleb Lawson looked unusual in comparison to the sparseness of the rest of the cathouse. The room was furnished in personal items. On the side tables next to her bed was a kerosene lamp. On a wall was a framed painting of a boat on a wave in a turbulent ocean somewhere. The room looked where Miss Mary slept and did not entertain. This was her personal room. She sat in a winged back chair and slowly packed a pipe that looked like it should be somewhere exotic. The bowl was small and the pipe three times as long as the bowl.

Miss Mary grabbed a long match and lit it. She placed the pipe in her mouth and drew to get the fire in the bowl of her pipe.

"Sit," Miss Mary said to Kate, pointing to her bedside. Kate sat. Miss Mary looked at Natalie, Elisabeth and Caleb Lawson and pointed to the two chairs along the side of the room. Elisabeth and Natalie shared a chair. Lawson sat in other chair just a few feet from Kate and listened.

Miss Mary pulled in the fire in the bowl of her pipe. Suddenly the small, intimate room had the hint of cherry smoke as the woman smoking the pipe exhaled. She studied the girl in front of her with her dark eyes.

"There's a bunch uv men come through my doors," Miss Mary said. "Black farmers, black fathers, black preachers, black thieves 'n drunks 'n black fighters," Miss Mary said.

"He's a Black cowboy wit an Injun named: Kaiyote," Kate said.

"I can't recall no Injun named: Kaiyote in this house," Miss Mary said.

"He was a bearded Black cowboy with two guns 'n dark," Kate said.

"You know me 'n my girls see all types," Miss Mary said, with a puff of smoke. "I seen long guns, shotguns, pistols, one-gun rigs, two-gun rigs," she smiled. "That don't limit the men none."

Kate looked from Miss Mary to Lawson and Elisabeth. Elisabeth nodded to Kate and urged her on.

"When I was here, he rode a black horse and dressed in a blue wool coat," Kate said. She wracked her brain. "He had one uv those Hardee hats he liked to wear."

Miss Mary nodded and thought about what Kate said.

"He was mean 'n dangerous 'n liked the plains more than the settlements," Kate said.

"The Freeman I knew was not much uv a talker. He was always tense, like a cat surrounded by dogs," Miss Mary said. "He was gentle. He never hurt any uv the girls."

Kate smiled and nodded at the picture Miss Mary painted of Freeman. She knew him as a thief, an outlaw, a killer and savior. He was all that Miss Mary said and the reason Kate was alive was because of the tough and dangerous Freeman.

"So, why do you want to know about Freeman? He your dad?"

"No," Kate said with a laugh. "I jus' owe him somethin'." The moody teen opened and closed her mouth not wanting to say anymore.

Kate smiled at the pear-shaped woman in the wing backed chair. Kate could not escape the cherry smoke flavor that filled the room. Caleb, Elisabeth and Natalie sat in the wooden chairs close to the only door in the small room.

Elisabeth smiled, awkwardly as Kate listened to Miss Mary. Natalie smiled and seemed hypnotized by all the unusual things in Miss Mary's room. Her uncle, Caleb, seemed to be antsy. Kate tilted her head to the woman smoking the long pipe.

Kate knew Freeman was this gruff and difficult man. Yet, he was also incredibly generous. He was a thief, but at the same time he had done more for Kate than anyone she knew outside of her family. He never raised a hand against her, she recalled. Freeman, when he spoke, was thoughtful and caring. At the same time, he threatened to leave Kate to the monsters pretending to be men, for as long as long as he knew her. Kate could not shake the fact that for all his bluster Freeman protected her from all those that dared hurt or harm her. It was those two sides of Freeman and all the shades of him in between that made the gruff cowboy memorable and admirable to Kate.

It was the distinct duality of Freeman that kept Kate at his side when things seemed bad. She innately knew that being near Freeman in any storm improved her odds of survival. Kate understood, subconsciously, the distinct nature of Freeman and the duality that Kaiyote spoke of. Freeman was a wolf through and through.  Yet, there were times when Freeman appeared human, if only for brief moments.

Miss Mary did not respond. Instead, she nodded.

"I don't know nobody that would come all this way jus' to pay someone back," Miss Mary said. "You sure he ain't your daddy?"

Kate laughed.

"I'm serious," Miss Mary said.

"I know 'n like I sed, he ain't my daddy," Kate said with a smirk. "I jus' owe him a lot 'n wanted to thank him."

Miss Mary looked at Kate skeptically.

"Thank him?" Why?"

Kate smiled but did not answer.

Miss Mary waited. Lawson and Elisabeth fidgeted. Natalie touched a piece of fabric that was covering a small table near her. Kate looked away and found two half dressed women in the doorway waving at Caleb Lawson. Kate shook her head. She wanted to laugh at the attention Mister Lawson was receiving from the girls in the house.

"Girls, scat," Miss Mary said, admonishing the two curious onlookers.

Hearing Miss Mary's voice the two disappeared from the doorway.

"Caleb, the girls miss you," Miss Mary said.

"I tol' you I ain't here fir that," Caleb Lawson said.

Miss Mary smiled at Caleb's awkwardness.

"Ain't no secrets that can be kept hid here," Miss Mary said with a crooked smile.

"Mary, focus on the girl's questions," Caleb Lawson said.

"I was," Miss Mary said.

Kate exhaled. She was visibly frustrated. Kate closed her eyes and went back in time to the ghost town where Freeman had appeared like an avenging angel to save her. Of course, saving her from one of the monsters was not saving her from all the monsters.

# Chapter 28.

Kate.
Day Three, Kansas territories, 1869

Freeman looked at the little girl. Kate looked left and then right, trying to decide where to hide. Where could she hide that was going to be safe?

Freeman looked back at the two men by the disused water trough and then to Kate before he walked toward the end of the ghost town where some weathered buildings still stood. He detoured just long enough to check on his horse and retrieve his rifle. Kaiyote had moved his horse closer to him, Freeman imagined. From his horse Freeman made his way to one of the three structures at the entrance to the ghost town. Freeman headed to what looked like a store of some kind because there were two shelves attached to a wall. The building had three walls still standing and of those two were falling apart but had a good vantage point of the mouth of the ghost town where the men would eventually appear.

"Mister Freeman," Kate said in the dimness of the building the ungentle cowboy had decided to make his stand. Her voice accompanied by her closeness and touch on his coat sleeve drew his attention. He stared at Kate's hand on his sleeve.

Kate removed her hand.

"I thought I tol' you to go 'n hide?"

"You did, but I figured the safest place was wit you," Kate confessed.

Freeman chuckled at the little girl's words. He immediately gritted his teeth and turned serious.

"This ain't no game," Freeman said. "The men playin' at bein' men comin' fir you ain't goin' to take no fir an answer," he continued. "This only ends in blood."

Kate nodded. Kate standing near Freeman was not sure what she should do. Kate looked out of the hole where a window would have been. She peered down the dirt trail which led back to the wagon trail and Stratton.

"They comin' to kill us?"

"They ain't comin' to kill us," Freeman said. "They comin' to try you out, I figure." The grim cowboy frowned. "They don't know 'bout us yet."

"They was goin' to kill me?"

"Think they was goin' to make you wish they killed you, but--" Freeman stopped. He looked at the shocked Kate, in the darkness. "They ain't comin' to give us peach cobbler," Freeman said. He looked at the little girl and scowled. "Get out uv sight. This ain't no schoolhouse 'n I ain't got time fir questions. This 'bout to be a fight."

Kate got quiet again. Freeman checked his rifle. He positioned his rifle close by. She looked at the trail for any signs.

"How much time we got?"

Freeman shrugged his shoulders.

"Still don't see nothin'," Kate said.

Freeman did not speak.

"This is bad?"

"I been in worse," Freeman said, trying to get comfortable.

The sound of horses and men talking stopped Freeman from talking. He was immediately focused on the dirt trail which led to the ghost town.

Freeman drew his pistol and prepared for the inevitable.

At the front of the group of men was Weaver and the pug-nosed Morris, Kate recognized from earlier, before they took her from Stratton. Behind them was Rulo and Lil' Ned, the square-faced kid from the general store. What surprised Kate was the sight of the deputy that had gone out to collect her family. The lawman was riding behind Lil' Ned, the gunmen, as if he was out for a Sunday stroll. The last two people were complete strangers to Kate. There was a pie-faced man wearing a slouch hat and a bandana covering most of his face. The stranger was wearing a dark blue long coat, with matching trousers and silver spurs and pointed black cowboy boots. Next to the stranger in the dark blue long coat was a long faced, pointy chinned man with blue eyes, a thin nose above a well-trimmed mustache, dressed all in black and wearing a brown wide brimmed hat that Kate had never seen before.

"Who's that?"

Freeman did not answer. Instead, Freeman hunkered down in the shadows of the building he and Kate were hiding in and waited. He watched as the five men from Stratton got closer.

"Where's this little piece of tail?" Rulo asked, looking back at Weaver.

"Tol' you I left her here wit Conway 'n the others. They prob'ly have her in one of the buildin's," Weaver said to Rulo and Lil' Ned.

They slowly moved down the little dirt trail, leading into the out of the way ghost town.

Morris was the first to slow and then pull up on his horse. Weaver looked at Morris and slowed.

"What's wrong?"

"Thought you sed that they was in a buildin'," Morris said, looking down the short trail. "What is that?" The horseman asked pointing down the trail toward the other end of the ghost town.

Rulo stood up in his stirrups and looked past Morris and Weaver with a smile.

"Maybe they done tuckered themselves out wit that little piece uv chocolate?"

"Yeah, maybe they fell asleep," Lil' Ned said with a grin.

Freeman stood up and aimed his rifle at Morris. Kate held her breath. The unsmiling cowboy pulled the trigger of the rifle.

The boom and crack of the rifle propelling the bullet through the long barrel was instantaneous. The horsemen watched as Morris was hit square in the chest and tilted backwards and to the right. He fell to the dirt without a word.

Instantly, all six riders drew their guns and looked for the source of the gunshot.

Rulo was the first to fire in the general direction of Freeman.

Freeman fired again and hit Weaver in the leg.

"Sunuvabitch," Weaver screamed. The shot grazed the gunman, hitting the side of his thigh. Weaver pulled back on the reins of his horse, and it jumped onto its two rear legs. For a moment, Weaver looked like he might tumble off his horse.

Without word, Freeman grabbed Kate and exited the building through the open wall. The pair had only exited when the first directed shots tore through the building. With the second shot Lil' Ned, Rulo, the deputy fired into the building where Freeman and Kate were hiding.

Freeman moved quickly, holding Kate by the shoulder, to the next building.

Rulo jumped off his horse and ran to the first building for cover. It was where Freeman and Kate had been only minutes before. The gunman peeked inside the clapboard building.

"Ain't nobody in there," Rulo said, looking back to the others.

"What the hell, Weave?" The deputy asked reining his horse in for control. He had his pistol in his free hand.

"What the hell is goin' on?" The stranger wearing the bandana asked pulling up on his reins as his horse wheeled around.

Before Weaver could speak another boom and crack was heard and Lil' Ned flipped off his horse. He was dead before he hit the ground. Lil' Ned lay on the ground with a hole in his chest.

All the men on horseback quickly slipped off their horses. They, all to a person, landing on the dirt pushed their horses out of the way or drew their weapons.

"Hey, pard'ner," Rulo said moving to the corner of the building where the shooting had begun and paused. He stuck his head out to look down the short distance between himself and the two hundred yards to the end of the quiet and forgotten town.

There was a boom and crack and the corner of the building where Rulo was looking splintered. Rulo ducked out of the way as the bullet tore through the corner of the building and disappeared into the plains behind him.

"What the hell?" The man wearing the bandana over his mouth asked.

"Hey! Pard'ner," Rulo said, from the cover of the shell of the building which offered little cover. "Why you shootin' at us?"

"You took the girl?"

Weaver limped to the side of the building with Rulo. He had his pistol out and ready to fire. He winced from the pain in his wounded leg.

"Well, hell, pard'ner that's what this is about?" Rulo asked with a dull smile. "I think you made a mistake," Rulo said with a smirk. "We ain't tryin' to keep her to ourselves. You welcome to her jus' as long as we all get a turn."

Scott, the deputy, slammed against the building beside Weaver.

"Lil' Ned's dead," Scott said.

"God damn it," Weaver said.

"Okay, pard'ner I think you need to stop shootin' 'n throw down that gun," Scott, the deputy yelled. "You shootin' at a duly deputized officer uv the law."

"What's that mean?"

"It means you shootin' at someone who got authority to be here," Scott said with a smirk.

There was a pause.

"I don't know 'bout authority or not, but I do know that you sonsuvbitches snatched the girl 'n now I'm plannin' on killin' ev'ryone who thought they could make a coin off 'n her or thought it was all right to come here fir a turn."

Kate felt a smile crease her lips. She could not suppress the joy she had in hearing Freeman threatening to kill everyone who dared think that they could abuse her. As she bathed in that reassurance Kate watched the two strangers climb off their horses and cut to the far side of the ghost town. Kate tapped Freeman and pointed. Freeman watched as the two strangers swung left and away from the place where the shooting took place.

Freeman nodded. He aimed and fired twice missing the pair as they ducked behind one of the standing structures.

"You thinkin' you can kill all uv us?" Asked Rulo from behind the building.

Freeman didn't speak. He grabbed Kate and moved back one more building. They did not have to go through doors of the first three shells. They simply moved through the openings of the shells of the structures. Freeman moved slowly backwards watching for movement in front of him or to the left and right.

"I asked a question," the deputy said, a little more aggressive than before. He pushed off the clapboard wall and stepped out into the open briefly. He stepped back close to the building but continued walking up the short trail of half a dozen derelict structures.

"The way I see it if you want to leave here alive you got one path," Scott, the deputy called, moving up the side of the street. "You leave that girl now 'n we'll let you ride out wit your skin," Scott said from behind a nearly collapsed wall of a small building.

Freeman didn't respond.

"There ain't no other choice fir you. We come here to get a turn at the girl 'n we ain't leavin' 'til we do," yelled Rulo from the corner of a building, his gun in hand and looking for targets. Rulo was maybe fifty feet behind the deputy.

The deputy stepped cautiously around the wall and moved up the short street with his gun at the ready. He moved shakily, using the sparse cover to protect himself. He had a scowl painted on his face as he continued walking up the overgrown grass street that divided one side of the ghost town from the other.

Freeman listened as the deputy slowly walked past the building Kate and he were hiding in. Freeman whistled and the deputy turned at the sound. In the dimness of the building the deputy hesitated, trying to locate the source of the sound. The hesitation was all the time the stony cowboy needed.

The deputy jerked back, as if he had been attached to an invisible rubber band stretched to its limits. The deputy fired his pistol but only as an afterthought. He disappeared from the open doorway.

The men on the street watched as the deputy looked as if he had been kicked by a horse. His gun still in his hand, but useless. He landed about ten feet from the door unmoving. He lay dead or dying in the middle of the ruts that had once been a division of the town but was now just a measure of the plains reclaiming the attempt at a town that had not seen any activity in years.

Freeman again grabbed Kate and exited the building where the gunmen believed they were hiding. Upon exiting the shell of a building Freeman stopped and placed his rifle just out of sight next to the building.

"What you doin'?"

Freeman put a finger to his lips.

"So, you goin' to die over some chocolate ass?" Rulo asked swinging into the empty building where Kate and Freeman had been.

"Chocolate ass?" Weaver repeated, limping behind Rulo at a safe distance.

"I don't think talkin' to you, whoever you are, matters anymo'," Rulo said. "I think we jus' kill you 'n take the girl." He laughed. "If there's any justice, we don't kill you outright 'n we make you watch us wit her 'fore you die."

Freeman and Kate entered one of the bigger buildings. It was bigger but still falling apart. The roof was half caved in and blocked half of the building. There was a rickety floor that was a patchwork of boards more than flooring.

"We comin' to get the girl," Rulo said with a smirk. "Ain't much goin' to stop this," the cowboy said standing a few feet from the dead deputy.

Freeman looked at Kate and smiled. He pointed to the ground where Kate was standing. He pointed three times to the ground and then raised a hand, before he spun on his heels and headed for the exit. At the exit he took a deep breath, shrugged his shoulders, and stepped out of the entrance of the small half collapsed general store.

Rulo, seeing Freeman appear, fired at the unflinching cowboy and missed. Rulo seemed surprised at his miss and fired again. The second shot was closer but not close enough to break Freeman's concentration.

Freeman leveled his pistol and calmly aimed and pulled the trigger of his Model 1860 Colt. The pistol kicked as the bullet tore out of the gun barrel and hurtled from Freeman to Rulo. Freeman watched as Rulo, the smirking cowboy, fell to his knees, holding his chest. As Rulo hit the ground Freeman fired again. Behind Rulo stood Weaver bleeding from his thigh. The menacing cowboy's bullet hit Weaver, the thick bearded man in his gray wool jacket, in the gut, spinning him around.

As Weaver was hit the gunman grimaced and let out a loud scream. Weaver like Rulo fell to his knees firing his pistol wildly in the direction of Freeman.

From the right side of the ghost town Freeman and Kate heard the first sounds of gunfire. Kate, still in the general store, watched as Freeman flinched getting nicked in the arm.

Freeman spun on the hiding shooter and searched for the gunman.

Another gunshot was heard, and Freeman watched as the bullet dug into the dirt at his feet. Instinctively, Freeman stepped back.

It was then, as Freeman stood in the middle of the ghost town, that he and Kate heard the crack and boom of a rifle. There was a pause and then another crack and boom.

Kate and Freeman waited.

From one of the weathered buildings on the right tumbled the stranger that the pair had seen earlier dressed all in black. He was holding his pistol toward the dirt. He moved as if he were drunk.

Kate scanned him for a bullet wound but saw none. As he moved away from the building it looked as if he was struggling to stand. His movement reminded Kate of how a chicken moved when looking for food. The man's head which was looking down moved first, then his feet and then his body. It was an odd thing to witness.

Freeman holding his pistol in his hand grimaced as he leveled his weapon on the approaching man in black. For the first time Kate noticed a tremor in Freeman's gun hand.

Behind the man dressed all black stumbled the man wearing the bandana. He stepped out of the same building but only made it to the threshold before collapsing dead there. His gun clattered across the wooden step and cartwheeled into the grass and dirt of the space between the two sides of the ghost town.

The chicken walking man continued walking forward and across the short distance from one side of the ghost town to the other. He could not lift the gun even as he tried to lift his head. He was an arm's length away from Freeman when his knees slammed into the dirt and then he fell face first into the ground dead.

Kaiyote appeared a few moments later with his rifle.

"Is that it?"

Kaiyote nodded. He raised two fingers.

Freeman holstered his gun. When the flinty cowboy put his gun away Kate dared to come out of the wreck that was once a store.

She slowly walked to the side of Freeman and Kaiyote. All around the ghost town were dead people. Kaiyote held his rifle in his arms like a baby. Freeman flexed his hand as Kate drew near. The little girl could see where the bullet had ripped through the fabric of Freeman's wool coat halfway up his right arm.

"Is it over?"

"Well, sort uv," Freeman said.

Kate frowned at Freeman's words.

"What's that mean?"

"I didn't kill Weaver or Conway," Freeman said.

Hearing those words Kate looked at the stern cowboy curiously.

"Why not?"

"Well, Conway," Freeman said with a tilt of his head. "I sort uv forgot about. 'N Weaver seemed someone you had a real reason to settle a score wit." Freeman paused. He flexed his gun hand and winced a little. He shrugged off his wool jacket and dropped it at his feet. Freeman lifted his arm and there was some visible pain, but the rugged cowboy did not let the pain stop his full extension of his arm.

"So, what?"

"So, you get to settle a score, I suppose," Freeman said.

Kate listened and thought about what Freeman was saying.

"You still have that belly buster I gave you?"

"No," Kate said, dejected. "Weaver took it from me."

Freeman nodded.

Freeman, Kaiyote and Kate walked back toward the entrance of the ghost town and past all the dead. The three moved to the only man alive on the dirt trail that had been the main drag of the ghost town.

Weaver, upon seeing Freeman and Kaiyote, reached for his pistol.

"You don't want to do that," Freeman said, reaching out and stepping on Weaver's extended forearm to stop him from grabbing his pistol.

Weaver groaned as Freeman applied pressure on his forearm. Freeman continued to keep his foot on Weaver's forearm as he bent down and braced him quickly. Freeman pulled a leather bag of coins from inside of Weaver's jacket pocket and quickly slipped that in his own pocket. In one of Weaver's pockets Freeman found Kate's loaded belly buster.

Freeman stood up and looked to Kate. The little girl looked at Freeman confused. The hardened cowboy looked to Kaiyote and spoke with his eyes, looking from Kaiyote to Weaver.

Kaiyote stepped away from Kate and to Weaver. He lifted the injured gunman onto his feet and pushed the only gunman, who was still alive, toward Freeman.

"Hol' him," Freeman said to Kaiyote.

Kaiyote held the bleeding gunman with one hand, by the collar of his coat.

"Here's your man," Freeman said. "You sed that he killed your family 'n that you wanted to have your revenge."

Kate looked at Freeman. The gunman had lost his hat and his greasy curly hair was plastered on his round head from sweat. He was bleeding from his stomach and leg. Weaver, that very moment, did not seem a threat or a killer. She looked from Weaver and to Freeman.

"So, here's your chance," Freeman said, handing Kate her derringer. Freeman smirked at Kate as she held the derringer in her small hands. "Jus' remember girl, that you take that step 'n you can't turn back." Freeman paused. "You sed I was diff'rent. I tol' you I wasn't. But I been thinkin' that I am."

Kate looked at Freeman and then at Weaver. The little girl looked at the deadly derringer in her hands. She tried to decide what she should do.

"I sed I can walk wit the monsters. I can. I know they evil. I think they wake up 'n have evil in their hearts. I think they go through they day wit that evil 'n they are jus' lookin' fir an excuse to do evil," Freeman said, standing in front of Weaver, Kaiyote and Kate. He shook his head. "I'm a killer. I ain't 'fraid to say that. But I don't wake up mad dog ready to kill." Freeman smiled at his words. "I think that is the diff'rence 'tween me 'n them. I'm a killer but I don't go to sleep thinkin' uv killin' or wake up wit killin' on my mind."

Kate smiled at Freeman.

"It ain't easy to take ev'rything from someone that they will ever have, if you have a heart," Freeman said with a shake of his head. "It is easy to make you feel better 'bout killin' if'n you think you protectin' yourself or your family, but what about now? He ain't doing nothing but dying. He ain't a threat. But you still want your revenge?" Freeman asked. He paused. He looked at the man Kaiyote had in hand. Weaver had been shot in the leg and stomach.

"Okay, Kate," Freeman said. "What will it be?"

Kate looked at Freeman and back to Weaver.

Kaiyote and Weaver stood watching quietly.

"You thinkin' 'bout killin' a dead man?"

Kate looked at Freeman confused.

"You see he's gut shot?"

Kate nodded.

"He ain't going to last very long," Freeman said.

Weaver moaned.

"So, it looks like I took care of the hard part," Freeman said, with a twisted smile. "So, if you jus' have to kill him, go 'head."

"You killed my family," Kate said to the curly-haired cowboy.

"What family?"

"On the waggun train from Kansas," Kate said.

Weaver smiled at the little girl.

"I tol' you I didn't kill your family," Weaver said. "That was Injuns. They was Apaches or one uv them killin' groups. They was wearin' warpaint 'n whoopin' 'n hollerin'. I barely got out uv there with my skin. I tried to tell the tenderfoots they was goin' in the wrong direction but they didn't listenin' to me," Weaver said in the hands of Kaiyote. The injured gunman struggled to stand. "Girl, you made a mistake. I ain't killed no one." He twisted in Kaiyote's grip. "It was Injuns."

Kate closed her eyes.

She closed her eyes and replayed the whole attack. There was no whooping and hollering. There were no Indians. She opened her eyes and looking at the curly-haired liar in front of her angered her.

She drew her derringer and aimed it at Weaver. Kate had a feral look about her all of a sudden.

"What you doin' girl? You want to kill me?" Weaver asked. He winced as if he had been touched with a white-hot poker. "You actin' crazy," Weaver said, blinking and his eyes tearing up. "I'm dying. Hell, I'm prob'ly already dead. I just ain't agreed to it yet."

Kate held the derringer close to Weaver. She tried to pull the trigger. At the last moment the nine-year-old was unable to pull the trigger. She spun on her heels and there was Freeman. The little girl was face-to-face with the dark cowboy. Up close, Freeman looked like he was made of aged walnut. His beard was sprinkled with bits of gray. Beneath his Hardee hat Kate saw the salt and pepper curls as well.

The cowboy reached out and redirected the belly buster from his chest. He held her wrist and studied the angry child. Freeman smiled at Kate, the nine-year-old who was suddenly full of emotions.

"Kate? What?"

Hearing her own name snapped the little girl out of her anger and inaction and made Kate look into the big and dark eyes of the man that saved her days before.

"It's okay," Freeman said. He rested a heavy hand on Kate's shoulder. "Don't beat yourself up 'bout it. Like I sed, it ain't easy to pull the trigger on someone 'n take ev'rythin' from a person he ever could be or would be," Freeman said. The dark cowboy paused. "Look at him. He ain't hurtin' you or doing nothin' but dyin' right now.  He ain't a threat." Freeman took the derringer from Kate. The little girl resisted. "You ain't a killer Kate. You ain't someone who needs to go to that dark place." Freeman studied Kate. "You want your revenge but sometimes it's jus' time that evens the scales."

Kaiyote walked away from the man who could barely stand on his own. He was the only one in motion. Weaver wobbled, like a baby trying to find its legs. The gunman fell to his knees and with the impact he breathed out and fell onto his side.

Freeman and Kate turned from Weaver and watched as Kaiyote walked away from them. He walked to the far end of the ghost town and stopped at the feet of the two gunmen tied to the base of the horse trough. Kaiyote looked back as Freeman and Kate slowly walked toward him.

Freeman winced. He flexed his hand and Kate noticed the first signs of blood appearing beneath his coat's cuff.

"We cleanin' up 'n leavin'," Freeman said. "When we head out you got one more chance to get your revenge," the dark-eyed cowboy said as the two of them arrived at the bodies and Kaiyote. Freeman looked down and kicked Conway.

The one-eyed gunman opened his eye slowly, as if he had been napping. He blinked and it seemed that meaningless action caused him pain. His face contorted in anguish.

Freeman smirked at Conway.

"So, what are you goin' to do wit him?"

Freeman reached for his gun with his injured arm and stopped. He grimaced and paused. The dark-eyed cowboy took a deep breath and pulled his heavier Dragoon from his other holster. Seeing Freeman armed with his pistol made Kate step back instinctively. She knew Freeman would not hurt her, but at the same time was aware of the violence of the man. He was like the wind. On a hot day his presence was appreciated. On a wet and windy day Freeman could add to the gloominess. Of course, he was dangerous, Kate thought, like a hurricane or tornado.

Freeman aimed his Dragoon at Conway and fired. The Dragoon was large and loud. The gun kicked in Freeman's hand as he pulled the trigger.

Kate clapped her hands against her ears surprised at the thunderous sound of the gunshot. Kaiyote flinched at the sound of the Dragoon as well. In the wake of the Freeman's shooting and killing Conway fell over but because he was tied to the frame of the horse trough could not fall completely to the ground.

Freeman braced Conway for any valuables. Kaiyote walked away while Freeman searches the dead man for valuables. Kate, her ears still ringing, watched as the quiet trail partner of Freeman walked into the feed store where Kate had been locked up initially.

"Why you do that?" Kate asked, her ears ringing.

"Do what?"

"Steal from them?"

"It ain't stealin' if they can't use it. They don't need it. I do," Freeman said.

"It don't seem right," Kate said.

"You tryin' to judge me? Judge me? The only one uv two people that gives a damn if you live or die out here," Freeman said. "Here we come to save you from God knows what 'n fir what? Fir you to judge me?" Freeman shook his head. Freeman stood up and looked at Kate with a smirk. "Come on, we're leavin'," Freeman said. "We need to get you a horse. Unless you think one uv them is gonna need it," Freeman said, waving to the dead around him.

Kate looked around the ghost town that when she had arrived tied and gagged there were only four horses. Now, there were twice as many pawing the dirt or snorting near their now dead owners.

By the time Kate and Freeman had walked to Weaver, the wounded gunman was lying on the ground motionless. Freeman kicked at Weaver only to hear a slight moan from the man on the dirt.

Freeman turned the nearly unconscious gunman over.

"Is he dead?"

"I don't think so," Freeman said.

Kate frowned.

"It ain't goin' to be that easy," Freeman said. "Not fir you."

Kate frowned at Freeman's words. She looked at the dark-eyed cowboy and tried to see if he was enjoying her inability to finish something she wanted him to finish.

Freeman turned and handed the derringer back to Kate. The nine-year-old took the weapon in hand but did nothing.

Freeman nodded. Freeman lifted his heavy pistol again and as he did Kate tried to cover her ears. Freeman reached out and grabbed Kate with his freehand.

"I sed it wasn't goin' to be easy fir you," Freeman said.

Kate looked at Freeman unsure.

"Take that belly buster 'n aim it at him," Freeman said.

Kate did as she was ordered. Shakily, Kate aimed the belly buster at the prone Weaver.

"Now, look at the man you sed killed your family," Freeman said.

Kate looked. Weaver laid on the ground on his back bleeding from his leg and gut. His hand was clutched against the gun shot just above his hip.

"Now, I'm goin' to countdown 'n you can pull the trigger 'n this whole thing will be over," Freeman said.

Kate listened, but the sound of her own heartbeat was loud in her ears. Her breathing was loud as well.

"Ready?" Freeman asked. "Three... Two... One," Freeman said slowly and unhurriedly.

Kate closed her eyes.

The boom of the gunshot roared and the bullet, a single bullet, tore through Weaver's chest. The gunman bucked on the ground in front of Freeman and Kate. Kate jumped and opened her eyes to look down and see a hole in Weaver's chest.

Freeman holstered his pistol and took Kate's derringer from her. Freeman popped out the two bullets in the derringer and pocketed them. Kaiyote stood to one side, holding his rifle as he had before, watching Kate and Freeman.

"Now, you can go home or to California 'n sleep at night," Freeman said.

Kate stood shocked at Freeman's violence. Freeman, as was his habit, reloaded Kate's derringer and then his pistol where he stood, before handing Kate back the belly buster. Kate took the gun and looked at Freeman speechless.

"What?" Freeman asked. Holstering his own pistol.

Kate shook her head.

Kaiyote appeared with their horses. He had another horse with him. The horse was unusual because it was not the strong quarter horse that Freeman rode or the Appaloosa that Kaiyote rode. It was a calm brown bodied Mustang. Kate noted that it had a white foreleg and tail.

"This is yours," Kaiyote said, handing the reins of the Mustang to the little girl.

Freeman, on his horse, looked at the two looking back toward the horizon. The bearded cowboy did not speak. He just waited for the two to mount their horses.

"What now?"

"Well, I think there's Garrett or the army outpost. The outpost is a couple uv days ride from here. Garrett is closer. If we get you there, I'm mighty sure that freedmen pass through there."

"You gonna leave me at another outpost?"

Freeman did not respond. He wheeled on his horse and led the slow march across the plains.

223

# Chapter 29.

Kate.
Day Four, Kansas territories, 1869

At nine, Kate left the Kansas territories with Thaddeus Monroe and a dozen others headed for Oregon and eventually California. That trip had taken nearly four months, but it was not in those one hundred and twenty-four days where Kate found her mind. The trip with Thaddeus Monroe, Kate had been numb and the trip unspectacular as Kate nursed her hurt and betrayal. She had hoped and dreamed that in those hundred plus days that Freeman would appear and take her to California.

Four months on the trail Kate rode, ate, slept and went through the motions but her mind continued to hope and dream that Freeman would show up. Every day on the trail to Oregon with Thaddeus Monroe and the four other families Kate found herself replaying the most significant four days of her life. Nearly one hundred hours, four days, a little under a week, Kate hoped and felt despite all the madness and chaos that she was safe as long as Freeman was around.

As a nine-year-old going on ten she could not explain the significance of Freeman. She simply thought him unique, gruff and dangerous. Freeman was her protector and unashamedly violent and dedicated to that task.

Four days she rode with the enigmatic Freeman and Kaiyote and no moment seemed lost on her. From the moment she had seen him to the moment he had left her made an indelible impression on the nine-year-old Kate.

His words rang in her ears as if Freeman was in Sacramento, where her father's people had taken her in.

"You want revenge," Freeman said in Kate's memories. "I can see that. You believe that man killed your family, 'n I would be a fool to try to convince you otherwise. But we in a lawless place. They would rather kill you 'n me than talk to us here. But you, little lady, they might not kill you right away. They might toy with you 'n

pass you around 'n mistreat so badly 'til you wanted to die."
Freeman paused and looked at Kate with his dark and unblinking
eyes. "All you can do now is get yourself in trouble. You might
want to die, but they might want to do worse. So, my advice is
keep living. Get older. If you want to kill someone, come back
when you learnt to shoot that Colt, we took off that pretend man.
Otherwise, you lookin' to destroy all you done to get this far."

Kate nodded.

"You get older 'n come back 'n you seek your revenge,"
Freeman said.

Thaddeus Monroe, the wagon train master, had taken
Kate to Oregon and then to California where her father's people
were supposed to live.

When Kate rode away from Garrett and Kansas by way of
the Oregon trail, she was nine years old. There were no tears.
There was no histrionics. Realizing that Freeman was leaving her
with Thaddeus Monroe and his wagon train she surrendered to the
idea. There was little she could do. She held onto her clothes bag
and all that was inside and watched as Mister Monroe smiled
behind his beard and showed his uneven teeth.

"Kate, you will be safe as you will be with this waggun
train," Freeman said, back then and he and Kaiyote turned and
rode away from the wagon train. It was the last time Kate had
talked to Freeman.

"Looks like you're my responsibility," Mister Monroe said
as Freeman mounted his horse and he and Kaiyote rode to the
Garrett saloon.

Kate did not respond. Instead, she looked at Freeman and
Kaiyote riding to the saloon, just two hundred yards away from her
and feeling as if it was two million miles away suddenly. She looked
back at Mister Monroe dressed in a thick jacket, button front shirt,
dark trousers and cowboy boots. On his hip was a pistol hanging
from a gun belt.

"You will be as safe as a cub with a mama bear," Mister
Monroe said, with a smile.

Kate knew the wagon master was trying to put her at ease before the long journey, but the more he talked the more Kate wished Freeman hadn't left her under the protection of Thaddeus Monroe.

She tried to smile, but her face fought her artifice. The smile looked more like a scowl. Kate gave up the effort to smile, looking at the wagon preparing to leave Garrett. She climbed aboard and tried to get comfortable in the rear amongst the supplies and clothing piled in the wagon.

Kate pouted and sulked, the only outward hint of the little girl's displeasure of being sent away from Kansas, Freeman and Kaiyote and all the good and bad memories that the nine-year-old could pack in just a handful of days with a Black cowboy and the silent warrior. In the rear of the covered wagon the nine-year-old tried to hide her pain and memories. Those memories circled her like a pack of wolves. They came in succession. The first memory was of the snippets of the wagon train ambush, then her mother's unmoving body and then the dark cowboy and the quiet and stoic partner. Her memories took her to camping overnight, then Stratton and the Stratton saloon. Kate had left Stratton and been ambushed again and nearly killed, only to kill the man that she believed had set up the ambush of her family.

As the wagon train made its way out of Garrett Kate did not look back to see if Freeman or Kaiyote watched. She did not want to believe that Freeman cared. More importantly, the little girl did not want to look and find that the stony cowboy who had protected her did not care at all.

Instead, Kate focused on the wagon train she was going to be a part of for the next four months as they rolled toward the Oregon trail. Thaddeus Monroe was a no-nonsense man who ran a tight wagon train. Kate learned she was part of a group of freedmen led by a firebrand named Thaddeus Monroe. Unlike Kate's father and a few on the first wagon train she ever was a part of, Thaddeus Monroe and all the men on the wagon train were well armed. They all had pistols. The person riding shotgun carried a scatter gun. There were twelve men to the four wagons. There were only five grown women on this first trip to Oregon. There were just eight children on the excursion to Oregon. None of the children was older than seven to Kate's dismay.

None of that mattered to the nine-year-old. She had to figure out how she would get from Oregon to Sacramento and find her father's people once she arrived in Oregon.

"Don't you worry, little lady, we'll get you to Oregon 'n once we get you there, we'll figure out how to get you to your father's people. It's the least I can do for Freeman, after he done saved my grits so many times."

That conversation came a couple of days outside of Garrett and in the Nebraska territories. The wagon train was bumping along, and some fakers rode by looking at the wagon train much the way wolves' nose around deer looking for an easy target. The wagon train drivers did not smile or give the fakers an opportunity to speak. They all placed hands on their pistols and watched as the fakers rode by. The wagoners were the shot first and asked questions after type.

"On the plains, it pays to not trust no one you don't know," Mister Monroe said. Sitting next to Mister Monroe was his son, John. The wagon train business was the idea of Mister Monroe and his son. They owned two of the four wagons in this train.

"How you know Mister Freeman?"

"Well," Thaddeus Monroe said, thinking.

# Chapter 30.

Kate.
Day Four, Kansas territories, 1869

Desmond "Dead Man" Freeman, before he became Desmond Freeman, went to sleep every night and wondered if he would live another day in the prison, he found himself imprisoned. The prison was vast. The prison was cruel. The prison was divided into prison yards and quarters, the working fields and the great house. Freeman, as a prisoner, only worked in the fields and lived, survived in the prison yards and quarters.

He had little memory of life as a child. The prison did not coddle to children. At an early age prison children were expected to work. So, Freeman worked from the time he could stand and hold things until he escaped. In between he witnessed incredible brutality, violence and inhuman acts that ripped the lives out of prisoners, men and women and child.

Now, Freeman got his unusual name after running away from the prison he escaped. What was the reason for his running away? What was the last straw? Freeman could not pinpoint that moment. In his head there were insufferable moments piled on top of unsufferable moments that began to weigh him down. Was he frustrated? Of course. Was he angry? Unquestionably. But it was perhaps the nightmares that visited him every night he closed his brown eyelids and there, where he sought sleep, instead, he found flashes of horrors he recalled and tried to bury in the day-to-day frustrations of his prison life.

*There were flashes, always just flashes, of a brown-skinned woman Freeman believed was his mother, running from a pale faced bearded menace with a belt. The pale faced bearded ghost swung the belt in the air and hit the brown woman and drove her to the ground. Once the woman was on the ground the bearded ghost leaped upon her.*

*The nightmare flashed forward and the brown-skinned woman, Freeman was sure was his mother, gathered Freeman and two other younger children that looked like Freeman in their prison cell. The woman was in tears. She showed her stomach to Freeman and the others and pulled a knife from beneath her dress.*

*She, crying and panicky, spoke in Freeman's dream.*

*"I can't let them take you frum me," she said to Freeman, and she reached out and grabbed one of the two other children.*

*"I should have dun this when he came the first time," the brown-skinned woman said.*

*The knife tore across the throat of the youngest of the small children.*

*The pale monster was suddenly at the door and snatching Freeman from the woman. The second child fell limp and bloody on the prison cell floor.*

*"You ain't gonna have no more uv me," the woman said, and Freeman watched as she dragged the knife across her own throat. The blood came gushing out like a fountain. In seconds, the woman slumped to the prison floor and was dead.*

A beaten and mistreated prisoner woke from a nightmare and found himself in the endless terror decided to run from the rickety shack where he slept. He ran from the constant beatings and attempts to break his will through the endless snarls, sidelong looks, condemnations and whippings. He ran from the whip and the chain. He ran into the unknown with the hope that there he might find something better.

Clothed with what he had on his back and a few scraps he had secreted away he left behind everything and nothing for something better. Anything was better he believed than the nightmare he woke up to everyday.

Almost immediately that unshackled prisoner got lost, but that feeling had been with him from the moment he realized he was imprisoned. He ran through the night. The stars above watched over him. The trees and night wildlife marked his passing.

He only stopped to rest and hide in the safety of logs, hollows and trees. The fugitive only had the stiff burlap trousers, heavy work shoes, and a thin shirt and a sack with his valuables. His valuables? The idea was laughable. In the sack was a dull knife, a length of rope, a flint, some bandages, and a hook and needle. He had taken some foodstuffs, but they ran out a day away from the big house and fields.

So, he ate berries. He ate roots. He made do. In the woods he found grubs, ants and worms to shove down his gullet. The food he found tasted better, the one-time prisoner thought, than the scraps the villains and evil men gave them grudgingly. In the wall-less prison, in the barely habitable prisoner quarters, he had eaten worse.

The scarred and whipped runaway looked for a river and picked up a fallen branch, which he tied the dull knife to making a makeshift spear. With that spear he hunted for fish and whatever could sustain him.

The first free food the escapee caught was a turtle. He was not a great cook, but the hunted runaway didn't care. He ate turtle that second and third day. The scarred prisoner had been forced to survive like an animal. So, he ate what he could.

On the fourth day of his escape the hunted runaway heard the sound of thunder in the distance over a hill. He did not look forward to what would come. But it was not rain that fell from the sky that day but more thunder. As the tired and hungry fugitive walked up a grade and through the woods looking for something to eat that day.

He stumbled over his first dead white man on the edge of the woods. The prisoner recoiled and immediately ran for cover thinking the man asleep. He looked and realized that the man was not asleep and more importantly not moving.

The escapee returned to the sight of the white man. The white man lay face down a hand stretched out like he was trying to grab something. Inches away from his hand was a rifle. The prisoner studied the dead man. His head was smashed like something heavy had fallen on it and left it caved in. The dark eyed self-willed soul studied the head because he had never seen a white man brutally killed.

The dead white man's head was what a watermelon looked like if dropped and split open on the ground. Instead of watermelon there was red, blue, purple and black liquid and ropy meat visible. The fugitive could not look away. He noticed that the white man's eyeball was somehow attached by a string of muscle to gray and pink ropy meat. It was not in his face, the runaway noted. It dangled inches from his shoulder on the ground.

The corpse was wearing a gray wool coat. His trousers were black. He had scuffed black boots and a wide leather belt. Well, he had all that before the nameless soul reached out and claimed what he wanted, without fight or sidelong look.

After the wanted runaway liberated those items the one-time fettered prisoner had a gray wool coat with a handful of bullets, a canvas shirt, trousers, some tight boots, which he discarded after trying them on, and the wide leather belt.

The rifle was heavy in the nameless prisoner's hand. He studied the heavy combination of metal and wood and all its mechanics. There were scribblings on the side of the weapon that the one-time imprisoned soul could not decipher. He did not need to know what the scratching's meant. He knew it was a rifle.

He had seen one back in the fields being carried by one of the fat, bearded criminals. One of the abusers had shot the rifle once or twice trying to kill a deer on the edge of the field but missed. The escaped runaway smiled at the memory.

The brutes always acted so superior to the men and women they abused, but, the one-time chained soul thought, it was only because they had guns and no hesitation with killing women and children. The males did not in large part revolt against them because of the abuser's bloodlust.

Yet, it had been the beating of Pock and taking of his woman that had made Dez, the runaway, run. He had watched as one of the villains came to the prisoner quarters and walked into Pock's shack and taken Nini from Pock. Pock had tried to defend his woman. For his attempt to protect his woman Pock was shot by the bearded offender and then, the next day, killed for fighting the oppressor.

He witnessed the whipping of Pock the villains called: Ben but all the beaten called: Pock. That day all the beaten from the fields were gathered together and made to watch the whipping. The traitor the lipless called: Sam and the beaten called: Soulless whipped Pock until he passed out. Soulless stopped and the lipless wrongdoer took the whip from him and whipped Pock until he stopped breathing.

"Let this be a lesson. You here 'til I say diff'rent. I take what I want. I own all uv you. You're my property. You're nothing more than the animals I use 'n replace. When you think you are more valuable than a horse, pig or cow then you end up like Ben," the bearded villain said.

That was the last day that the determined runaway slept in the prisoner quarters. He struggled in his cot after closing his eyes against the phantoms in his head. The image of Pock dead haunted his dreams that night. Dez, the prisoner, had woken from his fitful sleep and climbed out of his cot and left. He ran away first from his shack where six others slept. He then ran through the dozen buildings, shacks mostly, that made up the prisoner quarters. No one stopped him. No one seemed to be on guard. Dez, the prisoner, made his way to the fields where he had watched women give birth to the next generation of prisoners under the unblinking eyes of the oppressors and callous hearts of owners and the soulless. Dez, the prisoner, looked back thinking that at the edge of the field the oppressors and their horses would run him down, but all he saw was the silhouette of the big house standing there in the late night, a silent witness of his escape.

Now, dressed in dead man's clothes and four days away from those horrible prison memories he searched the smashed headed abuser twice to make sure he did not miss anything he might need. He found on the second search a wrapped piece of jerky. Of all the things the ex-prisoner, dressed in dead man's clothes, acquired he could not decide which he liked more the jerky or the rifle. They both were an acquired taste.

The unfettered prisoner ventured forward into the woods he was using to hide his progress. Along the edge of a trail the nameless prisoner found more dead men and liberated bullets for the rifle he now possessed. He took a belt off one of the lipless dead and quickly filled his gun belt with unspent rifle bullets.

Five days from the prisoner quarters he had escaped the runaway came upon a crater on the trail. Around the crater lay parts of five villains. All their rifles had been shattered. The bodies had been stripped down to their union suits and drawers. The paranoid runaway skirted the site of destruction and was surprised to find a heavy six-shooter, in good working condition, just a few feet from the trail that day.

That day, after finding the six-shooter, the tired runaway heard the first shots to restart the fight between the two groups. The runaway climbed over a small hill and found himself watching the lipless wrongdoers fighting. As best as the once shackled soul could tell they were fighting to possess the land between them.

There were hundreds of villains shooting at each other, charging and retreating and hiding behind trees and rocks. The exhausted runaway tried to figure out who was fighting who. One in grey and one in blue, fought each other. They shot their guns. The thunder or what Freeman had thought to be thunder came from the big guns. They charged and retreated. They retreated and surged. It was like some deadly tug-of-war, the opportunistic runaway dressed in dead man's clothes thought.

He sat and watched the battle. The fighting was intense. The one-time prisoner pulled out his recently found pistol and studied it above the fighting. The runaway aimed his pistol and acted like he had seen the villains below.

He had never fired a gun before and without much thought pulled the heavy trigger of the pistol. The pistol kicked out of the fugitive's hand and cartwheeled over his shoulder. Instantly, the prisoner backed away from the men below and hid in the closest trees.

His shooting had not drawn anyone's attention. The runaway pulled the trigger again and for the second time the six-shooter bucked in his hand, but this time he was able to hold onto it. The runaway pulled the trigger again and the third time the pulling of the trigger and the recoil was not as bad. The pistol moved a little in his hand, but not as violently as before. The runaway hid the pistol in his newly found jacket.

The fugitive did not care who won. He instead concentrated on the colors. The blue versus the gray was interesting.

Looking down and realizing he was wearing a gray jacket the runaway thought absently that he wanted the gray fighters to win for no other reason than that he was wearing their colors. Again, the colors, blue and gray, had no significance to the runaway. The men inside those colors looked exactly the same to him. They were the same faces that beat him and beat the men and women and children he knew and talked to before his escape.

The shooting went on until the sun began to sink in the sky. The men moved forward. The men moved back. At some predetermined time, the men backed away from each other.

He meandered and found a clearing where hundreds of men were standing around smoking, eating, drinking. Men wearing bandages laid on cots in and out of tents. There were all these men, horses, tents and flags. Men with beards and mustaches dressed in gray looked tired and defeated.

The unchained runaway studied from the shadows of the trees watching the white killers determined to kill other white killers. The idea of devils brutalizing each other was a foreign thought for the fugitive. He had never seen killers fight or harm one another. All violence he knew came at the hands of the lipless and aimed specifically at black men, women and children.

Sure, the one-time prisoner had to admit, he had seen black men fight with one another in the prisoner quarters over scraps thrown to them by the lipless or the soulless, what the beaten called those looking for favor from the lipless, but nothing on the scale of the skirmish he watched from the edge of the clearing. More importantly, the one-time prisoner wearing dead man's clothes had only seen the cruel men brutalize, humiliate, mistreat and kill black men, women and children.

So, as the runaway sat and leaned back against a tree and watched the battle below his feet and smiled. The idea of the battle was unusual. In his head the one-time prisoner imagined the cause of the fighting had to come back to some beaten or broken not doing something. It was always that way, the runaway knew. Yet, there was not a black face visible on the field. The unfettered soul shook his head at the idea of a beaten fighting with the white men who had brutalized him and everyone he knew for as long as he lived, seemed impossible. The idea of a good brutalizer, an honest brutalizer was an alien thought.

The unbound runaway looked and realized there was no need for a beaten to be present to make these criminals angry enough to cause violence against each other. They needed no excuse to use intense violence against the beaten and seemingly each other. That thought fascinated the beaten. It mesmerized the once broken.

The abusers were willingly killing each other. They were murdering each other for no real reason other than the colors of their coats. From the trees the one-time prisoner felt the smile broaden on his brown face at the deadly game below. The brutes were killers. He, who had no real given name, was called: Sonny by the abusers, but called: Dez by the beaten. He did not like either name or rarely answered to either.

Thinking, as he sat on the hill, he was not broken completely and did not recognize or accept the life and death power of the brutes. He knew they could kill him but if they did it would be on his terms. As for the others, his connection was like that of a rat in a in a sinking ship. He survived and got to know the other rats, but he did not see himself as the broken and defeated. He was neither Sonny nor Dez, but something distinct. He was thinking all sorts of thoughts and none of those thoughts involved being under the thumb of the brutalizers he had escaped. He looked across the plain where the fighting was going on and smiled at his freedom.

The runaway rubbed the back of his neck thinking he was now in control of his life. If he wanted to, he could walk down the hill and for the first time forfeit his newly liberated life if he wanted. His life was his to do with as he pleased. He knew that being no longer chained did not make him entirely free in this devilish land, he laughed at the idea. Was freedom portioned out? Were there small bits of freedom given, like food? The runaway wondered if he had just a taste of freedom compared to what he had before. The escapee shook his head behind the sound of death, dying and gun and cannon fire.

The fugitive knew that he should keep going. He had heard that the torturers would send killers to track down runaways, but he lingered. The brutes fighting, getting shot, wounded and killed amused him. Watching the lipless running forward, recoiling, retreating and battling made for great entertainment. Dez knew these criminals, who would beat, whip, humiliate and kill Dez if they knew he had runaway deserved the fate below. If it was in his power, Dez would not shed a tear if they all died there on the field.

Some, in their live-in prison, had tried to tell the fleeing escapee that some of the white brutalizers possessed the ability for kindness, but the one-time prisoner did not believe that. The escaped, newly freed soul instead believed them all killers. They were brutal. They were cruel. They abused the women and children. For the runaway there was nothing good or kind or human about them.

The groups of torturers did not possess the ability to care. They, men and women, were harmful, hurtful and violent and more inclined to violence than peace.

He climbed to his feet and leaned against a tree smiling and laughing at the losses below. They should die, the fleeing soul thought. All their beatings, threats, bootings were just cruelties. They were not superior. They were just brutal. Brutes.

As night fell the thunder from the cannons was replaced by a whining sound of those hundreds of killers retreating to the edge of the field they were fighting over, and a distinct smell of hundreds of men camped out at dozens of fires. The uncaged soul, climbed to his feet and moved away from the battle and through the woods. He skirted the camps and took a wide arc to avoid the white brutes, their wool coats, tents and guns.

The fleeing ex-prisoner, moved through the night knowing that the villains rested during that time. He figured during the dark and in the shadow of the night travel was easier and less likely to run into slavers, their catchers or villains in general.

He climbed a hill and stumbled over a root and tumbled headlong down the hill. At the bottom of the hill, he found himself face-to-heel with a young bearded white brute in a dark blue wool coat. The killer was watering a tree when the desperate fugitive nearly toppled him.

"Hey, now, boy," the soldier said, startled, holding himself and simultaneously reaching for his rifle as he did.

The startled fugitive, seeing the brute grab for his rifle panicked. He jumped to his feet and rushed the blue coat and slammed him back against the tree stunning him. The blue coat had been able to grab his rifle by the barrel but not been able to lift it above his waist when the one-time prisoner stopped him. Out of the corner of his eye, the unbroken saw the campfires just one hundred yards away. Just one hundred yards away, the unfettered also saw the dozens of villains moving on the outskirts of the camp.

"Boy I ain't the enemy," the white killer said through gritted teeth.

The scarred and untrusting runaway did not listen. The villain pushed against the stronger runaway. The ex-prisoner slammed the murderer against the tree again and again until he fell silent and limp in his hands. Scared and not wanting to be discovered the rattled runaway ran back up the hill and away from the unconscious murderer and the camp and fires.

A day later, the unchained individual found another blue coated killer. It happened quite by accident. The fugitive was moving through the quiet woods in the middle of the day and saw the blue coat. He thought it was abandoned and hoped it might fit better than the one he was wearing at the time. So, without any real concern, the ex-prisoner walked toward the blue coat, thinking it was draped over a boulder.

He was surprised to find a villain soldier kneeling against a tree with one pale hand against the gnarled bark. The escapee hesitated. In that hesitation the runaway weighed backing up and drawing attention from the still man. The cautious fugitive froze, not sure what to do. He was arm's reach from saplings that did not afford much cover.

"I'm not long fir this world," the brute said, and the fugitive was not sure the killer was talking to him. He did not lift his head.

The unsure runaway stopped breathing with the killer's words. He was in front of the kneeling man. He could see the brute in the blue coat was holding a pistol in his free hand.

"Why you wearin' that coat?"

The hunted ex-prisoner did not answer. He studied the white killer leaning against a tree. He had been gut shot. His shoulder was pressed against the trunk of the tree. It seemed that if he moved, he might collapse and die right there.

"You know that coat is the coat uv the enemy?" Asked the white brutalizer.

"You all my enemy," the one-time prisoner said. The runaway hesitated. It was the first time that he talked back to a brutalizer without fear.

"Not all uv us," the gut shot killer said.

"How you diff'rent?"

"If I was your enemy, I would've shot you," the brute said. He lifted his pistol but did not fire.

The cautious runaway nodded.

"That don't make you not my enemy," the fugitive said.

The killer nodded and winced in the effort.

"How's this?" Asked the gut shot brute. "If I was your enemy, I would have shot you knowin' you was an escaped runaway." The gut shot villain paused, breathing heavily. "Your enemy wants to keep you on that plantation. This war is to get you 'n your people free."

The fugitive smirked.

"You don't believe me?"

"Ain't a lot to believe," the runaway said. He studied the hunched over soldier.

"Well, we fightin' to keep all we got fir our people 'n yours," the brutalizer wearing a blue wool coat said, his voice strained.

"None uv you have that power," Freeman said. "Jus' because you done wrong 'n feel bad don't get rid uv the wrong."

The soldier, holding the pistol breathed raggedly.

"How long this fight been goin' on?"

"Nearly two years," the gut shot soldier said.

"You makin' headway? I mean, we still mistreated."

"It don't work like that," the gut shot brute said, with a small chuckle.

"How long you been here?" the runaway asked looking around the immediate area. There was no one around the two. The only witness to the conversation was the trees.

"I don't know," the killer said breathing as if the words exhausted him. "Maybe, a day," he wheezed.

"Why your people leave you?"

"They didn't leave me," the killer said. "I tol' them to go on." He paused, trying to catch his breath. "I tol' you. There's a war."

The runaway nodded. He didn't know what a nation was or care. All he cared about now was running away from the mistreatment with a hope of something better.

"That coat you wearing is worn by the traitors uv this nation," the white killer said. "They want to keep you in chains."

"A coat don't make you good or bad," the runaway said, looking at the gut shot man. "Your actions is all that matters."

The man in the blue coat wheezed. The sound was similar to the sound of a dying moose.

The unshackled ex-prisoner listened but suddenly became bored with the conversation. All the devils in this nation wanted to keep the runaway in chains. If they caught him now, in this forest, ex-prisoner imagined they would either kill him or beat him before putting him in chains and taking him back to the prisoner quarters.

The fugitive looked around, making sure no one was sneaking up on him from behind. Satisfied he was alone with the white killer he thought to say something. What should he say? Wearing a coat didn't make you good or evil, the unbound prisoner thought.

"So, if you 'n your blue coats win, what happens?"

"We goin' to free you 'n your people," the bearded killer said.

"How? You goin' to kill all the ones that want to keep us in chains?"

There was a pause. The gut shot villain took a breath. He seemed to be trying to claw himself back from the grips of death. The fugitive watched emotionless.

"We got the country's support. Too many feel this will tear us apart," the kneeling killer breathed. "There's the President 'n the government," the killer said, breathing harder than normal. "They been tryin' to fix this, but there are some that don't want this to change," he paused.

The fugitive smirked at the prison keeper dressed in a blue wool coat. He had said a lot of words, but none of them made sense. All the escaped prisoner knew was that for most of his life he woke in an endless nightmare of beatings, terror and abuse. He was fed scraps that no human would eat, even if starving. He was clothed grudgingly in the thinnest of fabrics to cover his nakedness and daily seen as a threat to the family of brutalizers watching over him and the other prisoners.

The runaway looked down and heard the wounded brutalizer wheeze. The sound got the runaway's attention.

"Boy, can you get me some water? I'm awful thirsty," the white killer said through parched lips.

The fugitive looked at the white brute wearing the blue wool coat and holding the pistol in his hand and smiled. He smiled at the brutalizer need of him then. The escapee wanted to laugh but instead thought how comical it was for someone that had beaten him, abused him, mistreated him and all those like him to ask for something and think it not far-fetched or idiotic. The one-time prisoner looked around and smirked.

"You want *me* to get you some water?"

"Yes," the gut shot killer said, not looking up.

The escaped prisoner looked at the killer leaning against the tree and tried to think. He thought if he was still in the prison, he grew up in the hesitance would have been followed with a beating. Yet, he hesitated and looked down at the back of the blue coat. He scanned the woods, looking for what he did not know. Not jumping at the words of a killer was an unusual and freeing thing indeed.

The gut shot killer did not move. The runaway did not move. In the silence and stillness, the sound of faraway shooting could be heard. The runaway knew that the big fights were far away from him and the wounded blue coat.

The runaway looked down on the prison keeper, unsure what he wanted to do. On the ground near the white killer was a canteen. The ex-prisoner stepped to the canteen. He hesitated. He looked at the canteen and then the killer. He picked up the canteen and studied it. He did not move into the thick woods and search for a small stream. He instead watched as the brute struggled to breathe. The breathing quieted. The killer's shoulders relaxed. The one-time prisoner listened.

Looking down on the brute it looked as if he had fallen asleep like the old did, the fugitive thought. He touched the villain lightly on the shoulder and found him unresponsive. The ex-prisoner placed a hand close to his nose and realized he was no longer pushing air out of his lungs.

"You don't need no water now," the runaway said.

The runaway walked away from the dead brutalizer with his Hardee hat on his head. The runaway figured that he wouldn't need it and the escaped prisoner definitely did. Though he did not know if he believed or understood what the dying killer had said, he did not have the heart to strip him of his jacket or disturb him against the tree. The runaway fugitive left the dead killer leaning and looking like he was watering the grass beside the tree.

That whole incident happened before the sun was at its highest. The two, a prison and a killer, were hidden beneath the canopy of trees. The one leaning against the tree dressed in a blue wool coat and braced by the tree and pistol had an oval shaped face and a beard. The other soul, dressed in a gray wool coat, shook his head at the unmoving brute against the tree.

The runaway walked away from the dead killer and made his way through the woods. It was unusual for the ex-prisoner to travel during the daylight hours, but it was an unusual situation. Just two or three miles away or less there was fighting, shooting and cannon fire.

The one-time prisoner walked on, and the gunfire diminished. Through the thick trees the fugitive walked looking for a place to hide until the sun went down. He found a hollow and was about to rest and wait out the day when he heard movement in the woods, he found himself in. It was not the normal sounds of the forest, or the animals usually found there. That day, the fugitive stopped and found a saddled horse standing the shadows of the woods he was traipsing through. The horse almost disappeared in the speckled light of the trees. It was a black quarter horse with intelligent eyes and a noble bearing. When the horse saw the fugitive, it looked up and nickered and paused.

"Hey, now," the runaway said, seeing the horse in the dappled sunlight of the woods and raising his hands, the rifle strapped across his back. He was maybe ten yards away from the horse and paused, giving the horse a chance to bolt if it wanted to bolt. The horse whinnied and snickered and took a few steps back but did not bolt.

"What you doin' out here all by yourself?"

The fugitive closed the distance on the horse and by the end of the day was riding slowly away from the battle and toward freedom.

A freeman rode west and into the hills and disappeared into the Kansas territories. While in the wilderness he met a group of Indians. Eight braves led by a long-haired leader appeared as the fugitive rode along the riverbank. Of the eight the leader, watched silently. Two braves lifted their rifles and the fugitive pulled up his horse.

That day he met Kaiyote and his scouting party. The quiet warrior, serious, stoic and fearless took the freed prisoner to their chief, Gray Hawk, and the tribe. For four summers the fugitive stayed with Kaiyote and his tribe.

The tribe, led by a tough but fair Gray Hawk, took the fugitive in and taught him their ways. It was there he received his name, which loosely translated to man wearing dead man's clothes, because he appeared wearing the clothes of dead men.

All those memories floated around Kate as she stood in the streets of Sacramento waiting for the wagon scheduled to take off to appear. The derringer, the belly buster, Freeman had given her for protection was a memento she cherished. She also had the modified Model 1860 Colt pistol she bought and both weapons sat in the clothes bag she had grabbed when the Marshall and deputy tried to arrest her the day before.

# Chapter 31.

Kate.
Kansas territories, 1877

Miss Mary puffed another small round cloud of cherry scented smoke into the air of the small room. The small pear-shaped woman looked at Kate evenly.

"I know you done tol' me you ain't Freeman's daughter 'n all, but you sort uv resemble him in a way," Miss Mary said, bringing Kate back to the small room on the edge of Curtis, Kansas.

Kate frowned.

"What? You think that is bad?"

Kate did not respond.

Mister Lawson cleared his throat. Miss Mary looked to Lawson.

"Need you to jus' answer the girl's question," Lawson said.

"Didn't I?" Miss Mary asked.

"Well, no ma'am," Kate said. "I wanted to know if you know Freeman or how or where I can find him?"

"So, why you lookin' fir someone so bad?"

"I didn't die when our wagon train was ambushed. I didn't die when I came to Stratton," Kate said. "I made some stupid mistakes. I was young, but that's no excuse. I didn't die when I thought I could kill someone 'n I wasn't ready." Kate paused. She took a breath. "All that was because uv that Black cowboy." Kate took a deep breath looking at Miss Mary who was studying her intently.

Miss Mary nodded. Natalie and Caleb Lawson listened quietly. Elisabeth of the people in the room knew the most of Kate's story.

"When all uv it was happenin' I was too young to understand. I was a nine-year-old brat. I had lost so much 'n didn't know how to thank 'em fir what they did. So, when they took me to Garrett 'n found me a waggun train uv freedmen I didn't want to go. I thought Mister Monroe was like all the other men. Mister

Monroe tol' me he was friends wit Freeman 'n I was safe. Freeman paid Mister Monroe 'n put me on a waggun headed to Oregun."

Miss Mary raised a hand.

"I get it girl," the woman with the floral scarf on her head said. "I take it back. You got a good reason to come back 'n repay Freeman." Miss Mary frowned. "When was the last time you saw him?"

"I haven't been back here in almost seven years," Kate said.

Miss Mary nodded. She drew another puff of smoke and let it out easily from the corner of her mouth. She nodded again, slowly.

"Like I said, I get it. He seems to be all that I was tol'. The only problem is you came too late."

"What do you mean too late?"

Miss Mary pulled on her pipe and blew out a cloud of cherry scented smoke.

"My girls hear ev'rythin'. They listen to every man's secret. They tol' me that they heard Freeman was shot down dead in a small town not too far from here," Miss Mary said, getting serious.

Kate listened. She could not hide the shock of the news Miss Mary announced. The teenager frowned at the weight of the words.

"A few uv my girl's tol' me a month or so ago they heard a Black cowboy was finally killed in some small town between here 'n Coffeyville," Miss Mary said. She sat with her legs crossed, smoking on her long pipe and filling the room with the hint of cherry smoke.

"You know the name uv the town?"

"No, but it don't matter," Miss Mary said. "My girls tell me news since news matters here," Miss Mary said, with her pipe in her hand.

Kate twisted her lips, thinking about what Miss Mary said.

Mister Lawson climbed to his feet. He crossed the distance from the chair to Kate. Caleb placed a hand on Kate's shoulder.

Natalie and Elisabeth climbed to their feet as well and knelt beside Kate.

The five people in the small room fell silent. Caleb Lawson patted Kate's shoulder gently. He looked to Miss Mary and lowered his head. After a beat, Caleb Lawson looked up and into the eyes of the dark eyes of Miss Mary.

"Well, thank you Mary fir your time," Caleb Lawson said.

Miss Mary examined Caleb Lawson and nodded. She did not smile. Instead, she frowned, sadly.

Lawson reached out and placed a hand on Kate's back, getting her attention and urging her to stand. Kate, Natalie and Elisabeth slowly climbed to their feet.

"Freeman was def'nitely one uv a kind," Miss Mary said from her chair.

As the four exited the cathouse and found themselves in the darkness on the edge of Curtis Elisabeth reached out and put her arm around Kate's shoulder. Natalie stood awkwardly. Kate looked at Elisabeth and smiled.

"Sorry, that didn't end the way you 'spected," Lawson said.

"It's fine," Kate said. She walked in the darkness back to Bucktown. Natalie walked along side of Elisabeth quiet. Elisabeth and Lawson talked in low tones along the way. In a few minutes they were back in the small section of Bucktown.

"So, what are you gonna do?"

"I'm not sure. I had planned on findin' Freeman 'n maybe Kaiyote," Kate said, unsure. "Now, I'm not sure."

"You can stay wit us 'til you figure it out," Elisabeth said, with a smile.

Caleb Lawson nodded.

"I wouldn't want to be a burden," Kate said.

"No burden," Lawson said.

"No burden," Elisabeth said with a slight smile. "We're stayin' wit my aunt 'n uncle Caleb on their ranch. It ain't much but it's better than bumpin' 'round tryin' to think what you're goin' to do next," Elisabeth said, grabbing Kate by the hand.

"The ranch is ten acres," Caleb Lawson said.

"Well, it's ten acres of land," Elisabeth said.

Kate nodded.

"Before we go to your daddy 'n tell him what you're thinkin' let's go and see when the next waggun is headin' back to Oregun," Kate said.

Elisabeth laughed.

"What you laughin' at?"

"My dad, after he goes to Coffeyville, he turnin' 'round 'n headin' back to Stratton fir supplies," Elisabeth said. "So, we can talk to my daddy," Elisabeth smiled. "He's the next waggun goin' east."

Kate nodded and chuckled.

The three teenagers walked back to the Bucktown camp where there were still a few people dancing. There was a man dressed in a wool coat playing a violin softly. About a dozen men and women were sitting around a small bonfire.

That night, in the glow of the bonfire, Kate was invited to the Lawson ranch. She accepted the invitation, not because she wanted to stay with the Lawsons but because they were headed to Coffeyville and the mopey teen hoped to find the town where Freeman had been gunned down. In her seventeen-year-old mind Kate imagined that someone in one of the towns they rode through on the way to Coffeyville would recall Freeman and she would find his last resting place.

"Daddy can we stop here?" Elisabeth asked.

They were just a few hours out of Coffeyville. There was a small nameless town just to the left. At the edge of the small town near Coffeyville Elisabeth's father stopped the wagon and the two girls sought out anyone that might have met the dark-eyed, bearded cowboy.

"Stay close," Mister Lawson said.

Of course, Kate's reality was that she and Elisabeth searched the small town for anyone that might have met Freeman. The two girls went in opposite directions and asked everyone they ran into if they knew of the tough, dark cowboy. Several men had met Freeman but did not know where he was let alone believed he was dead.

It was an old man named: Isaiah Plum, who said he knew Freeman. He was a small shouldered little man with a salt and peppered beard and mustache. Plum wore a checkered collarless shirt, a loose-fitting leather jacket with fringes, leather belt and dark trousers. He had a triangular head and wore a flat-topped brimmed hat made fabric.

Isaiah Plum was sitting on a bench when Elisabeth brought Kate to the one man that said he knew Freeman, the dangerous cowboy.

"Before you start," Isaiah Plum said, tilting his triangular head to the left at the appearance of Kate. "I ain't a close friend of that Freeman your friend was talkin' 'bout. I tried to tell her that, but she got all excited once I sed I knew him."

"So, do you know him?"

Isaiah Plum nodded.

"So, when was the last time you seen him alive?"

"Last time I seen him alive was here, in this town," Isaiah Plum said.

"Is there another town between here 'n Coffeyville?"

"I don't think so," Isaiah Plum said.

"Someone sed he was killed in a little town near Coffeyville," Kate said.

"I can't say if I know anything 'bout that," Isaiah Plum said.

"Where's the cemetery?"

Isaiah Plum pointed to the right and the two girls looked in the direction Plum indicated.

"Thank you," Elisabeth said as she and Kate left the old man.

The two girls walked slowly toward the far end of the small town.

"You know we should have gone and talked to the undertaker," Elisabeth said as they walked to the far end of the small town and the whitewashed building in front of it.

"You think they have an undertaker here?"

"I don't know," Elisabeth said, with a shrug. "I was just thinkin' if anyone would know who died it would be the undertaker."

"I think the preacher might know too," Kate said.

Kate and Elisabeth walked to the small plot of land dedicated to those that had died and scanned the thirty or so graves, tombstones and wooden crosses.

Some of the grave markers had names. Some did not. Elisabeth began to walk the perimeter of the plot of land that held some of the dead. Kate walked up and down the rows trying to see if there was a gravestone or wooden cross with Freeman's name on it.

Kate stopped near the rear of the graveyard and looked at a nameless grave marker. She studied the wooden cross that was sticking up from the ground. The cross was weathered and gray and held together with two bent nails. Kate reached out and placed a hand on the arm of the cross.

Elisabeth walked up and stopped.

"Is this it?"

Kate shrugged her shoulders.

"You know, if it is or isn't," Elisabeth said. "It doesn't matter." She smiled. "You looked. You heard the stories. Like my mom sed, you know how this story ends."

Kate nodded and the two girls walked back to Elisabeth's father's wagon. Eventually, they would ride out of the small town and reach Coffeyville by nightfall. Elisabeth and Kate would return to Bucktown and Caleb Lawson. Kate would become a part of the Lawson family and on the small ranch she could start over again.